To die for...

Ramirez excused herself and went outside. Just a cigarette break or was she up to something like knocking on doors to interview my neighbors, asking things like, "Does Ms. Jewel practice martial arts in the patio behind her house?" "Does she hang out with lowlifes?" "Does she throw loud parties while wearing stolen shoes?" "Would she kill for a pair of Louboutin shoes? Manolo Blahniks? Roger Viviers?"

Now I was alone with sexy detective Jack Wall. The room seemed smaller. The atmosphere heavy with unspoken questions. Mine and his. Finally he spoke. "Regarding the shoes Ms. Jensen was wearing. Any idea what happened to them?" he asked. "Do you know anyone who would murder someone to get a pair of shoes?"

"Most women love shoes. I'm no exception," I confessed. "But murder? I can't imagine going that far. Although they were silver."

"Were they worth stealing?" Jack asked.

I shrugged. What was the right answer? I had no idea. "Depends."

"Worth killing for?"

I blinked. What could I say?

Shoe Done It

GRACE CARROLL

BERKLEY PRIME CRIME, NEW YORK

THE BERKLEY PUBLISHING GROUP
Published by the Penguin Group
Penguin Group (USA) Inc.
375 Hudson Street, New York, New York 10014, USA
Penguin Group (Canada), 90 Eglinton Avenue East, Suite 700, Toronto, Ontario M4P 2Y3, Canada
(a division of Pearson Penguin Canada Inc.)
Penguin Books Ltd., 80 Strand, London WC2R 0RL, England
Penguin Group Ireland, 25 St. Stephen's Green, Dublin 2, Ireland (a division of Penguin Books Ltd.)
Penguin Group (Australia), 250 Camberwell Road, Camberwell, Victoria 3124, Australia
(a division of Pearson Australia Group Pty. Ltd.)
Penguin Books India Pvt. Ltd., 11 Community Centre, Panchsheel Park, New Delhi—110 017, India
Penguin Group (NZ), 67 Apollo Drive, Rosedale, Auckland 0632, New Zealand
(a division of Pearson New Zealand Ltd.)
Penguin Books (South Africa) (Pty.) Ltd., 24 Sturdee Avenue, Rosebank, Johannesburg 2196,
South Africa

Penguin Books Ltd., Registered Offices: 80 Strand, London WC2R 0RL, England

This is a work of fiction. Names, characters, places, and incidents either are the product of the author's
imagination or are used fictitiously, and any resemblance to actual persons, living or dead, business
establishments, events, or locales is entirely coincidental. The publisher does not have any control
over and does not assume any responsibility for author or third-party websites or their content.

PUBLISHER'S NOTE: The recipes contained in this book are to be followed exactly as written. The
publisher is not responsible for your specific health or allergy needs that may require medical supervi-
sion. The publisher is not responsible for any adverse reactions to the recipes contained in this book.

SHOE DONE IT

A Berkley Prime Crime Book / published by arrangement with the author

PRINTING HISTORY
Berkley Prime Crime mass-market edition / October 2011

Copyright © 2011 by Penguin Group (USA) Inc.
Cover illustration by Jennifer Taylor / Paperdog Studio.
Cover design by Rita Frangie.
Interior text design by Tiffany Estreicher.

ISBN: 978-0-425-24403-6

BERKLEY® PRIME CRIME
Berkley Prime Crime Books are published by The Berkley Publishing Group,
a division of Penguin Group (USA) Inc.,
375 Hudson Street, New York, New York 10014.
BERKLEY® PRIME CRIME and the PRIME CRIME logo are trademarks of Penguin Group
(USA) Inc.

PRINTED IN THE UNITED STATES OF AMERICA

10 9 8 7 6 5 4 3 2 1

Acknowledgments

With thanks to my wonderful agent, Jessica Faust, for her unwavering support, sense of humor and always helpful suggestions.

A special mention for a devoted reader and expert bridge player, my neighbor Dorothy Greenberg.

This book is for my editor, Emily Rapoport, without whom I would never have met Rita Jewel: fashionista, solver of crimes and super salesgirl. Thanks, Emily!

One

When I arrived in steamy Miami Beach that morning, it was already ninety degrees with matching humidity. Before I melted away, I headed straight for Collins Avenue and bought a vintage Lilly Pulitzer floral halter dress and wedge sandals with studded leather accents. After stuffing my old clothes in my Heys USA Exotic polka-dot carry-on bag, I walked out of the store in my new outfit feeling more like a native and less like a clueless tourist from San Francisco. In fact, I was there on business. To pick up a pair of shoes from a shop in South Beach for my boss Dolce of Dolce's Boutique.

The stilettos for her special customer were on hold at an exclusive atelier tucked between two other stores on a side street. The dazzling handmade silver shoes were safely wrapped in yards of white tissue paper, stowed in their box in a large shopping bag. Dolce had told me not to let them out of my sight.

"Must be a *very* special customer," I'd said, trying not to act too curious, which I was. Especially after I saw the hand-spun silver heels. How many people could afford gorgeous, expensive, one-of-a-kind shoes like these?

"All my customers are very special," Dolce had told me. Why all the secrecy? Dolce followed a code of ethics when it came to her customers that rivaled anything the AMA required. She expected me to do the same. No one was supposed to know what any customer bought, wore or how much they paid for it. But she couldn't stop the customers from talking among themselves, comparing shoes and jewelry, which I was sure they did. The important part of my mission to South Beach was to get the shoes back to San Francisco in time for the annual Golden Gate Garden Benefit tomorrow night—the event that kicked off the fall social scene.

I made time to stop off at the popular Not Your Mother's Underwear Shop where the clerk talked me into the latest trend, high-waisted undies inspired by a popular TV show that takes place in the 1960s, along with some other to-die-for lingerie I couldn't resist. She assured me my selections "will make you feel beautiful even if no one knows you're wearing them." Given my Spartan social life, no one would. But *I'd* know, I thought as I put all the intimate items into my black-and-white polka-dot carry-on. Then I was back at the airport on my way home. San Francisco had been my home for only half a year during which I'd been lucky enough to land my dream job through a friend of my aunt back in Columbus—which was selling clothes and accessories to the rich and well connected at Dolce's.

Five hours, two glasses of Chardonnay and a bag of complimentary pretzels later I stood outside the San Francisco Airport Arrivals waiting for Dolce to pick me up. I was shivering, wishing I'd had time to change back into my old clothes, when my phone rang. It was my boss.

"Rita, I can't believe this. Some idiot just ran into me on Van Ness. My car is totaled."

"What? Dolce, are you all right?" I asked anxiously.

"I'm okay. Just shaken up a little. Get in a cab and go straight home. See you first thing in the morning. Eight o'clock or earlier. And don't let those shoes out of your sight."

I hung up, unzipped my bag, pulled out a cashmere scarf and wrapped it around my shoulders. Poor Dolce. She sounded really upset. Who wouldn't be? Now, of all times. I just hoped she wasn't injured. Sometimes you're in shock and you don't know how badly you're hurt until later.

From out of nowhere a tall, rakish-looking guy pulling a Prada men's rollaway crashed head-on into me. I stumbled, and my open carry-on bag banged into his, flipped over and spilled my lingerie on the sidewalk.

"Damn, damn, damn," I cried as the one-of-a-kind silver shoes popped out of their shopping bag, broke out of the shoe box and skidded away in opposite directions.

"Sorry," he said.

"Sorry? Sorry doesn't do it," I blurted. My face flamed, my eyes smarted with angry tears. First, I went after the shoes. They must be worth at least a half year's salary and were only available from that one shop in South Miami Beach. After I retrieved them and put them carefully into their box inside the shopping bag, I scooped up my new sexy underwear from the ground and shoved it back into my carry-on bag. When I looked up, I realized how many people had stopped to stare as if they'd never seen lacy thongs or an underwire bra spilled at a taxi stand before. Miffed at the invasion of my privacy, I muttered, "I hope you all miss your connections." What a way to end an overnight business trip. My first and probably my last.

"Can I help you?" the guy who'd bumped into me asked in a strong foreign accent.

"You could help by watching where you're going," I said. But it wasn't his fault, not completely. I was the one who hadn't zipped up my bag when I took out my scarf. And he *was* pretty hot looking in a trench coat, knockoff designer jeans and wraparound shades. He could have been a member of Interpol or an international spy if his accent was genuine. So many guys faked it these days, their background, their education, their jobs. You never knew.

I gave him points for having politely averted his eyes from my underwear and focused on the shoes instead. They were definitely eye-catching. He looked genuinely concerned at my plight.

"Let me help you," he said.

What could he do? I'd already stowed the shoes back in the box and zipped my bag shut.

"You are going in to the city, yes?" he asked.

"Yes. I'm going to take a taxi."

"Me too. We can take together. It would be for me my pleasure." With that, he picked up my bag, bypassed the line and whistled for a taxi, which screeched to a halt two feet from the curb. It did occur to me as I got into the cab that he might be a homicidal maniac looking to kidnap innocent women like myself and sell them into slavery in his country. But avoiding that official taxi line was especially appealing given that I was on the verge of freezing my butt off. Sharing a cab would be cheaper than taking one by myself even though I could expense the cost. Dolce would appreciate my being frugal when possible. I decided to take my chances.

"My name is Nick Petrescu," he said.

"Rita Jewel," I said. We shook hands in the backseat of the cab.

"You're a tourist, yes?" he asked.

How galling to be mistaken for a tourist in my own town. Probably because my clothes were so glaringly inappropriate for this chilly City by the Bay. As Mark Twain said so aptly, "The coldest winter I ever spent was summer in San Francisco." I sighed.

"No, I live here," I said. "What about you?"

"I am here to work a new job."

Because of his accent and being naturally curious, I asked, "Where are you from?"

"I am coming from New York. Oh, you mean originally. I am coming from Romania."

"Romania? *Salut cum esti?*" I couldn't help showing off what few words I remembered in Romanian, my minor in college.

He turned to me with a look of surprise on his rugged Romanian features. "You speak my language."

"Only a little. I'm afraid I can't remember much more than that. The classes I took were mostly reading and writing." I only hoped he wouldn't ask what I'd read or written. The truth was I'd only taken the classes to read about vampires, which I found fascinating, but the courses were harder than they looked.

"Your accent is excellent," Nick said.

"Thank you." I felt a glow of satisfaction. No one had ever praised my effort to speak Romanian before, certainly not my professors or my family, who were forever asking me, "What are you going to do with it?" If I'd known I was going to run into an honest-to-God attractive Romanian one day, I might have hit the language lab more often.

"Where you will wear the beautiful shoes?" he asked with a glance at the shopping bag on my lap.

"I won't. They're not for me. Much too . . . too much." I bit my tongue. I almost said "expensive." I knew I shouldn't discuss the shoes at all. But surely Dolce didn't mean don't even mention them to Romanians you meet at the airport. "I just picked them up for a customer where I work," I explained. Blame my loose tongue on my chattering teeth, goose bumps or lack of sleep.

"You work for a shoe store?"

"It's a boutique in Hayes Valley. We carry upscale shoes, clothes and accessories. What kind of work do you do?" I asked, finally able to change the subject.

"I am gymnastics coach for children," he said. "Do you know the Ocean View Gymnastics School on Vista Avenue? I came here to be teaching there."

"Never heard of it," I admitted. I hated the thought of exercising unnecessarily. "I take kung fu classes. My boss is a fitness freak, and she insists I know how to defend myself." From what or whom I had no idea. But working at Dolce's had so many perks that I would have signed up for skydiving if Dolce wanted me to.

"Your work is so dangerous then?" he asked, a frown on his face.

"The only danger is when two customers fight over the same item." No danger with the shoes I was hand-carrying. They were so pricey only one of Dolce's customers could afford them. Besides, the benefits of buying clothes and accessories with my employee discount were worth any danger I might encounter.

"The shop is just for women?"

"Women with lots of money and time on their hands. It's very exclusive."

"Like those shoes."

I shrugged in a noncommittal way. I'd already said too much. I was proud of myself for not spewing, "Yes. They're one of a kind." I didn't know any straight men who were the least interested in fashion. Was this that rare man who noticed what women wore or knew the difference between Dior and Chanel and wasn't gay?

I gave the taxi driver directions to my flat on Telegraph Hill. When the taxi stopped in front of the two-story building on the edge of the hill I sublet from a friend of a friend who got transferred to LA, Nick got out to carry my bag and walk me to the door. He offered to carry the shopping bag too, but I remembered my promise to Dolce.

"You must see my gymnastics class," he said, handing me a brochure from the studio. "Maybe I can change you from kung fu to our gym. Not only for children, but good for all ages. We learn handsprings, trampoline, tucks and how to say . . . cartwheels. Very important cartwheels to stay in shape. Not that you are not." He carefully looked me up and down. I hoped he was satisfied I didn't need any cartwheels. The thought of turning upside down made me dizzy. "Here is my card. Call for free lesson, okay?"

"Okay." I put the card in my purse and thanked him. Inside my dark, chilly flat, I was immediately hit with a bad case of post-assignment travel letdown syndrome. Sure it was great to meet a hunk in the airport, one who was an athlete and cared about his body and maybe mine too. But he hadn't asked for my number. He'd only given me his. So it was up to me to make the first move, which is not something I would ever do. If he wanted to see me again, he'd find a way.

A girl has to have principles and mine were handed to me by my aunt, Grace. She's my mother's older sister who while still unmarried has a much busier social life than I

do, which isn't saying much. "Don't call him back." "Don't
accept an impromptu invitation like 'Call for a free lesson,
okay?'" And, "Don't *ever* ask *him* out." So where had these
rules gotten me? Nowhere. Call me cynical, but Petrescu
probably got a commission on any new students he enrolled.

I sighed and switched on the gas logs in my faux fireplace
as the fog crept up the hill toward my house. Then I brewed
myself a Cuban-style coffee from the bag of ground beans
I bought at the airport in Miami and bit the head off a chocolate alligator I'd planned to give Dolce as a souvenir. Finally
warm in a fleece Snuggie, the blanket with sleeves my mother
gave me last Christmas that I would never wear unless I was
really, really cold and completely alone, along with a pair of
sheepskin UGGs, I played my phone messages.

The first was from Dolce.

"Rita, I'm sorry about tonight. I got hung up with the
police, who blamed me for the accident. When the asshole
hit me! Needless to say I'm going to fight it. I hope you got
home okay. I never would have sent you for the shoes if it
wasn't important. The shop has been crazy busy these last
two days and I really missed you. It's not only the Benefit,
but the opera season starting in a few weeks, the symphony
gala, and you know how it is. Everybody's just got to have
whatever it is they've got to have. As long as it's one of a
kind. Which is the whole reason for the shoes. Sometimes
I wonder if it's worth it. It gets to be too much. Yesterday
I had to reorder those tights you like so much. You were right
about those. They're so hot I can't keep them in stock. So
glad you didn't have a problem picking up the shoes. I'm in
a bind here with those frigging shoes. If I had to do it over,
I'm not sure . . . I have to tell you-know-who tomorrow she
has to pay up or forget the shoes. I'm not running a charity
here. Can you possibly do me a huge favor and come in even

earlier tomorrow? Don't say anything to anyone about the shoes. Take a taxi to work and guard them with your life. If word gets out, it could be bad, you know? I'm rambling. I've taken a painkiller and I'm washing it down with some Scotch. Uh-oh, someone's at the door. Tell me it's not her. See you tomorrow."

I was confused and worried about Dolce. Usually crisp and focused, she sounded scattered. I wondered if she should have gone to the emergency room to be checked out. Of course I was dying to know who she was talking about. And why the hush-hush about the shoes? One thing was for sure. Dolce, the consummate coolheaded businesswoman, was not her usual self. She needed her assistant, and I admit I liked to be needed. Who didn't? I'd go in at seven thirty, deliver the shoes, and finally find out who'd ordered them and why it was a secret. My own problem of whether or not to call the buff Romanian was too trivial to think about.

I looked at my "California the Beautiful" calendar on the wall. I had no problem with a crowded fall schedule. I didn't have tickets to the opera, the symphony or the charity affairs. But I loved finding just the right dress and shoes for someone who did have a full calendar. Not just the dress and shoes, but the right bag and jewelry to go with it. I'd always loved it. As a child I used to dress my dolls, then accessorize them. When they were completely decked out in shoes, hats, necklaces and stockings and dresses, I'd drag them around to the neighbors to see and be seen.

Now I got paid to dress socialites. And I was able to purchase whatever I just had to have with a hefty discount. It was the best job ever. The only downside was I never met any men at work. Or anywhere. The only man in my kung fu class was the teacher, Yen Poo Wing, who was always yelling at me to kick harder, jump higher and turn more

gracefully. The only eligible man I'd met in months was
Nick the gymnast. At least I assumed he was eligible.

Despite the strong Cuban coffee, I fell asleep on the
couch, warm and secure in the knowledge I hadn't broken
any of Aunt Grace's rules and wasn't going to. When I woke
up the next morning, I went to my closet to find just the right
outfit. It was Saturday and I knew the shop would be packed
with last-minute shoppers with big plans for Saturday
night—the Benefit, the parties, whatever. I decided to wear
a knit dress from the Marc Jacobs spring collection. It was
no longer spring, but hopefully no one would notice. Dolce
had special ordered the dress for a customer who then
decided not to buy it.

When it arrived, the woman shuddered. "I had no idea the
colors would be so bright. I'm getting a headache just looking at them."

Dolce never broke a sweat or lost her cool. All she did
was turn around and insist I try on the blue vertical striped
skirt with attached checkered blouse. The red blazer thrown
casually over my shoulders completed the ensemble. "I
know it's bright, but you've got the shoulders to pull it off,"
Dolce said, patting me on the back. When she said that, I
wondered if maybe it was too bright and called attention to
my shoulders that were admittedly a tad broad. "It's yours,"
she said. "Pay me when you can." That's the kind of warm-
hearted, generous woman my boss was. How could I refuse
her anything she asked?

Today was the perfect day to wear the outfit with my new
push-up bra and some hip-hugger panties. I buckled a wide
belt around my waist, snapped on a vintage Bakelite bracelet, slipped into a pair of metallic ballet flats and called a cab.

"Lady, you got an hour wait at least," the dispatcher said.
"Busy day today."

Dolce badly needed me to come early, so I took the bus. Some day I'd save enough for the Chevy Corvette I'd always coveted, but fortunately San Francisco was basically a small, pedestrian-friendly city and the bus took me almost to my door. One thing was for sure: I was the only person on the Nineteen Polk who was wearing Marc Jacobs and carrying a pair of handmade silver shoes in a shopping bag.

More than a few heads turned as I lurched down the aisle toward an empty seat by the window. Admiring glances I was sure. I was feeling good until I sat down, opened the *Chronicle*'s fashion section and read that "Muted colors are fall's key look." I frowned, then folded the newspaper and stuffed it under the seat. No one could say I was muted today. Far from it. Ah well. It wasn't fall yet, not officially. But if I were in Florida now, I'd fit in perfectly. No muted colors in South Beach.

Just before eight I arrived at the Victorian mansion that Dolce's great-aunt had left her over a year ago. My boss had done a fabulous job converting it into Dolce's Boutique. I let myself in with my own key. The twelve-foot-tall entry hall with the original crown molding was lined with racks of filmy scarves and clunky costume jewelry. The real stuff was locked up in a glass case in the great room. That was the room with the marble fireplace and a curved bay window where the morning sun streamed in on the racks of gorgeous dresses. The kind of dresses suitable for evenings at the theatre, the symphony and coming-out parties in Pacific Heights.

Dolce must be in her office, the converted closet under the grand staircase that led to her charming quarters on the second floor.

"I love living above the store," Dolce always said. "How else could I live in an 1800s house in a happening neighborhood?" She never got a break, but maybe she didn't want one. She was totally dedicated to fashion and her customers.

I was about to knock on the closet-turned-office door when I heard voices. Dolce was not alone. I dropped my hand and stood shamelessly listening.

"I can't let you have the shoes before you pay for them, MarySue. What if something happened to them? A spill, a crack?" Dolce asked in a firm voice.

I was so shocked, I almost dropped my bag. First, I couldn't believe a Dolce customer wouldn't have paid in full for the shoes. And second, that the customer was MarySue Jensen, who was originally a Garibaldi, an old San Francisco family.

"Dolce, I've got to have the shoes. I've scrimped. I've saved. I've sweated for those shoes. I gave you a sizable deposit." MarySue sounded desperate.

"But MarySue . . ."

"I'm the cochair. I can't go without my shoes, can I? You know I can't. My dress is nothing without the shoes. You know it's true. When I saw the picture of them in *Vogue*, it was love at first sight. I had to have them. My picture will be in the paper tomorrow. And you'll be mentioned. Don't forget that."

"Publicity is nice, but money makes the world turn," Dolce said.

I nodded. I'd heard my boss say that before.

"We had a deal," Dolce continued. "You told me you'd have the rest of the money by today, so I ordered the shoes for you. You give me the money, I give you the shoes. Rita is on her way as we speak with the shoes in hand. You know I can sell those shoes ten times over, but I'm giving you first crack at them. But I have to have the money you owe me today. No checks. Cash or credit card."

I gripped the handle of the shopping bag tightly. I pictured MarySue, a tall, statuesque blond who was one of Dolce's best customers, facing off with my boss. It wasn't a pretty picture.

"I can't," MarySue said. "Not today. Things happen, Dolce, can't you understand? I thought I'd have the rest of the money today, but . . ." Her voice broke and there was a long silence. I wondered if MarySue was crying. I imagined her tears running down her face, smearing her mascara and leaving a streaky trail on her perfect skin.

"I'll hold them for you until six o'clock tonight," Dolce said. "I'll stay open late if that helps. As soon as you get the money, they're yours."

"You don't understand. I have to be there at six thirty with my shoes on. I'm the cochair. I can't appear in anything else. I *have* to have those shoes now." MarySue's voice rose.

"MarySue, stop, you're hurting me," Dolce said loudly. "Let go."

I froze. I leaned against the door wondering if I should burst in or call 911.

"Sorry. I didn't mean it. I'm not myself, Dolce. I've got a lot on my mind. If Jim finds out how much they cost, he'll kill me."

"There's no way he'll find out. My lips are sealed. Everything that goes on at Dolce's stays here. You know that. I took over the shop because this place is a safe haven just like it was for my great-aunt. I want my customers to feel the same."

"I know. They do. I love coming here. Everyone does. The atmosphere. Everything. I'll have the rest of the money next week, I swear I will. I just wish you'd trust me."

"Of course I trust you, but I'm running a business, Mary-Sue. I want you to have the shoes, but I have expenses. The property taxes alone are out of sight."

"Your taxes are not my problem, Dolce."

"The shoes are your problem, MarySue."

I heard the sound of a chair being scraped across the refinished hardwood floor, then a loud thump like something or someone had fallen on the floor. I pressed my ear against the door. All I heard was the whir of a ceiling fan. I reached for the antique doorknob, but it wouldn't turn.

From inside I heard a cry. "Help!"

Two

============

I reached for my cell phone, but my hands were shaking so much I couldn't even dial 911. Face it, I was no good in a crisis.

Finally I heard MarySue's voice on the other side of the door.

"Sorry," she said. "I didn't mean it. Give me the shoes and I'll forget we had this conversation."

I heaved a sigh of relief.

"No," Dolce said. She sounded tired.

"Yes," MarySue shouted. "I'll have the money for you on Monday."

"Now," Dolce said.

The door jerked open and MarySue stormed out. I jumped out of the way, fearing another collision. MarySue stopped and stared at me, her steely blue eyes riveted on mine. I swallowed hard over a lump in my throat. Her gaze swerved to the bag with the logo of the atelier in bold letters. Her eyes lit up as she realized what was in the bag. She grabbed it out of my hand. Then she brushed past me as if I were no more than a shadow and ran for the door like a filly out of the gate. Her heels clicked on the polished floorboards.

I ran after her, but with her long legs she was too fast. The front door slammed in my face. The sound bounced off the walls. I yanked at the doorknob and stood on the steps swiveling my head to the right and then the left. Frantic, I ran down the stairs. But there was no MarySue in sight. Nowhere. Not on the street, not in a car. She was gone and the shoes gone with her.

I trudged back up the steps, feeling hollow and desperate. I blinked back tears of frustration. Dolce stood in the hall-way looking as stunned as if MarySue had hit her over the head with an antique andiron. Her face was as white as her cruise-wear collection. This on top of her accident last night.

"Don't tell me the shoes were in that bag," she said.

I nodded. "I'm sorry." My voice cracked and I broke down and sobbed. I couldn't stop myself. I'd failed. "She's gone. I lost her." How could I have survived a collision at the airport only to lose the damn shoes right here in the shop?

Dolce shook her head. "She won't get away with this. If I have to hunt her down."

"No, I will." I took a tissue from my pocket and blew my nose. "It's my fault."

Dolce's eyes narrowed. "I should have gotten the full amount instead of a down payment. I'm ruined," she said quietly.

Ruined? Was she being overdramatic? "They're worth a lot, aren't they?" I asked. Of course they were worth a lot. Why else would Dolce say she was ruined?

"Shoe-making is more than a craft, it's an art. Take those

shoes you picked up. They're stilettos, but they're like walking on a cloud; they cradle your feet and yet they're the height of fashion, the ultimate luxury."

"No wonder she—"

"She wanted them so badly that she stole them? Yes, no wonder," Dolce said bitterly. "I'm just glad I got some of the money up front." My boss looked like she'd aged ten years since I left two days ago. Her forehead was etched with deep lines, her shoulders sagged.

"This is my fault," I said. "I let her take the bag out of my hand. I should have brought them in a plain grocery bag. Or come in later. Or earlier. I'll get them back for you," I promised. "Or the rest of the money."

"How?"

"I . . . I'll go to her house. I'll demand she return them." The more I thought about it the more I knew I had no choice. MarySue couldn't grab those shoes and get away with it. She didn't know who she'd just ripped off. It was me, Rita Jewel, she'd ripped off: a tough chick and protector of the working girl. "I'll reason with her," I assured Dolce. "I can't believe she'd keep them if she knew we were going to call the authorities. We are, aren't we? Think of the scene. The patrol car arrives at her house. Her neighbors come out to gawk, and she's cuffed and hauled away in broad daylight. She misses the Benefit altogether. Everyone in town knows what happened. She'll beg us not to tell anyone. And we won't if she gives back the shoes. Because if she doesn't, then we have no choice. We'll call the cops. You said it yourself, she stole them. This is theft, pure and simple." I might not have convinced Dolce, but I'd talked myself into it.

"I'm on my way," I said. "Where does she live?"

"No." Dolce grabbed my arm. She squeezed it so hard I

gasped. "I need you here. Today of all days. Besides, there are other ways. There are professionals who do this kind of work. Repossession agents."

She turned and walked toward her office. I followed her, intent on carrying out my plan. But she stopped me with a hand gesture that meant "stay where you are." "Open the front door. We have a big day ahead of us. I need you to wait on customers. Act like nothing has happened. You can do that, can't you?"

I nodded. Dolce went into her office, and I stood there wavering between obeying my boss and charging after the shoe thief. I wanted to go after MarySue more than anything. I wanted to wrest those shoes from her multiringed fingers and hold onto them until she coughed up the money. And I would just as soon as I could. Professional repo agents or not. They couldn't possibly want to recapture the shoes as much as I did.

Standing in her office doorway, Dolce looked at me as if seeing me for the first time since I arrived. She tilted her head to one side. "You look fabulous. I knew that outfit would work for you, the crazy patterns and the wild colors. They're so you."

I didn't feel wild or crazy in the least. I felt stupid and naïve for letting MarySue snatch the shoes. One good thing, my boss had at least partly recovered her poise.

"Take care of things, will you?" Dolce asked me while rubbing her arm. Was that a black-and-blue spot she had courtesy of MarySue? "And not a word about the shoes. I have a call to make." Without waiting for an answer, Dolce closed the door to her office.

I was flattered Dolce trusted me with her best customers. If it weren't for the shoes, she'd be out there full steam ahead. With all the events and parties coming up, sales were

sure to be brisk today. Maybe brisk enough to make up for
the shoes. Dolce was the world's greatest saleswoman.

Patti French, MarySue's cochair for the Garden Benefit,
was the first customer in the store. She was waiting on the
porch when I opened the door. If MarySue planned to wear
those silver, one-of-a-kind shoes tonight, what would Patti,
her blond, whippet-thin sister-in-law wear to outdo her?
Maybe that's why she was here, looking for a last-minute
purchase so she could match her sister-in-law in money
and taste.

"Hi, Rita," Patti said with a glance at my colorful ensemble. "Great outfit. How are you?"

"Fine, fine. Big day, right?"

"Right." She smiled and craned her swanlike neck. "Is
Dolce here?"

"She's tied up right now. What can I do for you? We just
got some new tights in. They're the latest celebrity trend,
which you've probably already seen in *Star* or *OK!*"

"I don't think I have," she confessed.

"You'll love the sun-kissed, polished effect you get with
them. Let me show you a pair in tan."

"Wait, I don't want to look too polished." Patti seemed
distracted as she glanced around the room, which was now
slowly filling up with the usual crowd as well as some faces
I hadn't seen before. In a low voice she said, "I was wondering if MarySue was here. She won't tell me what she's wearing tonight. All I know is that it probably cost a fortune. Her
spending is out of control. Jim is furious with her. He cut
up her credit cards last week. And if that doesn't work . . .
Where did you say Dolce was?"

"I didn't. I just said . . . Oh, there she is."

Dolce seemed to be her old smiling, self-confident self
in a new outfit—a pair of black trousers from British

designer Maggie Hu, a deep maroon sweater that might be covering her bruises, and ropes of beads.

"Dolce dear," Patti said, hugging her as if she hadn't seen her for years, "you look divinely casual and understated as usual. I was just doing some last-minute shopping. I don't want to show up for the benefit dressed like MarySue, or anyone else for that matter."

"You won't," Dolce assured her smoothly, although just the name MarySue must have sent a tremor through her as it did me. I wanted to ask if the repo people were on their way. Until then I couldn't relax. "Your sister-in-law's taste is absolutely light years from yours."

"Thank you," Patti said. "But you never know. Except you do know. You know what she's wearing and I don't. Just a warning." Patti paused and looked around to see if there was anyone in hearing distance. "MarySue is, well, let's just say she needs help to curb her compulsive spending. I just hope no one we know will turn into an en: ler and let her charge things she can't afford."

My eyes widened. I was flattered to be let in on the gossip, but now I was even more worried about recovering the shoes. To her credit, Dolce looked serene and unperturbed even though Patti had as good as accused her of encouraging MarySue's shopping addiction.

"I don't expect you to tell me what MarySue's wearing tonight," Patti said.

"That's good, because I can't. I'm sworn to secrecy," Dolce said as she pressed her finger against her lips. "She wants to surprise you."

Patti sighed and Dolce nodded at me. "Would you check on the customers in the great room?" she asked.

"Of course." I left the room, sorry I couldn't continue to watch Dolce in action. And wondering what she was going to say that she didn't want me to hear. She was such a pro. The word on the street was that Dolce Loren could sell water to a drowning man. I wanted to be like that. Dolce was my role model, my idol and my inspiration. I had to get the shoes back or Dolce would be ruined. Plus she'd never trust me again.

Three

·····················

The rest of the day we were so busy I didn't even have time to wonder "how" or "when." I didn't even have time for lunch. Several times I stopped in the hallway to ask Dolce, "Any word?" But she just shook her head and hurried away. What did it mean? Had she called the repo people or not? Were they doing their job, or had they even agreed to take the job? At five o'clock Dolce closed the front door and hung the "Closed" sign in the window.

When I tried to ask her what was happening, she told me not to worry about it. "I've put the matter in the hands of professionals, Rita," she said. "If they can't retrieve them, no one can. Go home and get some rest. I'll see you Monday."

"But it will be too late," I protested. "We have to get the shoes back before she wears them to the benefit." I looked at my watch. We only had an hour.

"There's nothing more I can do," she said, brushing her hands together. "Either they get them or they don't. Frankly, right now I have other things on my mind. Would you mind locking up on your way out?"

Of course I agreed, then I stood watching while she walked slowly up the stairs to her apartment. I couldn't believe she'd just turn her back on the whole thing. That accident last night must have been more serious than she let on. Maybe it had affected her brain. Or sapped her of her will. I had enough will left for both of us, and some to spare. Maybe it was my expensive colorful outfit that made me feel so confident and determined to get revenge on MarySue. Had I been wearing muted colors, I might have let the repo agents take over. Who knows? Maybe it was just a strong inner resolve I'd just discovered that I had. Whatever it was, I was going to get those shoes if it was the last thing I ever did.

First, I stopped in the office, which Dolce had uncharacteristically left unlocked, and I flipped through her Rolodex to find MarySue's address in Pacific Heights.

When my cab pulled up to MarySue's, I saw the house on upper Broadway was an Italian Renaissance hilltop mansion. The views they had of the Bay and the Golden Gate Bridge must be spectacular. I got out of the cab and stood there on the sidewalk, breathless and awestruck. I shouldn't have been surprised. Many of Dolce's clients lived in houses like this, I supposed. But most of them paid their bills on time and didn't order shoes they couldn't afford. No time to stand and gawk and envy the rich and overdrawn big spenders who breathed the rarified air around here.

I opened the gate and walked up a winding path between the furry green foliage and vivid red flowers of the California fuchsia on the right and blue-flowering Ceanothus maritimus on the left. Obviously someone here cared enough about the environment to stick to native plants. Then I saw it. A small discreet "For Sale" sign at the front entrance. I stopped dead in my tracks. How long had that been there? Was there any connection between the shoe theft and the selling their McMansion?

I rang the bell and knocked on the door so hard I bruised my knuckles. Nothing. I pressed a button next to an intercom.

"Yes?"

I took a deep breath.

"Rita Jewel here to see MarySue Jensen."

"Who?"

"Rita from Dolce's Boutique. It's about the shoes." No sense in pussyfooting around. Come out with it. Give her a chance to hand over the shoes before she was in real trouble.

"Sorry, Mrs. Jensen isn't here."

I rocked back on my heels. I could have sworn that voice sounded like MarySue herself.

"Could you tell her she's in serious legal trouble if she doesn't return the shoes to me right now? Otherwise I'll be forced to call the police."

The answer was a firm click. She'd hung up on me. So, it *was* her. She was in there. I went back down the path and looked up and down the street. A few houses away there was a van in the driveway with "Smythe's Landscape Service—Water-wise Garden Gems" painted on the side. I looked around, not a landscape artist to be seen on the street. Probably all busy pruning or planting Garden Gems or whatever out of sight. I looked back at the Jensen house. On the third floor I saw the outline of a figure. Someone was looking out. Was it MarySue or maybe an accomplice? It was getting late. If she was in there, she'd have to leave soon for the Benefit. Should I wait for her to come out and tackle her and take her shoes? Or would she run me down first in her Mercedes on her way out? I contemplated hiding in the backseat of her car and surprising her when she got in, but when I tried the door to the three-car garage, it was locked.

I went back to the front door and pushed the intercom again.

"Yes?"

"Smythe's Landscape Service and Garden Gems here to do the yard maintenance," I chirped.

"Go to hell. Back where you came from, toady sycophant."

I didn't even blanch. That was MarySue all right. I smiled with satisfaction despite the insult. I'd rather be a sycophant than a shoe thief. Now I knew two things. She hadn't left yet. And she had the shoes.

I walked around the side of the house, pushed open a gate and found myself in the middle of a Japanese garden. A waterfall cascaded over a rocky precipice and into a small pond filled with colorful koi. A small wooden bridge arched over a stream lined with rocks. If this was his work, I must remember to hire Smythe when I made my first million. Then I saw it. A tall ladder propped against a sick old oak tree. The oak trees of California were under attack from sudden oak death. I knew the symptoms—yellowish brown leaves, stains and lichens on the bark. They were all there. This tree would have to come down. Maybe that's the reason the ladder and the chain saw were resting against the tree trunk.

My heart was racing. I knew I didn't have much time. I knew if I didn't get those shoes back before the benefit, MarySue would return them tomorrow damaged or stained and she'd never pay Dolce the money she owed her. Or she'd sell her house and leave town with the shoes on her feet. Dolce would face financial ruin, I'd be out of work and . . . I . . . I didn't know what I'd do.

Right now I had to do what I could to stop MarySue. I dragged the ladder from the tree to the back of the house. I climbed up a few steps and paused, my fingers gripping the steel rungs. I half expected someone to pull it out from under me. Maybe Smythe, maybe Jim Jensen, MarySue's husband. Maybe MarySue herself. But nothing happened except the ladder wobbled. I leaned into the house and grabbed a handful of the ivy that covered the wall. I took a deep breath and climbed higher. My fingers were so stiff I could barely hold on to the rungs of the ladder.

I was opposite a window level with the second floor. Afraid of heights, I didn't dare look down or I'd get dizzy and fall. Where was MarySue? Where were her shoes? No, not *her* shoes, she hadn't paid for them.

A moment later I had the answer to my questions. Mary-Sue came to the window. Her eyes bulged when she saw me looking in at her. She was wearing a simple but costly black beaded sweater dress by Chloé. She was right. She needed those silver shoes to set it off. But from that angle I couldn't tell if she was wearing them now or not. I almost felt for her. The fashionista in me almost wanted her to have them. I almost felt like climbing down the ladder and going home. No one would blame me. No one would know I'd failed except MarySue, and she'd be glad I had. But I didn't. I rapped on the window. "Give me the shoes," I shouted.

She shook her head. Then she opened the window. Her cool blue eyes darted from my face to my shoulders to my white knuckles. She put both hands on my shoulders and pushed. The ladder tilted backward. I reached out to grab something, anything. Preferably MarySue. The ladder swayed forward then backward again. I swayed with it. I screamed as I felt myself falling, falling backward into the branches of the dead oak tree. Then everything went black.

"Dr. Foster. Calling Dr. Foster. Report to the ER. Marjorie Lambert, fourth-floor Obstetrics stat. Dr. Kramer, you have a call on line three."

The voices were so loud they penetrated my poor brain. Where in the hell was I, and how did I get there? I opened my eyes, but the lights were so bright I quickly closed them. All I knew was I was flat on my back in a hallway and people were rushing past me shouting out instructions. Suddenly I was moving too. Someone was pushing me down the hall.

"How are we feeling?" the woman asked.

"Terrible," I mumbled. "My head hurts. Who are you? Where am I? Where are we going?"

"I'm Winnie Bijou, LVN. We're at San Francisco General Hospital. You might have a slight concussion and trauma to an extremity, but we've been busy with other more serious stuff. Don't worry, you're next. Lucky you, you get to see Dr. Rhodes. Trust me, it's worth the wait." Winnie Bijou giggled.

Worth the wait? How long had I been waiting? So I had a concussion? The last thing I remembered was falling off a ladder into a tree. But where and why I had no idea. Why would I climb up a ladder when I was scared to death of heights?

"Nurse Bijou," I said with a shiver of apprehension. "Do I have amnesia?"

"Possible," she said as we turned the corner and headed down another hall. "Doesn't say anything about it on your chart. Says you were brought in wearing ballet flats by someone who didn't leave a name. Remember who that was?"

"Not really, no. I mean I don't know who it could have been because . . ." I drifted off, not able to think clearly.

"Here we are." She went around the gurney and pushed open the door to a small examining room. I saw she was someone about my age in a crisp white uniform—admirable,

I thought, for someone working the ER on a long, injury-filled Saturday night.

Once in the small room, Nurse Bijou propped up my head on a pillow. She asked me for some personal information for my chart, then she wrapped a cuff around my arm, gave a cursory glance at my Bakelite bracelet and stuck a thermometer in my mouth. There was a knock on the door and another nurse whose badge said "Opal Chasseure RN" came in.

"Dr. Rhodes is on his way," she said. "He works the ER, but he's a specialist in sports injuries."

"This isn't a sports injury," I said when Nurse Bijou had removed the thermometer from my mouth and the cuff from my arm. "I mean, I don't think it is because I don't do sports, except for kung fu." Maybe my memory was coming back to me by inches. They say your long-term memory returns first. Maybe that's all I'd ever get back.

"We'll let Dr. Rhodes decide what it is or it isn't," Nurse Chasseure said briskly. "Nurse Bijou, I have everything covered here."

By her tone I gathered she meant, "Butt out."

Nurse Bijou got the message and when the door opened to admit Dr. Jonathan Rhodes, she scurried out. That left the three of us, one tall, strapping, sun-bleached blond-haired god of a doctor, one starchy nurse and me, half out of my mind but still able to appreciate a gorgeous man. My head floated somewhere above me and I closed my eyes. The smell of antiseptic hung in the air. Maybe I'd gotten too big a whiff. Or maybe this was all a dream. If it wasn't, I was hoping I was wearing my new lingerie just in case Dr. Rhodes had me strip down for a full-body scan. It had been so long since I'd gotten dressed, I couldn't remember. After my accident, I was lucky to remember my name. It turned out all the doctor cared about was my ankle.

"How did this happen?" Dr. Rhodes said. His deep voice cut through the fog of my brain. He put his hand on my forehead. I opened my eyes and then it all came back to me in a blinding flash. MarySue, the shoes and the ladder. The shoes. Where were they?

"I fell off a ladder. It's my foot. I think I sprained my ankle."

Dr. Rhodes carefully removed one metallic ballet flat and wrapped his strong, caring fingers around my ankle. I winced. "Nurse Chasseure, would you get an ACE bandage and wrap the patient's ankle?"

Opal left and I was alone with Dr. McDreamy Rhodes.

"You have a grade-one sprain and a mild concussion," he said. "I'm prescribing some anti-inflammatory medicine along with cold packs for your ankle. As for your concussion, these things usually go away by themselves. I recommend monitoring and rest at least for a few days."

I felt better just hearing his voice and was reassured by his bedside manner. Combined with his looks, this guy was going far. I wouldn't be surprised to see him rise to be surgeon general or at least get his own reality TV program.

"So, Ms. Rita Jewel," he said, looking up from where he was writing on my chart. "Not where you thought you'd end up on a Saturday night."

"No," I said. "I was actually on my way somewhere when I got sidetracked and fell into a dead oak tree. That's all I remember until I got here." What I remembered was I was on my way to get the silver shoes back when I ran into trouble. But why bore the doctor with irrelevant details like that? I looked at my watch. It was four o'clock in the morning. The Benefit was over. MarySue had gotten away with the shoes. I felt weak and helpless. My ankle was throbbing.

Dr. Rhodes chuckled as if I'd been joking about the oak tree debacle. I smiled weakly. Nurse Chasseure came in with the bandage and silently and sullenly began to wrap my ankle. What was her problem? Didn't nurses have to take some kind of oath like "Look like you like your job even though you're stuck treating gunshot wounds on Saturday night instead of clubbing in SoMa." Apparently a sympathetic demeanor was not a requirement for all nurses these days.

"I'll need to see you again in a few days," Dr. Rhodes told me. He looked down at my chart. "Is this your current phone number and address?"

I nodded. He wanted to see me again. Of course, his interest in me was purely professional. Still, I felt lucky because he could have passed me off to an assistant.

"Hold on," Dr. Rhodes said. "Wait here while I get you a few pain pills and an ice pack to tide you over until the pharmacy opens tomorrow." He left me, and a minute later Nurse McCranky left too without a word.

I sat up then and the room spun around. It was a strange feeling. No one knew where I was or what happened to me. Except MarySue. Had she called an ambulance? Was there an ambulance? Had she brought me here in her Mercedes on her way to the Benefit? Or had she left me lying on the ground while she dashed off to the party in her silver shoes hoping I wouldn't recover. At least not until the party was over. She got her wish. But who brought me then, Smythe's Landscape Service? If so, I wanted to call and thank them.

I stared at the wall as I waited for my pain pills. Lightheaded and dizzy, I wondered how I'd fit my foot back into my shoes. Any shoes. I shuddered to think of having to wear some kind of ugly orthopedic shoes with support hose. I might have slipped out of consciousness for a moment until I heard the voices in the hall. It was Nurses Bijou and Chasseure.

"Saturday nights are the pits," Winnie said. "Last time

I'm working this shift. I don't care if I get time and a half. I'm dead on my feet."

"At least you're not *dead* dead," Opal said. "Like that woman they brought in from some big high-society charity thing."

I blinked. High-society charity thing? I opened my mouth to ask who it was, but my mouth was so dry no sound came out.

"Yeah, you catch her dress?" Winnie asked. "Plain black. Looked like a long sweater. If I had that kind of money, I'd wear Marc Bouwer."

"Who's that?"

"Who's that? Don't you read *Entertainment Weekly*? He's the designer to the stars, that's all. If I had MarySue Jensen's money, I'd be wearing . . ." Her voice faded as I grabbed the edge of the pad and slid off the table. Pain shot through my ankle, and my knees buckled. I fell onto a chair and tried to catch my breath.

"Just thought those society types had better clothes, that's all," Nurse Bijou said. "If I was her, I'd wear—"

"I know, I know, Marc Bouwer, whoever that is."

"And my shoes? Guess what I'd wear."

"Manolos?"

"I don't know. Maybe. I can tell you Ms. MarySue wasn't wearing any shoes at all. Not when I saw her. She was covered with a sheet except for her feet. They were bare. No shoes. Nada. Zilch."

"How'd she die? You hear?"

"Maybe she was murdered. There are plenty of people who'd kill for a pair of Manolos."

"Would you?"

"Wouldn't I!"

I heard muffled laughter and then nothing. I hobbled to the door and looked out. The hall was empty except for

Dr. Rhodes on his way back with my medicine. He gave me more instructions along with the ice pack and the meds and said he had an emergency but he'd see me later that week. "Oh, and Rita . . . stay off of ladders," he added with a twinkle in his cobalt blue eyes.

"I will," I promised. I would have promised him anything at that point.

I clomped out to the waiting room barefoot on crutches the nurses had left for me, my shoes in a plastic bag, and made an appointment to see Dr. Rhodes in three days at four in the afternoon, which I was already looking forward to. I was intending to call a cab when I saw Nick Petrescu leaning against the counter chatting up the receptionist. What was he doing here?

"There you are now," he said. "I am waiting for you."

"But . . . it's still early morning. How did you know I was here?"

"They called me after finding my card in your possession. Perhaps thinking I am next of kin? How is your feeling?"

"I'm okay." I wasn't okay. I was weak and tired and in pain. I needed one of my pain pills, and I needed to go home. "I just need some rest."

"What happened?"

"I fell off a ladder. It could happen to anyone."

He looked confused, as if his English wasn't quite good enough to figure it out.

"I will bring my car around to the front of building."

I nodded. I didn't know he had a car, and I didn't know the emergency people would go through your purse to see if there was a business card with the number of a gymnastics coach they should call. But they'd obviously done just that.

A half hour later Nick dropped me off at my house. He looked worried when I collapsed on my living room couch and propped my bandaged foot on the coffee table. I told him I was fine and I just needed to lie there for a day or two. It was true. I didn't want anyone hovering around watching me while I recovered. I knew what I had to do. Take my medicine and follow Dr. Rhodes's instructions for RICE: R—rest, I—ice, C—compression and E—elevate.

"I am sorry I have advanced tumbling class today or I could cook something for you. Some *sarmalute* or—"

"Thanks, Nick, I couldn't eat a thing right now, but I appreciate it." All I wanted to do was lie there and watch some mindless program on TV. My brain wasn't working very well. I guess I was lucky to be alive, all things considered. It seemed MarySue hadn't been so lucky. Brain or no brain, I had to find out what really happened last night. Was it true MarySue was dead?

"If you are not better tomorrow, I think you should see a different doctor. I don't believe this Dr. Rhodes is very good, and he is not a specialist in brain injuries."

"My brain is fine," I insisted. How did he know anything about Dr. Rhodes? Or anything about my brain? Had he met my doctor? Had he overheard some gossip? No way was I going to change doctors. "I'm sure I'll be better tomorrow."

Nick finally left after promising to come by tomorrow with a bowl of his grandmother's *zama* for me. A dish that was guaranteed to cure any and all ills.

As soon as he left, I hopped on one foot to the kitchen. I put the cold pack they'd given me in the freezer and took out a bag of frozen peas to wrap around my ankle until the real thing was ready. I don't eat frozen peas or any kind of peas. They'd been left there by the previous tenant and I'd forgotten completely about them until now when they sure came in handy. Back on the couch, I slapped the bag of peas on my ankle, propped my foot above my heart, clutched my remote control and watched the local news.

When the news anchors finished with the weather report, they got to the juicy stuff.

"Police are calling socialite MarySue Jensen's death a possible homicide," said the attractive dark-haired anchorwoman.

The peas rolled off onto the floor as I swung my legs around, leaned forward and turned up the volume.

"Here's what we know, Amy. Well-known society maven MarySue Jensen, wife of California Airlines exec Jim Jensen, was taken to San Francisco General Hospital last night after she hosted the Golden Gate Garden Benefit at the Lakeside Nature Reserve in Golden Gate Park. Her lifeless body was found in an Adirondack chair late last night by park rangers who called the authorities. Her grief-stricken husband Jim Jensen didn't realize her expensive and one-of-a-kind hand-spun silver shoes were missing until hours later. The case is now being treated as a possible homicide-robbery."

The male co-anchor paused and then asked Amy, "The question is, would someone kill for a pair of shoes?"

"Well, Larry, it depends on the shoes. We have a photo of the shoes here, and you be the judge. To the best of our knowledge, these were custom, hand-spun silver stiletto heels."

Larry gave an appreciative whistle. "Those must be worth a large chunk of change, Amy."

"Indeed they are. I've done a little digging and found they were purchased at Dolce's, the upscale Hayes Valley boutique owned by Dolce Loren. Ms. Loren is the niece of San Francisco native daughter Lauren Loren. Here they are in an old photo pictured in front of the landmark building before the elder Loren died a year ago. How many women at that Benefit were dressed and accessorized by Dolce, do you think?"

"I have no idea," Larry confessed.

"Probably half of the guests," Amy said. "I'm hoping to have an in-depth interview with Dolce Loren on our news program tonight. Stay tuned for more on this disturbing story."

I turned down the volume when they moved on to another story, and stared at the screen without seeing anything. Homicide? Someone killed MarySue for her shoes? My boss Dolce interviewed on TV? What would she say?

Under the influence of my painkillers I unfortunately dozed off and on all day and missed the news. What had Dolce said? I woke up feeling empty. No wonder, I hadn't eaten anything for hours, maybe days. I reached for the menu from a Cambodian restaurant in the Mission, knowing they delivered. Everything sounded good, especially my favorite, the tofu crepe stuffed with bean sprouts, ground pork and coconut smothered in a lemon-garlic sauce. Something we never had back in Columbus, I can tell you. The hostess in her charming Cambodian accent assured me it would be delivered within the hour.

I'd just hung up when the phone rang. I looked at the screen. Dolce!

"Rita, where are you?"

"I'm at home. I have a grade-one concussion and a sprained ankle. What's happening? How was your interview?"

"Fine, fine. Rita, the police are here. They're asking questions nonstop. It's been awful. Now they want to know about you."

I gripped the phone tighter. "Is it regarding MarySue?"

"Yes. What were you doing at her house last night?"

"I . . . I went to get the shoes back." No sense pretending

I wasn't there. Someone picked me up there and brought me to the hospital. But who? How did Dolce know about it?

"I told you not to."

"I know, but I couldn't let her get away with them."

"Did you kill her?"

I gasped. "Of course not. How could you even ask?"

"It's not me who's asking. It's the police. They need to talk to you. They're on their way to your house."

"What?" I shrieked. I dropped the phone and staggered to my feet. The police. At my house. On Sunday. Asking questions. What would I say? And more important, what would I wear?

Four

:::::::::::::::::::::::

I hopped on one foot to my walk-in closet and flipped past a boxy red military-inspired jacket from Ralph Lauren that would look terrific over a feathered gown if I had one. But hardly appropriate for a police interrogation. I dug out a pair of shiny cocoa-colored leggings that were meant to be tucked into a pair of Gucci over-the-knee fringed boots. Or how about a pair of kitten heels? I shook my head. Not for a housebound invalid with a sprained ankle.

I briefly considered the olive green Theory dress from my latest buying spree, which just happened to occur while I was in my quasimilitary phase. "No, no," I muttered and tossed it on top of the pile on my bed. Wrong, all wrong. What was I thinking? I was not the military type, no matter what I wore. And olive green would make me look even sicker than I was. On an ordinary day I wanted to be tough and vulnerable at the same time. Today I needed something to make me look pale, casual, and of course, innocent. But stylish too. In an understated way.

Denim? It was casual all right, and never out of style, but the Ralph Lauren jeans and the Gap shirt in my closet conveyed a kind of sloppiness. I tried tucking the shirt into the jeans, but the overall effect was way too preppy. I'd be arrested on the spot by the fashion police or the real ones for looking like I just got off my motorcycle after killing someone for her shoes.

Aha, there it was. Soft pants with a drawstring waist from Rebecca Taylor that I'd picked up at Neiman Marcus in their semiannual sale. Paired with a comfy knit tank, I had the look I wanted. Like I just tumbled out of my sickbed. Too ill to remember what happened the night MarySue was murdered but cooperative and helpful as possible to the authorities. I pulled my hair back in a casually messy updo, scrubbed my face and added a touch of mascara. A pair of cashmere socks completed my ensemble, and exhausted from all the preparation, I sank back onto the couch, waiting. And waiting. Wondering if my food would arrive before the gendarmes. Or simultaneously. Nervously I gnawed on a fingernail. Then I staggered to the freezer and replaced the peas with the regulation cold pack.

Finally two plainclothes detectives arrived at my door. I could see through the window one was young, one was older. One was short and was tall. One was a woman, the other a man.

They rang the bell and I called "Come in." I was determined not to move off the couch and to play the invalid role to the hilt.

"Ms. Jewel?" the tall man asked as he came through the door. "I'm Detective Jack Wall, San Francisco PD." He and his partner Sylvia Ramirez both flashed their IDs. Actually, "plainclothes" was not the right word for what Detective

Wall wore. I didn't have to see the label to know he was sporting a Ralph Lauren two-button, single-breasted suit with a striped shirt and tie that shouted Wilkes Bashford, the guy who'd been dressing San Francisco men practically since the earthquake. How in hell did a public servant afford clothes like that? Looking so gorgeous, was he on his way to somewhere like a wedding or a funeral?

"I'm Rita Jewel," I said. "Won't you come in and sit down?" Aunt Grace would have been so proud hearing me in my gracious-hostess mode. "Tea, coffee?"

They both declined my offer of a beverage. No tea- or coffee-drinking allowed on the job, probably. Just as well since I was hardly up to brewing anything for them. Then Detective Ramirez, with her long curly hair and her pear-shaped figure wrapped in a long flowered skirt designed by Isaac Mizrahi for Liz Claiborne, looked around my living room. Her outfit was absolutely wrong for her body shape, which she would know if she ever read a fashion magazine, which she probably didn't. Such a shame. Now if she'd been in uniform, I wouldn't have even noticed. Detective Wall explained they were investigating the death of MarySue Jensen. I looked up at him and nodded. As if I sort of knew but didn't really know much at all.

"You were acquainted with the deceased?" Detective Wall asked as he eased his long frame into the chair opposite the coffee table where I'd propped my foot, making sure my ACE bandage and cold pack were visible. I'm not sure he noticed. Instead, his gaze lingered on my soft, Balmain plain gray tank top I'd picked up on sale last month. I felt a shiver of awareness go up my spine. Was it the presence of the long arm of the law? Or was it the arrival of a bona fide sexy barracuda in my living room? Or was it just my medication that made my heart race?

I'd been in the city for months without meeting one attractive man. In the past two and a half days I'd met a gymnast, a doctor and now a cop. All in my target age bracket and all definitely worthy of a second glance. I couldn't believe my luck. Of course, this cop was made of steel and the gymnast was from another culture and the doctor might be unavailable and laden with med-school debt, but none of them was wearing a ring. It gets to be a habit, looking at ring fingers.

"MarySue—Mrs. Jensen, that is—was a customer at the boutique where I work." I knew the rules from watching crime shows on TV. When interrogated, don't ever say any more than you absolutely have to.

"A good customer?" he asked and crossed his legs. I had a glimpse of black calf Stamford loafers.

"Yes, I mean she came in often and she appreciated fine jewelry and clothes. She had excellent taste. With her height she could wear anything and look great. French Connection bodysuit or a little dress by Missoni. If that's what you mean," I said. Now why did I go on and on about MarySue? Unnecessary information.

"What I mean is did she have trouble paying her bills?"

"You'd have to ask my boss Dolce," I said primly. "I'm just a sales assistant." I tried to look modest and humble. If that's possible while wearing new high-waisted underwear.

"Tell us about her shoes," Detective Wall said.

"Her shoes?" I repeated, sounding like a parrot.

"The shoes you picked up in Florida that she was wearing the night of her death," said the short detective in the yellow cardigan that matched the flowers in her skirt.

"But I thought she wasn't—"

"She wasn't wearing them when she was found," the tall, extremely well-dressed cop said. "That's right. How did you know that?"

I froze. Wasn't I supposed to know that? "I heard someone say so. A nurse in the hospital who was there when she was brought in. Plus I heard it on the news. Why, is it a secret?"

He ignored my question. Instead the female detective jumped in. "So you yourself just *happened* to be in the same hospital when Ms. Jensen was brought in?" she asked, her voice dripping with sarcasm, her dark eyes locked on mine.

"It's a big hospital, San Francisco General. They have an excellent trauma center. That's why I—"

"That's why you ended up there the same night as Mary-Sue Jensen. Quite a coincidence, wasn't it?" Detective Wall asked. His name suited him, I thought, as he zeroed in on me. His face had became a wall keeping out any sign of empathy or emotion. Which made me try even harder to win him over. I focused on stopping my brain from rambling when it should have been focused on telling these guys what they wanted to know without telling them more than they needed to know. But I was having trouble staying on task. "Or was it?"

"Was it?" There I went repeating again. I honestly forgot what the subject was. I was recovering from a concussion, for God's sake. Didn't they know that?

"A coincidence," he said.

"Yes," I agreed. "Absolutely."

"Can you describe the incident that brought you to the hospital?"

"Concussion and sprained ankle," I said, wiggling my foot.

"I didn't ask for the diagnosis, I asked you about the incident," Detective Wall said coolly.

Okay, I could play it cool too. I'd give him the facts and nothing but the facts. "I fell off a ladder. I blacked out. And I woke up in the hospital."

"What time was that?" he asked, taking out a small notepad. Didn't the police have access to laptop computers or the latest iPad? Or did this guy spend all his high-tech allowance on his clothes?

"I don't know. I mean, I left the hospital in the early morning. But I don't know what time I arrived at night. Or how I got there. I had a concussion. I was unconscious." I didn't want his pity, and I was grateful he hadn't asked why I was on a ladder or the location of the ladder. Did he know I went to get the shoes back or not? If not, I wasn't going to tell him. "You can check with the hospital. They will have a record." Did I have to suggest this to a cop?

That's when Detective Ramirez excused herself and went outside. I watched her light a cigarette just outside the window and walk around the side of the house. Just a cigarette break or was she up to something like knocking on doors to interview my neighbors, asking things like, "Does Ms. Jewel practice martial arts in the patio behind her house?" "Does she hang out with lowlifes?" "Does she throw loud parties while wearing stolen shoes?" "Would she kill for a pair of Louboutin shoes? Manolo Blahniks? Roger Viviers? Or was I reading too much into her absence? Sometimes a cigarette is just a cigarette.

Now I was alone with the detective. The room seemed smaller. The atmosphere heavy with unspoken questions. Mine and his. Finally he spoke. "Regarding the shoes Ms. Jensen was wearing. Any idea what happened to them?" he asked. "Do you know anyone who would murder someone to get a pair of shoes?"

"Most women love shoes. I'm no exception," I confessed. "But murder? I can't imagine going that far. Although they were silver."

"Were they worth stealing?" Detective Wall asked.

I shrugged. What was the right answer? I had no idea. "Depends."

"Worth killing for?"

I blinked. What could I say? I thought I'd already answered that.

"Do you know how much they're worth?"

I shook my head.

"Are you sure?" the tall, smooth detective asked.

I wanted to say, "Come on, tell me how much they're worth. You know. You must know," but I didn't. Of course I had an idea. But why should I share it with him?

He turned over a page in his notebook. Perhaps signaling a different topic or at least a new approach since he wasn't making much progress this way.

"I have a few names here. Customers or others in the fashion business. I'd like to get your impression of them. Don't think too hard. After all, you've just had a concussion." He looked at me and I didn't see a shred of compassion in those dark eyes. After all I'd been through. It was as if daring me to contradict him or make an excuse. I didn't. "Just tell me the first thing that comes into your mind."

I sat up straight and tried to prepare myself for his little game.

"Dolce Loren."

"My boss. A wonderful woman. Kind and caring." I paused. He was sitting there staring at me. "Smart and savvy," I added.

"Patti French."

"Patti has a great fashion sense. She loves Tom Ford, Prada, and Louis Vuitton. She's MarySue's sister-in-law." Like he didn't know that. "I mean she was or she still is now that MarySue is dead. I'm not sure how that works."

"Jim Jensen."

"I don't know him."

"Did MarySue ever mention him?"

"Not to me." *If Jim finds out how much they cost, he'll kill me.* Isn't that what MarySue said to Dolce? Did he do it?

"Peter Butinski."

"Peter is our new shoe supplier." I felt my mouth twisting and my eyes narrowing despite my effort to stay neutral. The shoe guy was a little too high on himself, in my opinion, but what he had to do with MarySue was beyond me.

"Was he acquainted with Ms. Jensen?"

"I don't think so, unless she special ordered shoes from him."

"It sounds like there was a possible connection there. Would you agree they were both interested in shoes?" he asked.

I sighed. "Who isn't?"

The detective had just flipped another page in his notebook when the front door opened and his cohort burst in looking like she'd just won the lottery. She was wearing rubber gloves that did not match her outfit and holding a shoe box in her hand. My eyes widened. My heart pounded. It was the brown cardboard box the silver stilettos came in. Where in the world did she get it? And were the shoes inside? If so, mystery solved, or at least part of it.

"I found this box in your garbage," she said, her eyes gleaming. "Recognize it?"

"I . . . I don't know," I said as calmly as I possibly could while my mind spun in circles. After all it wasn't necessarily *the* shoe box I'd brought on the plane. Though the resemblance was striking. It was brown with an abstract ink drawing and the name of the shop stamped on the top. I squinted and held out my hands to have a closer look. But Detective Ramirez had no intention of letting me put my prints on the box.

"Come now, Ms. Jewel," she said, holding the box away from me as if she was afraid I would contaminate the evidence. "Tell the truth. Did you or did you not transport this box and the shoes inside it across the country last Friday?"

"The shoes are inside the box?" I asked eagerly.

"I'm asking the questions," she said curtly.

I glanced at Detective Wall. Where did he stand in this confrontation between his cohort and myself? He was inscrutable as usual, watching the dialog play out as if the two of us women were actors in some existential drama.

"I transported *a* shoe box and *a* pair of shoes across country, that is correct," I said brusquely. "Whether that is the box or not, I can't say."

"Can't or won't?" she asked.

"I'm sorry," I said weakly, leaning back on the couch, "I'm feeling faint, and since I'm under a doctor's care who has prescribed rest and ice packs for the next few days, I'll have to stop now and . . ." I closed my eyes as if it was all too much for me to handle in my current weakened state. When no one said anything, I opened my eyes again. "I'm so sorry. Really. But my memory isn't very good right now. Not unusual in these cases. I'm afraid I'll have to postpone our conversation, as interesting as it is."

Ramirez was not unaware of how sarcastic my comment was. She glared at me. "We are not here to converse with you," she said. "We are here to investigate a murder."

"I understand that," I said, "but your questions are upsetting me. Exactly what my doctor warned me about. No agitation. No commotion, no excitement. Or there may be complications," I warned. I stared at Detective Ramirez, daring her to continue. After knowing what the risk was. I paused to let the significance of complications sink in.

"I hardly think a few questions . . ." she said, obviously unwilling to give up and go away just because I was suffering the effects of a fall from a two-story building into a tree.

"I would love to answer however many questions you have at some later date when my head clears. Right now I'm at risk for a relapse, and I know you wouldn't want to be responsible for it." Besides, I thought I saw the Angkor Wat delivery truck outside and I was eager to get rid of these two.

Ramirez darted a glance at Wall, who shook his head, and she bit her lip. Probably furious and frustrated she couldn't nail me. Did she really think that after I stole Mary-Sue's shoes and killed her, or killed her and then stole her shoes, that I would then check into the hospital with a concussion and a sprained ankle, return home and toss the shoe box in my garbage can? It boggled the mind.

"Of course, if you'd care to look in my closet for the silver shoes before you leave . . ." I cocked my head in the direction of my bedroom, knowing she'd decline.

Again she looked at her partner, who again shook his head. It was too bad in a way because I would have liked to show off my shoe collection. I had no silver shoes, but I was proud of my taste in footwear, ranging from sporty two-tone brogues to a pair of brand-new leather t-straps and everything in between. It seemed to me that choosing the right footwear was almost the most important decision a girl could make. Did Ramirez want to see my shoe collection just out of curiosity or did she think she'd find the silver shoes in my closet, arrest me and get a promotion? I'd like to see her face when she came up empty.

"No?" I said when she didn't respond to my offer. "I can only assume that the shoes are back in their box safe and sound."

If looks could kill I would have been dead meat. We all

remained where we were, frozen in place for thirty seconds at least. The delivery van was looking for a parking spot. Detective Ramirez was staring at me with the unopened box in her hands, Detective Wall was standing in the middle of my living room looking like he wanted to be somewhere else, and I was still sitting on the couch, leaning back, my head cushioned on a pillow.

Finally Jack Wall took the shoe box from his assistant detective and opened it. It was empty. Just as we thought.

"Believe me," I said to Wall, "I have as much reason to find the shoes as you do. Maybe more so. My boss Dolce entrusted them to me. MarySue snatched them out of my hands without paying for them so she could wear them to the Benefit and now they're gone. As soon as I recover"—I glanced at my swollen, bandaged ankle—"and I will recover, God willing, then I will recover the shoes. If I don't, my job, my boss, our shop . . . we're all in trouble."

"We appreciate your *help*," Jack Wall said and maybe he meant it. I hoped so. "But recovering stolen property is the job of the police. When amateurs attempt to circumvent the appropriate procedures, accidents can and will happen." That's when he looked pointedly at my ankle. Did he know? And if so, how? "If it wouldn't upset you too much, we would like to hear how the shoe box got into your garbage can," he continued.

"You'd like to hear? I'd like to hear too," I said. "But if I were in law enforcement instead of a simple salesgirl, I'd say that whoever did steal the shoes put it there to frame me for the theft and maybe even the murder. Which is crazy because I was in the hospital when the crimes were committed."

There, I'd given them the motive for the placement of the shoe box, and I'd included my alibi so they could narrow their search and quit wasting their time and mine. But not a word

of thanks did I get. What I got instead was a scolding for trying to recover the shoes on my own. The odd couple didn't
even seem slightly grateful. I mean, what more did they want?
It was so obvious what had happened. All they had to do was
dust the box for fingerprints and presto—they'd have the
answers they were looking for. Did I dare suggest it? No, I
didn't. Let them fumble their way to solving this crime.

"Now if you'll excuse me," I said with a glance out the
window. "I do hope you'll keep in touch, but it's time for my
medicine." And my dinner. Or was it lunch? My inner clock
was seriously screwed up. I looked anxiously at my watch
as if I might lapse into a coma without my medication. Not
to mention the harassment I was getting from these two. That
was enough to set me back days in my recovery program.

Before they left, Detective Wall handed me his card. "If
you have any more information for me, give me a call. Any-
time. When you're better, of course, and thinking more
clearly. That's my cell phone number on the back. We're
anxious to get this high-profile society-type story solved
and off of the front page and let the community know about
the good works we're doing."

With the delivery man coming up the walk, my stomach
rumbled, and I wanted them to leave in the worst way, but
I couldn't resist seeing if he could back up his claim, by asking, "Which good works are those?"

"The Wilderness Program for City Kids, the Celebrity
Tennis Tournament Fund-Raiser, Saint Anthony's Dining
Room . . ."

He must have noticed that my forehead was furrowed as
I tried to picture this suave detective serving the homeless
at St. Anthony's in the crime-ridden Tenderloin district.

"I work the line on Saturday nights," he said as if he'd
read my mind.

Not sure what that meant. Maybe he had no social life. Maybe he was devoted to serving the poor. He just didn't look the type in that expensive suit. I started to think they'd never leave and it was my fault asking him about his charity work when it was murder we needed to discuss. Not just discuss, but do something about.

They did finally leave. They crossed paths with the delivery man, and Detective Wall noted the van and wrote something on his famous notepad. Then he turned and looked back at my house. As if he might wonder just how sick I was if I could handle a tofu crepe stuffed with bean sprouts.

It turned out I could handle it just fine. After polishing off every single delicious bite, I drifted off again. When I woke up, I read a few chapters from a well-regarded vampire novel (not in the original, but translated from Romanian into English) guaranteed to put me to sleep again. The book probably gives some readers nightmares, but I don't scare easily. The next thing I knew it was Monday morning, and after I had a cup of coffee and the rest of the chocolate alligator, I called Dolce to report to her about my interview and ask her about hers. And explain why I wasn't at work today.

Five

"Dolce," I said.

"Rita," she said. "What happened? I tried to call you last night and again this morning."

"Sorry, I turned off my phone." I stretched my leg out and critically surveyed my ankle. I thought the swelling had gone done a little. "My doctor wants me to rest."

"You had me worried. I thought they might have arrested you and hauled you off to the new county jail."

"The one they call the San Francisco Hilton South? No they didn't, but I'm sure the detective in the long flowered skirt would have liked to."

"That skirt," Dolce said with an audible shudder, "was bad enough. Then there was her sweater. Jones New York if I'm not mistaken. Someone should tell her to avoid raglan sleeves or at least wear a scarf tossed over the sweater to broaden her shoulders. I'm telling you, if the fashion police had been on duty that woman would be behind bars."

"Was it that bad?" I asked. "I didn't notice."

"Didn't notice her sloped shoulders? Rita, you must really be sick. Now don't even think about coming in today."

"I have to. I can't sit here with my foot up another day of watching TV and reading Romanian vampire novels or I'll go mad, I swear. How was your interview on TV?"

"Fine, in fact we got some free publicity from it. We've been mobbed so far today."

"I wish I'd seen it," I said.

"I TiVo-ed it so I can play it for you. Of course they tried to get me to say something incriminating, but I think I did pretty well dodging the questions. 'How well did I know the deceased? What kind of clothes and accessories did she purchase? Any financial problems? When was the last time I saw her?' You should have heard me doing a sidestep. How about you? Did you tell the police you went to get the shoes back from MarySue?"

"They didn't ask. Either they already knew, or they still don't know or don't care."

"What did you think of Detective Wall? Quite a hunk, as you girls would say, or were you too sick to notice? Can't complain about his taste in clothes. I hope he didn't give you a bad time."

"He asked questions, but I think I convinced him I couldn't have killed MarySue or stolen her shoes. The bad thing is they found the shoe box in my garbage can."

"*The* shoe box?" Dolce said. "The one the silver shoes came in?"

"That's the one," I said. "Needless to say I have no idea how it got there except that whoever put it there is someone who wants to frame me."

"Who would want to frame you? Everyone likes you. Except MarySue of course and she's dead. Why, everyone's asking about you. Claire Timkin is here now. On her way to a teachers' meeting."

"Don't tell me she's actually buying something?"

"No, of course not. How can she even look at our merchandise on her salary? And why waste high fashion on the fourth-graders in her classroom? But she tries to keep up. She does. She comes in and she looks. Then she goes to Macy's and buys her clothes." I could just picture Dolce shaking her head at the tragedy of it all. A woman with solid-gold taste forced to shop at a department store. "At least that's my theory."

"You sound better, Dolce. How do you feel?"

"Physically I'm fine, but I can't help think about the shoes . . ." Her voice dropped as I reminded her of the trouble she was in. Both of us actually.

"That's what I wanted to ask you about. Any word from the repo people?" I asked. "I was hoping they'd found them and somehow later dumped the box in my garbage."

"No such luck. If only I'd never ordered them, never sent you to get them, . . . Never mind, I'm afraid the shoes are gone for good," she said sadly.

"Maybe not," I said, feeling the medicine kick in and elevate my mood as well as relieving my pain. "No one could wear those shoes in this city without being noticed. And once they are noticed, the police will be all over them. I've got Detective Wall's card here with his cell phone number." I didn't tell her I wouldn't mind calling him with some information just to see how he took it. Would he really be grateful enough to change his opinion of me as a dimwit, treat me with respect, maybe even give me a medal or a certificate the police hand out to citizens who help solve crimes? Or would he just dismiss me with a curt thank-you and hang up. I was a little intrigued and very curious about how he planned to solve this murder case. The sooner the better. "Who else was in? Was everyone talking about MarySue?"

"Not everyone, no. Some people avoid the subject like the plague, but it's on everyone's minds, that's for sure. Harrington Harris dropped in and said he'd be back with his sister a little later so she can see our fall collection. He won't buy anything, of course. Why do I cater to these deadbeats?" She sighed. "Here I am with another penny-pinching schoolteacher taking time off so he can troll the shop for ideas for his drama productions. Says it's part of his job. Never buys a thing, just steals ideas. Guess I can't prosecute him for that. But funny thing, he did ask about MarySue's silver shoes. Probably hoped to get his hands on them."

"Wouldn't we all," I said. "How did he know what she was wearing? Was he at the Benefit?"

"I don't think so. He said he saw them in a magazine last month and he's the one who showed the picture to MarySue. Then she got us to order them for her. So in a way he's responsible for her death, am I right?"

"I suppose . . ." I said. Suddenly it was all too confusing. "Time for my medicine, Dolce. I'll come in as soon as I can pull myself together." By that I meant as soon as I found an appropriate outfit to wear.

"Are you sure?" she asked anxiously.

"Absolutely. I'll come in even if I'm on crutches. I have to get out of the house."

"If you think you're up to it. I really need you, so I won't say no. I wouldn't mind if sales were up, but it seems like everyone just wants to drop in hoping to hear some gossip. But they're not buying. They all want to know what she was wearing. Why she was murdered. Who killed her. I wish I'd never ordered those shoes for her. It was my fault. I was too trusting. I'm going crazy."

I was feeling a little crazy myself, so I hung up, took a pain pill and still hungry, found a fortune cookie in the bottom of the take-out bag I'd thrown away. Cambodians made fortune cookies? Who knew. Anyway, mine said, "You cannot step in the same river twice without getting your feet twice as wet." I puzzled over this for a few minutes, knowing I'd heard it before. But where? In my dreams or in my college class on pre-Socratic philosophy? Greek thinkers are sometimes hard for me to follow, which is why I took Romanian in college instead of Greek. I put the fortune aside to try again later.

Before I left for the shop, I had to check on MarySue's house. I started to wonder how much of Saturday night was real and how much was a nightmare. I scrolled through "Houses for Sale" on my BlackBerry and found the Jensen house with the number of the realtor. So it really was for sale. I really did see that sign. I called the real estate office.

"Sorry, ma'am," said the real estate agent on desk duty, "the house is no longer on the market."

"But I just saw the sign on Saturday."

"The owner has decided not to sell. Just got a call on that. Circumstances have changed. It happens. Sorry about that. We have some other listings in the Pacific Heights neighborhood I'd be happy to show you. Some with fantastic views, high ceilings, hardwood floors, spas, offices, skylights . . . You name it, we've got it."

"Never mind." Just got a call? From whom? Jim Jensen? Now that he had the life insurance on his wife to collect he could afford to stay in the house, was that it? It was no secret to Dolce or to me that they were in financial trouble. Enough to cause Jim to cut up MarySue's credit cards. Was Jim mad enough at his wife for her free-spending habits to kill her, and take her shoes to get a refund or just toss them in the

Bay and collect her life insurance? And then take down the "For Sale" sign. It all made a kind of terrible sense. If it was this apparent to me, why didn't the police follow up on it? I thought about calling Detective Wall to find out if he'd heard about the house, but I didn't. I had to get to work. I had to see people. I had to get back to the real world . . . or was it?

But first I had to get dressed. It took forever. Partly because of my injuries. Have you ever tried on your new thong while avoiding putting weight on your ankle, the one with the ACE bandage? It wasn't easy, but even harder was trying to decide what looked right over the new lingerie. I was so tired of looking like an invalid, I wanted a complete change. I had to look professional, but maybe a little more casual than usual.

I peered out the back window at the view of the East Bay to see that the sun was out. Back in my closet I pulled out a pair of gray Kasbah pants made of natural fibers that had a relaxed fit but a sophisticated look at the same time. With the pants I chose a quiche-colored Tencel and cotton ribbed top. No Louboutins today, nothing with a heel at all. I'd be lucky to squeeze my poor feet into anything but an orthopedic boot. But I did. Before I stuffed both feet into retrofitted floral sling-back flats, I rewrapped my ankle, grabbed an oversize granny sweater and my bag and called a cab. No way was I up to fighting the crowd on the bus with my crutches. It took me about ten minutes just to climb the stairs to the front doors of Dolce's boutique one step at a time. In my commodious tote bag were all my supplies—extra cold packs and ACE bandages and my meds.

As soon as I opened the front door of the boutique, the whole shop full of customers turned to look at me. I must say I made a grand entrance. And even if my ankle was going to take an extra week to recover, it was worth it.

Apparently Dolce had alerted all the regular customers, who couldn't have been nicer. Before I could say "I'm back," they'd taken my sweater, my purse and my bag out of my hands and I was eased onto the big overstuffed chair in the great room with an antique mahogany footstool for my bandaged ankle.

"Poor you," said Claire Timkin, who was still hanging out wearing an oversize crimson shirt with a pair of skinny boot-cut jeans, the brand that costs at least two hundred dollars. She got those at Macy's? She'd never get away with jeans in her classroom, but for a teachers' meeting she'd be fine. Better than fine, the older, stodgy, less-stylish faculty members would either be all green with envy or shake their heads with disapproval. While in between summer and fall, Claire was obviously taking advantage of not having any dress code enforced by her principal. Not today, anyway.

Dolce saw me giving Claire the once-over and sent me a brief wink as if she knew exactly what I was thinking.

I looked around the room. After my initial splash, the customers drifted away to look at racks of scarves, stacks of T-shirts and piles of gypsy ruffled skirts. Now that the Benefit was over, it was time for some casual wear.

I was just about to get up from my comfortable chair and try to help Dolce wait on customers, when Harrington Harris came back with his sister as promised. He was dressed just as you'd expect from the extremely dramatic drama teacher with a huge wardrobe of his own. He sported a hopsack blazer, tight jeans and a shirt open a little too far at the neck.

"Back to window shop and steal more ideas," Dolce whispered to me on her way to look for a medallion necklace in the jewelry department. "Earlier he was wearing a snakeskin vest." She rolled her eyes. "What next?"

I shook my head in dismay. I asked myself if he only stole ideas, or would he steal a pair of shoes if he had the chance?

"I want you to meet my sister, Marsha," Harrington said to me. "Marsha loves fashion too. It must be genetic. I've told her so much about Dolce's, I had to bring her by. She's a hairstylist. Absolutely passionate about hair, am I right?" He fondly ruffled her supershort, silver-blond hair. "She trained with Vidal Sassoon," he added.

I ran a hand through my hair, conscious that she must be horrified to see what shape my hair was in, which was no shape at all.

"What with my injury I haven't had time to do a thing about my hair," I said.

She nodded. Then she reached into her pocket and pulled out her card and gave it to me. "Give me a call," she said. "I think I can help you."

No doubt she could, I thought when I saw the name of the salon and the location. But at what cost?

"So tell me, Rita," Harrington said, "I hear you've actually seen the fabulous silver shoes."

"Well, yes, but only briefly," I said. What was he getting at?

"What did you think? Worth the money?"

"They were beautiful all right," I said. But how did I know what they were worth? I didn't know how much they cost. Did he? I didn't know where they were now either—did he?

"Are you enjoying the summer off?" I asked him, to change the subject.

"Summer off? Not for me," he said. "It may look like I'm not working, but I am. Call it a sick day or call it research. I need it. You know I've been busy at school all summer, and starting tomorrow I'm in full fall season mode. Besides rehearsals, I've got meetings, meetings and more meetings. I tell you it's all too much. I have two classes of remedial English to teach along with the plays I direct. The worst part is I'm under the thumb of a principal with the most sophomoric taste. We're doing *Bye Bye Birdie* this fall and *High School Musical* in the spring. Can you imagine anything more banal? I make all the costumes, props and you name it."

I tried to look sympathetic, but my head was starting to ache. I wanted to say, "Then hadn't you better hustle on back to the scene shop at your high school and get busy cutting and stitching costumes, or pounding nails together for a set?" Instead, I reached into my bag for my pain pills and my bottled water.

Harrington and his sister both watched as if they'd never seen someone popping pills before. Not the ones prescribed by a doctor anyway. I hoped he'd take the hint and take his sister to lunch or at least go look at this season's costume jewelry in the back room.

"Heard you had an accident. What happened to you?" he asked, his eyes on my bandaged ankle.

"Just a slight sprain." I held my breath, expecting him to pursue the topic as Detective Wall had done by saying, "I didn't ask for a diagnosis, I asked what happened," but he didn't. "I guess I'd better quit malingering and get up to help Dolce." I struggled to get out of the chair, and Harrington took my hand and pulled me up. With hands that smooth, how was he going to construct sets and paint scenery?

I murmured something about how good it was to see them both before they wandered over to Dolce's casual wear collection. Now what would I do? I could hardly stand around with one sprained ankle trying to help customers. Maybe I shouldn't have come back to work so soon after all. Fortunately Dolce realized how awkward my position was, and she asked me to hang out in her office and answer the phone, which was ringing off the hook today.

"Is it because of MarySue?" I asked after gathering up my stuff and plopping myself into the chair behind her desk.

She said she didn't know and closed the door behind her. "I wouldn't mind the extra traffic and calls if they added up to sales, but as you saw out there, everyone just wants to talk about the murder. I'm going back and try to actually sell something. If anyone asks for me, just say I'm with a customer and take a message. Or better yet, try to solve their problem, whatever it is. An order for something special? Take it. Store hours? Tell them. Directions? Give them. What I hate is when they just want to ask about MarySue. If they do, just say she was a valued customer and I'm devastated. So upset I can't talk about it. But I'm open for business. How does that sound?"

"Makes sense to me," I assured her. But I hoped no one would ask. What if I said the wrong thing? What if someone really tried to pin me down about my relationship with MarySue, like the detective had? Maybe I could pretend to be the answering service.

"Take a break," I said to Dolce. "I'm fine in here with my leg up on the desk. Don't worry about a thing. Go mingle with the customers. I'll handle all the calls." I smiled and shooed her out. She closed the door behind her and immediately the phone started ringing.

"Good morning, you've reached Dolce's," I said.

"Ms. Loren? This is Detective Jack Wall. I have a few questions for you regarding the case of Ms. Jensen. I wonder if this is a convenient time to come by?"

"Ms. Loren is not available to come to the phone or for interviews," I said, trying to sound like a temp who knew nothing about anything. "She's extremely busy. Perhaps another day."

"Is this Ms. Jewel by any chance?" he asked in a voice that said he knew damn well it was me and that he found it suspicious and almost criminal that I didn't tell him up front who I was.

"Yes, it's me," I admitted with a sigh.

"I thought you were laid up for the duration. It's good to know you've recovered enough to go to work. If Ms. Loren isn't available, I have a few follow-up questions for you if you're up to it."

"We're running a business here," I said. "Customers might be put off by the presence of the police. It's bad enough one of our customers is murdered, but to have the police hanging around makes people nervous."

"Do I make you nervous, Ms. Jewel?" he asked in that deep voice of his that caused my hand to shake.

"I have nothing to be nervous about," I said. Then why was my throat dry and my voice trembling?

"Then you won't mind my dropping by."

"I'd rather you didn't," I said. All I needed was another interrogation. "As I said, the presence of the police tends to freak out some people."

"I know what you said," he said. "I understand that you prefer our interview occur away from your place of work. Since it's almost lunchtime and we both have to eat, I propose we consider this a business lunch. I will provide the food, you will provide certain information."

I didn't know what to say. It sounded vaguely illegal or at least immoral to exchange lunch for ratting on someone, if that's what he meant. On the other hand, I was so hungry my stomach was growling. It must be the pain pills.

"Do I have a choice?"

"Yes, you do. I can ask questions at the central police station, your home, or we can eat lunch in some outdoor facility nearby. It's your choice."

"Fine," I said, wishing I knew where he meant. Lafayette Park? Ocean Beach? He said he'd be by at twelve thirty to pick me up.

When Dolce popped into the office to get her appointment book from her desk drawer, she was surprised to hear about my lunch date, as she called it. I didn't tell her he'd originally asked to speak to her about the murder. I was sure she was still on his to-do list.

"The man is good-looking, no doubt about that. And if he wants to buy you lunch, why not go?"

I was glad to hear she approved. Then she said, "I wonder what he wants in exchange."

"I thought I'd already told him everything I know," I said. "Except the part about going to MarySue's house that night. I suppose I'll have to come clean about that."

"Why shouldn't you? You're the victim there. Aren't you?" she asked with a frown.

"That's right," I said. It was time to level with Dolce. "MarySue almost killed me when I tried to get the shoes back."

"What? That's terrible."

"But I didn't kill her," I insisted. "There I was on the top of a ladder outside her bedroom because she refused to let me in. She's inside dressed for the Benefit. I yell at her to give me back the shoes. She is not happy to see me. In fact, she opens her window and gives me a shove, right into her dead oak tree. You see, I am not just falling from a tall ladder. That's bad enough. What's worse is that she is furious. She reaches out. She pushes me. I fall. The next thing I know, I am waking up in the hospital with a concussion and a sprained ankle."

"But how did you get there?"

I shook my head. "I have no idea. Maybe Detective Wall will enlighten me. I owe someone unless it was MarySue who dropped me off on her way to the park."

"Doesn't seem likely," Dolce said. "I picture MarySue hoping you wouldn't wake up until the Benefit was over."

"Which I didn't. Which was good because I have an alibi for MarySue's murder."

Dolce looked thoughtful. "But I don't."

"You don't have a motive either," I reminded her. "What good would it do you to kill MarySue? To get the shoes back? Somebody wanted those shoes. But not you. Especially after they'd been worn; we'd never be able to return them."

I pictured myself flying back to Miami with the shoes, begging the artisans at the atelier to give us back the money in exchange for the slightly worn shoes. Maybe I could clean the dirt off the soles. If it would do any good, I'd volunteer for the job.

Someone knocked on the office door. "Dolce, are you in there? I desperately need your advice on this little Ellen Tracy coat. Is it me or not?"

Dolce patted me on the head and went out to help her customer. How like her to want to comfort me when she was the one who needed reassurance. The rest of the morning flew by. There I was, cozily ensconced in the office with my foot wrapped in ice on the desk, taking calls and feeling useful. Best of all, I was not feeling lonely and unwanted. Everyone who called, no matter what they wanted, asked me how I felt. What I felt was a warm, appreciated glow that counteracted the pain in my ankle and my head.

I was taking a break to take my pill and thumb through

the latest *Vogue* when there was another knock on the office door.

"Are you in there Rita? It's Peter, and I've got a surprise for you."

Peter Butinski, the shoe supplier? Oh, no. I wasn't up to being nice to anyone I didn't like. But what could I say?

Six

::::::::::::

"Come in," I said reluctantly.

I couldn't believe he, someone in the upscale shoe business, would be wearing Crocs on the job. With all the great men's shoes out there . . . sport or dress, leather or suede, why choose plastic or rubber shoes or whatever they're made of, they're just plain ugly. What was wrong with him? Not only was he clueless about his shoe choice, he wore his thinning hair in a comb-over. I forced a smile. After all, this was business and Dolce trusted me to deal with everyone—whether I liked them or not. "Hi, Peter, how are you?"

"Heard you had quite a weekend," he said, looking at my ankle.

"Oh, that," I said, wondering what he'd heard exactly. "Just took a tumble. It's nothing really. What's new in the shoe biz?"

"Glad you asked," he said, setting a stack of shoe boxes on Dolce's desk. "Have I got something for you with your bum foot. Perfect for those days you don't want to teeter in to work, when you're wearing an ACE bandage, for example." He gave a nod at my ankle and whipped off the cover to a shoe box to reveal a pair of sandals.

"Warm weather must-haves," Peter said.

"Nice," I said politely. Then I caught a glimpse of the price tag and I gasped.

"Too much? Okay, let's see what else I have for you."

I tried to be patient as he flipped open box after box, but I knew I wasn't going to buy a single shoe, no "caged" booties and no ankle-tie stilettos and definitely no wooden wedge with a Mary Jane strap. Nothing from this guy no matter how much I loved them or how good a deal they were.

"Sorry, Peter, with my bad ankle I can't wear any of these gorgeous shoes until I recover. Besides, I'm not in the same league with the customers here. I'm a working girl."

"Got it," he said. "Anyway, I'm leaving them here with you and Dolce on spec. If you sell them, you get the usual fifteen percent. So get out there and hustle," he said with a toothy grin. "When you're up to it, I mean."

My cell phone rang and I expected him to leave, but he didn't. He picked up the same magazine I'd been reading and stood there leafing through it while I answered the phone. Even though I shot him a get-lost look, he didn't seem to notice.

"Ms. Jewel? This is Jonathan Rhodes."

I spun around in Dolce's office chair so fast I almost fell on the floor.

"Dr. Rhodes, how are you?"

"Fine, thanks. Calling to see how you're doing. Taking it easy, I hope."

"Oh, absolutely. Actually I had to come in to work, but I have a desk job for today with my foot elevated and an ice pack on my ankle."

"Excellent," he said. "Not too much pain?"

"I'm managing," I said bravely.

"Good girl. I'm actually calling on a personal matter."

A personal matter? My heart pounded and I reached for my water bottle to soothe my dry throat. What did that mean?

"One of my patients plays in a trio at the Café Henri—it's a little French bistro kind of place."

"I've heard of it," I said. What I'd heard from customers was that it was small, elegant, pricey and a place I could never afford to go to. I gripped my phone tightly, still breathless from the shock of having my Greek god doctor actually call me. I wondered what was coming next. Maybe instructions to change my bandage. No, he said it was personal. Maybe he wanted me to pick out something for his mother's birthday from our jewelry collection.

"I promised Daniel I'd go hear him play this weekend," he said. "I wondered if you'd like to go with me Sunday night. If you like jazz and French food, that is."

"I love jazz and all kinds of food," I said. "And I'd love to go." A date. An actual date with an eligible professional man. If I'd had two good ankles, I would have stood up and shouted it to the skies. I wanted to phone Aunt Grace. I had to tell Dolce first.

Dr. Rhodes, Jonathan that is, said he wouldn't be at the hospital on Wednesday for my follow-up appointment, but he took my address and said he'd pick me up at seven on Sunday.

After I hung up, I sat there staring at the wall in a state of semishock. Unlike my so-called lunch date today where Detective Wall was no doubt going to soften me up then try to find out who killed MarySue, this was a real date. With no hidden agenda as far as I knew. My first date in a whole year. It had nothing to do with shoes, murder or anything.

Except for the fact that because of the shoes, I'd gone to MarySue's that night, then fallen off the ladder, then was taken to the ER. If not for those events, I'd be sitting at home on Sunday night as usual. So though I was sorry MarySue had stolen the shoes, and sorry I had a sprained ankle, and sorry MarySue had been murdered in the park, I was glad I hadn't broken my neck when I fell off the ladder and even happier that I'd met Dr. Rhodes. What would those two chatty nurses say if they knew?

I couldn't wait to tell Dolce. When I swiveled around, I realized Peter had finally left. The stack of shoes and the issue of *Vogue* he'd been looking at were gone too. Couldn't he buy his own magazine?

I hobbled to the door and waved to Dolce, who was artfully tying a silk scarf around the neck of a customer. A few minutes later, she entered the office.

"Dolce, you won't believe who just called and asked me out."

"Jim Jensen?" she asked.

My eyes widened. "Jim? You don't think . . . I mean, MarySue is barely cold in her grave, if she's even in her grave yet. He couldn't possibly be . . ." The idea of dating Jim Jensen whether he was a wife-murderer or not made me a little nauseous.

"Of course not," she said soothingly. "I don't know why I said that. It's just that I can't help thinking about him. And wondering . . ."

"If he killed her?" I said.

She didn't say anything, just stared off in space for a long moment. Then she said, "I don't know if you heard Mary-Sue say that Jim would kill her if he found out she'd bought the shoes."

I nodded. "But people say things like that all the time."

"And sometimes they mean it."

"Should I tell the detective?"

"I don't know. I just don't know," Dolce said. "I do know withholding evidence is a crime."

I shivered, picturing myself in the county jail awaiting trial, missing my date . . . I had to tell the detective what I'd heard. It was just crazy not to. If Jim killed his wife, it was better to find out as soon as possible.

"Dolce, my doctor just called me."

"Is it bad news?" she asked, leaning down to grasp my hand, mistaking my trembling voice for fear instead of excitement.

"No, no, he asked me out on a date. Is that . . . I mean is that in violation of some kind of code? I don't know."

"I don't think so," she said, blinking rapidly. "Where else would doctors meet women if not in their clinics?"

"I thought maybe in med school."

She shook her head. "Too ingrown. Too incestuous. I would think they'd want to meet someone in another line of work."

"Like fashion?" I asked.

She smiled. "Exactly."

"Where are you going?" she asked.

"Café Henri on Sunday night."

She raised her well-shaped eyebrows. "We'll find you something spectacular to wear, understated but elegant, like the café."

Just as I was going to ask her what Peter Butinski had done with the shoes he'd brought, there was a knock on the door.

"Detective Wall to see Rita Jewel," he said.

I locked eyes with Dolce. I had a feeling she wanted to

tell me something or warn me not to say something to the detective. Whatever it was she wanted to communicate, it was too late. He was here. But Dolce knew me well enough to know I wasn't the type to blab.

Dolce opened the door with a smile and the kind of greeting she reserved for her best customers. Jack Wall looked like the type who'd shop at Dolce's if we had a men's section. I noticed, and I'm sure Dolce did too, that he was wearing a J.Crew Ludlow slim-cut suit. After all, fashion was our business and our passion. Even though J.Crew is an all-American brand, the suit had a definite Italian flavor. All that just to take me to a bucolic lunch, or was this his usual official business attire?

I grabbed my crutches and we walked out of the shop. There was a hush that fell over the crowd in the great room. I could just imagine them saying once I was out of sight, "Who's that with Rita?"

"Sorry to have to take you in a government-issued cop car," Jack Wall said as he opened the car door for me. "But this is official business."

"No problem," I said. At least I hoped there was no problem. It depended on what kind of official business this was going to be.

Before he got in the car, he took off his suit jacket, loosened his tie and rolled up his shirt sleeves. I tried not to stare, but I have a thing for muscular arms. "I hope you like eating outside."

"Of course," I said. "As long as there's room for me to prop up my ankle."

"I guarantee it." He drove his so-called cop car to the Embarcadero and stopped at Pier 39, where, fortunately, they had valet parking since the place is always crowded with tourists gawking at the spectacular views of the Alcatraz Island, the Golden Gate Bridge and the sparkling blue waters of San Francisco Bay. Since I'd pictured sitting on the lawn in a public park as befitted a policeman's picnic, this was a big and welcome surprise.

With his hand under my elbow, Detective Wall helped me climb the steps to the second floor of Neptune's Bounty Restaurant and out to the deck with a sweeping panorama, where he then asked for a table off to the side and out of earshot from the other customers.

"What a fabulous view," I said, dazzled by the sun shining on the Bay.

"San Francisco at its best," he said, pulling out a chair for me and taking my crutches. "I recommend the Hog Island oysters on the half shell, the crab cakes and the clam chowder."

"You've been here before?"

He nodded.

I didn't even look at the menu. Sometimes it's good to have someone else make the decisions. Like now. So I said, "Sounds good to me." They say there's no such thing as a free lunch. I knew there'd be a price to pay, but at the moment I didn't care. The sun on my back, my foot resting on the chair next to Jack Wall, the lapping of the waves against the pilings beneath the restaurant and a basket of freshly baked sourdough bread on the table added up to pure heaven. Then there was the suave detective across the table. Just a glance around the deck told me he was the best-looking man in the whole place by a long shot. I would have to remember every detail to tell Dolce.

"How long have you known Ms. Loren?" Jack Wall asked after he'd ordered the items he'd suggested along with a bottle of white wine. The San Francisco police drank on the job? Or wasn't he on the job? Or didn't he care? Or did he intend to abstain and get me to talk while under the influence. I told myself to be careful, but it was hard not to relax—the sun, the scene, the food, the undeniably good-looking man across the table. All calculated to make me loosen up and forget to be on my guard? Maybe, but I didn't care. At the moment I didn't want to be on my guard. I didn't care why he'd brought me here. This was the San Francisco I'd dreamed about back in Columbus. This was the kind of life I wanted. Lunch alfresco with a well-dressed professional man who hung on my every word. Why worry? What did I have to hide anyway?

For a moment when he mentioned Dolce, I thought he must be a mind reader. Then I got hold of myself, gave myself a mental shake and reminded myself this was an official interview even though it felt like a social occasion, which I knew it probably wasn't. Not for him. He probably took his informants out for expensive meals every other day to extract important information from them. No wonder he was so knowledgeable about the menu at this restaurant. I could see how it could work. I hadn't even had a sip of wine and I was ready to squeal. Most likely he was right now biding his time before he pinned me with the hard questions he had to ask. Anyone who spent this much time and money on lunch was not going to let me off the hook.

"I met Dolce some months ago," I said. "She's an old friend of my aunt, so I looked her up when I first came to town and she gave me a job."

"You had experience in the fashion field?" he asked as he poured some California Pinot Grigio into my glass.

"Not really. Columbus doesn't actually have a fashion field. But clothes and jewelry have always been my hobby.

I was working in an office, doing data processing. Unfortunately no one there appreciated my clothes sense. In fact, I got some pretty strange looks at the office sometimes. And even a few comments like 'Is it Halloween already?' So I jumped at the chance to leave."

Jack Wall glanced at my ribbed top. I hoped there was admiration in his glance, both for my fashion sense as well as my body. But maybe he was just trying to imagine how anything I wore could be considered bizarre or avant-garde in Columbus, Ohio. I had no idea what he really thought, which was probably why he was such a good detective.

"It wasn't until I arrived in California that I finally felt at home in my clothes, even though I was far from home, if you know what I mean," I continued. "I can't believe what people wear out here, I mean every day. Harem pants, watercolor prints, boho jewelry, cropped leather jackets, boots with shorts . . ." I could have gone on and on about how I sometimes felt like I'd landed in a fashion free-for-all wonderland, but maybe the detective wasn't as interested in the latest trends as I was. Who was besides Dolce? No one I knew.

Interested or not, he nodded politely. Anyone who dressed like he did would know exactly what I meant.

"Are you from around here?" I asked. If we kept talking about clothes and personal stuff, maybe he'd never force me to say anything I didn't want to. After all, hadn't we already had a conversation during which he pumped me for information right in my house? What more could I tell him? I took a sip of wine, enjoying the floral, smoky, honey-tinged flavor.

"Oregon," he said. "I've been here for almost ten years. I started a small software company in Silicon Valley, but after it took off I got bored and sold it. Then I went into law enforcement. It's a new challenge, and I like living and working in the city. Helping people for a change instead of selling them things they don't need."

"I like living here too," I said. I liked helping people too, but I was also guilty of selling them things they didn't need. I told myself that even if the customers didn't NEED a new camisole or a trendy fringed bag, they felt better after they bought it and just wearing something new gives a person a psychological lift. Our merchandise, while expensive, was cheaper than therapy, wasn't it? No wonder he could afford to dress like a dot-com millionaire: that's probably what he was before he became a cop. It seemed like an unusual background for a detective, but what did I know? I was from Ohio.

When the oysters came, they were briny and smelled fresh from the sea.

"We don't have these in Columbus," I said, dipping mine in hot sauce. In fact most of my old friends back in Ohio might have shuddered at the very thought of eating a bivalve, especially if it wasn't cooked. But I've always been a little different, willing to try something new and I was glad I was. Especially today. If I hadn't been willing to take a chance and move across the country to take a new job, where would I be today? I wouldn't be having lunch on a terrace with a hot cop in one of the world's most beautiful cities. Of course I wouldn't be worried about fending off murder accusations either, but you can't have it all, as Aunt Grace would say. So far it was worth the trade-off.

Instead of commenting on the availability of fresh seafood or something more appropriate, he went back to the subject of Dolce. I should have known it was coming.

"Do you have any idea where your boss was the night of the Benefit in the park?" Detective Wall asked.

I shifted my foot and straightened my shoulders. I sighed. I'd almost forgotten why we were here. This was not a date, no matter how much I pretended it was. I was only here to give or take away any alibi for my boss. Which made me wonder, was she really a suspect?

"Why don't you ask her?" I asked.

"I did. She said she was at home."

"Then she probably was. The last time I saw her that night was when we closed the shop. I left in a cab. I assume she was upstairs in her apartment."

When the waiter took away the oyster shells, Detective Wall took out his notepad and wrote something. "She hasn't been able to verify her whereabouts. Can you?"

"As you know, I was unconscious and in the hospital for most of the night. I didn't see her again until today. But she wasn't at the Benefit. I'm sure she wasn't. She couldn't have been. She doesn't do benefits. She dressed half the people there. She was exhausted. Besides, she didn't have a ticket. They were expensive."

"How would you describe the relationship between Ms. Loren and MarySue Jensen?"

"Fine until Saturday. Dolce gets along with everyone. She has to. She sells clothes and accessories. Everyone loves her. Just ask them. MarySue had ordered a pair of expensive shoes from Dolce. Dolce wanted MarySue to pay for the shoes on arrival, which is totally reasonable, but MarySue said she didn't have the money. MarySue was angry. She said she had to have the shoes. Dolce said no, but MarySue took them anyway. Naturally Dolce was upset. MarySue had put a deposit on the shoes but that's all. Now Dolce was out . . . I don't know how much money."

"So you took it upon yourself to retrieve the shoes, is that correct? Or did Ms. Loren ask you to do it?"

"No, in fact she definitely told me to forget about the shoes."

"Was that because she was dealing with the matter herself?"

"She said she'd called a repo company." I paused. "Is this about me or about Dolce or—"

"This is about the murder of MarySue Jensen," he said, pausing only when the waiter came with the crab cakes and offered me some spicy remoulade sauce.

"I realize that this is all about MarySue," I said, lowering my voice just in case the waiter was listening. "But I don't know how I can help you find her murderer." From out of the blue, I remembered what Dolce had said, that she'd get the shoes back from MarySue if she had to "hunt her down." But she hadn't really meant that, had she?

"Just answer my questions," he said, picking up his fork. As if it was the simplest thing in the world.

"I will if I can," I assured him. "But . . ."

"Back to the shoes," he said.

"It's all about the shoes, isn't it?" I said. "Speaking of shoes, our supplier, Peter Butinski, was in today."

"And?"

"I just thought you might want to talk to him. Ask him about the shoes. Any shoes. All shoes. Maybe he knows something we don't know. He's an odd one; something about him strikes me as not quite right."

Jack Wall jotted something down on his notepad. Was it Peter's name or was it my name with a question mark after it because he thought I was a little too eager to put the blame on someone else, anyone else but me and my boss? I stared at his notepad, wishing I had the X-ray vision of Superman. If only I'd had some practice reading upside-down.

"As for the shoes," he said, "any idea where they might be at this point in time?"

"At the park?" I asked brightly, hoping he'd get the impression I was being helpful.

"Possibly, since that's where they were last seen," he admitted. "Let's look at it this way. Who wanted the shoes, besides MarySue?"

I chewed my crab cake thoughtfully, trying to look like I was concentrating while I was savoring every bite. "Not Dolce. What good were they to her once they'd been worn? None at all. They were spoiled, used goods. But someone else might have seen them and wanted them—even worn, they were beautiful. It could have been anyone."

"Could it have been Ms. Jensen's sister-in-law?"

I shook my head. "Not her style."

He wrote something on his notepad.

"Her husband Jim?" he asked.

"Why would he want the shoes?"

"To return them?" he asked. "I understand he wasn't happy about her overspending at Dolce's."

"I guess it could have been him. But why didn't he just wait until she got home that night, take them from her closet and return them to Dolce's for a refund on Monday?"

"Would Dolce have given it to him?"

"Well, no, since MarySue never paid for them in full and they'd been worn, but he didn't know that." I bit my lip. "There is something strange. The night I went to get the shoes back, I saw a 'For Sale' sign in front of the Jensens' house. Today when I called the real estate agent, he said it had been taken off the market."

The detective raised his eyebrows and made a note of it.

"Do you think it means anything, Detective Wall?" I asked.

"Call me Jack," he said.

I nodded. "Well, Jack, maybe MarySue wanted to sell, but Jim didn't. So now he doesn't have to. Or . . ." I paused to get a breath. "I don't know if MarySue had life insurance, but if she did and Jim was the benefactor . . ."

"Ramirez is checking on that," he said. "You're thinking like a detective, Rita, which is good. It's all about motives, probability and opportunity."

Motives, probability and opportunity. If I'd had a notepad myself I would have written the words down so I could ponder them later. I knew they were important in the effort to find the killer, so I tried to burn them into my brain. I was flattered by Wall's words, but even better, I was glad to shift the emphasis away from Dolce to almost anyone else as long as it wasn't me. Even better, I was able to shift the emphasis to the clam chowder when it arrived, rich, creamy and chock-full of clams.

"What I'd like to do," he said, "is concentrate on those who were at the Benefit who had a motive to either steal the shoes or kill MarySue or both."

I agreed to concentrate, but I was getting tired of playing this game of who killed MarySue. It could have been Jim, it could have been Patti, her sister-in-law, or . . . "It could have been just about anybody but me, of course. Mary-Sue wasn't a lovable person," I said. "I don't even know how she died, how she was murdered, I mean."

"Her champagne was drugged," he said.

"Maybe it was an accident," I suggested. "Maybe the perpetrator, if that's what you call them, only meant to drug her but gave her an overdose. Would the charge still be murder?"

"Interesting thought—we'll let the jury decide that," he said.

I decided to stop making suggestions. The thought of a jury deliberating the case gave me the chills. What if the defendant on the stand was someone I knew? One of our customers? Someone I liked? If it was, I knew what she ought to wear. Something subdued, a suit that didn't cry out money. Nothing too fashionable. Something from last year's collection in a neutral color. Jewelry? Maybe a plain gold band on her finger. No diamonds. Unless it was just a pair of diamond studs in her ears. Hair? A tight chignon and no makeup unless it was just a light dusting of a pale powder.

Jack passed on the dessert and I did too, a little reluctantly, but he ordered café mochas, my favorite after-lunch drink, for both of us. I breathed a sigh of pure pleasure. If this guy weren't a cop, he'd be the perfect date. He anticipated my every wish, and he kept up a lively conversation. Too bad it was about murder, but then I was getting used to thinking, talking and speculating about MarySue's murder wherever I went.

The lunch was winding down, I hadn't given away any secrets that I knew about, and in a few minutes we'd be drinking espresso coffee laced with chocolate syrup, steamed milk and whipped cream. But when I glanced up, I was shocked to see Patti French at a table across the room.

"Oh my God," I said under my breath. "It's Patti, Mary-Sue's sister-in-law. Having lunch with some man. I don't think that's her husband, although . . ." I knew I'd vowed to stop speculating, but I couldn't help it. "What if she's having an affair? What if MarySue threatened to tell her brother about it, and Patti killed her and dumped her shoes in the duck pond? Or what if she's having an affair with Jim, and they killed MarySue so they could be together? She sees me. She's getting up and coming over here. Do you know her? Who shall I say you are?"

"I haven't met her yet. But I think it would be helpful if I did. Introduce me as Jack Wall."

"Good to see you, Patti," I said when she stopped at our

table. My gaze rapidly took in her Louis Vuitton blazer over
a silk halter wrap dress, both of which were top-of-the-line
and I knew had come from Dolce's.

"Rita, what are you doing here?" she asked, plainly surprised to see me out of the shop with what appeared to be
a date. "I heard you hurt your ankle."

"That's right, but I'm feeling better. Patti, this is Jack
Wall. Jack, Patti French."

Patti positively beamed at Jack. Sooner or later she was
going to find out he was not my date. He was the detective
on the MarySue case, and then what would she say? "Rita,
you should have told me"? But how could I? And why should
I? If she had something to hide, it was time to bring it out
into the open.

We exchanged a few more remarks before she said it was
good to see me.

Then I said, "Love your shoes," and she blushed. Why?
Because they cost an arm and a leg? Because she didn't get
them at Dolce's? Then she said, "Good-bye," and turned and
headed for the door before I could ask where she got them.
I watched her go, my eyes fastened on her feet as she walked
away in her silver Jimmy Choo sandals and a pair of striped
stockings I'd never seen before. Silver shoes seemed to be
the hot item this season. But then Patti and MarySue had
always been rivals. Anything one had, the other had to outdo
her. Was that what this was about?

Jack Wall was studying me over his coffee with narrowed
eyes. "Well?" he said. "You've made quite a case against Ms.
French."

"I shouldn't have said anything. I was just speculating. I
could be wrong," I said. "I probably am. I just got carried away
for a moment. Patti buys a lot from Dolce, like the whole out-

fit she was wearing just now, but not the shoes. I don't get it. We could have ordered them for her. Where did she get them?"

"Aren't there any other high-end shoe stores in town?"

"Of course, but none are as good as Dolce's. Take the infamous missing silver stilettos for example. Who else would send their assistant to Florida to pick them up for a customer but Dolce? And that's exactly what she did. You don't get service like that at Macy's."

"I'm not talking about a department store," Jack said. "I'm talking about other boutiques."

"Like Janice Powers's Glass Slipper?" Her shop was only a few blocks away from Dolce's, but it didn't have the same cache. "I suppose . . . But why go there when you've got Dolce?" That's what I had to find out. If I had to hobble over there to see what Janice had that Dolce didn't. I owed it to my boss.

A few minutes later we finished our coffee, my new friend Jack paid the bill with his credit card, and we went out to his car. He thanked me for my time, and I thanked him for the lunch. Did he get what he wanted? Did he learn anything he didn't know before? Did he take my harangue about Patti seriously? He didn't say. As for me I got a delicious lunch and a look at Patti's shoes. What now? I couldn't go back to Dolce's right away so I asked Jack to let me off at Janice's shoe shop.

"How will you get back?" he asked with a glance at my foot.

"I have my crutches," I said. "It won't hurt me to walk. In fact, my doctor wants me to get some exercise." I wasn't sure my doctor wanted me to hobble two blocks on my crutches, but I'd do anything to get a look at the shoes at the Glass Slipper. Dolce couldn't go there, that would be awkward, but Janice didn't know me, so I could stop by for a look at her inventory without setting off any alarm bells. If Dolce's customers were shoe shopping elsewhere, I had to find out why.

I didn't even have to go inside the store to see several Dolce regulars sitting in large comfy chairs sipping coffee and trying on shoes. In fact, I definitely did not want to go in and have them see me. Instead, I did a quick survey of the shoes in the window, then I headed back to Dolce's, keeping in mind the instructions that came with my crutches.

"Head held high," I told myself. "Shoulders back. Stomach and buttocks in." As I walked ever so slowly to the shop, I muttered, "Left crutch, right foot. Right crutch, left foot. Repeat." By the time I got up the steps at Dolce's, about half a lifetime later, my whole body was screaming in pain. I could barely manage a feeble smile for the few customers in the great room as I stumbled into Dolce's office and fell into her swivel chair.

I took a pain pill and laid my head on Dolce's desk and fell asleep. I dreamed that Patti French told me to butt out of the investigation of MarySue's death. When I refused, she threw a glass of champagne in my face. I woke up with a start completely confused. I had no idea what time it was or where I was until Dolce slowly opened the door and looked in on me with an anxious expression.

"How are you?" she asked.

"I don't know," I said. "I must have fallen asleep." I shook my head to erase the vision of Patti's angry face. Then I raised my head and looked at my stainless steel wide-band watch. "I can't believe it's five o'clock. What happened?"

"You fell asleep. I disconnected the phone. I was sick of hearing it ring anyway."

"Thanks," I said. Where else would your boss turn off the

phone in the middle of a busy afternoon so it wouldn't wake you up? I was so lucky to work here. It was more than a job. It was a way of life. It was a glimpse into a world I didn't really belong in. A world where a woman could be murdered for a pair of shoes she hadn't even paid for.

"What's this?" I asked, pointing to a package wrapped in brown paper.

"Your Romanian friend brought it for you. It's called *zama*, a native soup made of green beans, which is supposed to make you feel better. He said not to disturb you. How was your lunch?"

"Wonderful. We went to a great restaurant at Pier 39. Great food and a beautiful view."

"Let me see if I've got this right," Dolce said, leaning against her office door. "Last week you were complaining that you never met any men. That you had nothing to do on Saturday nights but watch old vampire movies by yourself. Then I sent you to Florida. You met this Romanian on the plane who has now cooked up some soup for you. When you got back, MarySue stole a pair of shoes from us. You were injured trying to retrieve them. You mysteriously ended up at the hospital where you met a doctor. MarySue was murdered. You met a detective. And now all three men are feeding you either their grandmother's *zama* or lunch overlooking the Bay or dinner at a posh bistro. Have I missed anything?"

I shook my head. It did sound pretty impressive and in some ways improbable. "I know it sounds like I'm some kind of socialite myself, but I'm not. I'm the new girl in town, that's all. You're right, something happened. Mary-Sue got killed and I got popular. Why? I don't know for sure. All I can say is that for now I'm having a great time and I owe it all to you, Dolce. If you hadn't sent me to pick up the shoes . . ."

"You don't owe me, you owe MarySue," Dolce said. "Don't forget she's the one who started this whole thing. Those were her shoes. That was her house. There's her husband and her sister-in-law. Everything goes back to Mary-Sue. She's not here anymore, so you have to enjoy life while you can, because no one knows how long it lasts. You deserve it. If I didn't know better, I'd think you killed Mary-Sue. Who else has benefited as much as you?"

"Good question," I said, leaning one arm on the desk and cupping my chin in my palm so I wouldn't end up facedown on the desk again. "If we knew the answer to who wanted MarySue dead, we could probably solve this murder without the help of the detective, his assistant or anybody. Who do you think did it?" I asked her.

"I'm not saying I know who did it, but isn't it obvious that Jim was not happy with her? Or Patti?" Dolce said.

I nodded. "I do have some bad news for you."

Dolce pulled up a folding chair and sat down, the better to receive bad news. There wasn't a sound from the showrooms. I assumed she'd closed up. She looked tired and so subdued, I hated to tell her what I'd seen at Janice Powers's shop.

"I stopped at the Glass Slipper on my way back from lunch."

"But that's two blocks from here. No wonder you had to take a nap."

"I was a wreck," I said. "My ankle was killing me, and I couldn't keep my eyes open."

"You should never have come to work today."

"But if I hadn't I wouldn't have had lunch at Pier 39 with the detective. I wouldn't have seen Patti French at lunch."

Dolce leaned forward. "How did she look?"

"She was wearing the wraparound dress and the blazer you sold her. A dynamite outfit."

Dolce nodded and smiled proudly. I wished she'd seen her too. Those are the moments we live for. "But here's the weird thing. She was wearing a pair of silver Jimmy Choo sandals with striped hose."

Dolce frowned. "I didn't sell her those."

"I know. Which is why I stopped at the Glass Slipper, and guess what I saw?"

"The shoes?"

I shook my head. "No. I saw several of your best customers."

"But . . . but why?" Dolce looked like she was going to cry. Her voice quavered and her eyes watered. I should never have told her, but she's usually so strong, so tough. I realized I'd gone too far.

"I don't know," I said. "The world has gone crazy. Why buy your clothes here and your shoes somewhere else when we've got the best selection of designer footwear anywhere. And if we don't have it, you know where to get it."

Dolce stood up, but she didn't look too steady on her feet.

"Of course it may be because word is out that one of your best customers was murdered and none of the Glass Slipper customers were. As soon as the case is solved, they'll all be back," I assured her with more assurance than I actually felt.

She didn't look assured. "I can't think about this now," she said. "I've had enough for one day. And you've got to go home and get some rest. But first check your messages. Your kung fu instructor called about your class. He wants to move you to a lower level on Thursday nights. I told him you had an accident and were on crutches."

"Thanks," I said. On the plus side, falling off a ladder was one way of getting out of class for at least a week. I used Dolce's pewter letter opener to open the sealed note from Nick that came with the soup. After I scanned it, I said, "Nick, the guy with the *zama* wants me to take his gymnastics class."

"But will it teach you to defend yourself like kung fu does? I'm worried, Rita. There's a murderer out there. First MarySue, who knows who's next?"

I couldn't believe my boss thought I was in danger. What did I have that someone would kill for? Of course I had a great shoe collection and a closet full of designer clothes, but nothing like any of our customers. I was happy with my wardrobe, but my clothes and shoes were last year's models or returns or on sale.

"Dolce, we don't even know if MarySue was killed for her shoes. I know she wasn't wearing them when they found her body, but they may still be in the park. She may have been killed for an entirely different reason. A personal reason like envy or revenge, jealousy, lust, fear, insanity or . . ."

"Rita, calm down," Dolce said, raising her hand. "Finding MarySue's killer is not our job. At the moment I'm more worried about my car. I'm supposed to stop at the repair shop to see if by some miracle they've been able to fix it. I'm afraid they just want to sell me a new car, which I can't afford." She looked at her watch, then she slung her Prada brown leather satchel over her shoulder and asked if I'd be all right if she took off.

"Go ahead," I said, sorry I'd gone off on a tangent like that. "I'll call a cab and lock up."

After Dolce left, I waited for at least a half hour for the cab while keeping my foot up on the desk as prescribed. Finally, I heard a knock on the big front door. I was just gathering my paraphernalia together when the knocking got louder and a man shouted, "Dolce, are you there? Let me in."

Even though it was probably just a last-minute customer, I was a little nervous. Dolce's words, "There's a murderer out there. Who knows who's next?" rang in my ears. And even though I'd been taking martial arts for the past three months, I was hardly in shape to defend myself from a determined killer.

But just in case, I slipped Dolce's letter opener into my pocket and went with my crutches to open the heavy solid-wood front door.

Seven

Jim Jensen stood on the threshold looking like he was out for blood. I knew it was him from the photo in the newspaper of him in his airline pilot uniform. His eyes were bloodshot and blazing, and his short-cropped hair was standing on end. His face was flushed, and it flashed on me instantly that he must be his wife's killer. He looked like a killer. Who else wanted the spendthrift MarySue out of his life more than he did? Had he been hiding outside until Dolce left, knowing I was alone inside? Was he waiting his chance to kill me next? Because he thought I was responsible for MarySue's murder? Or he thought I knew that he was the murderer? I tried to stay calm and focused, but my mind was spinning and my ankle was throbbing.

Subtly, carefully, I reached into my pocket and fingered the letter opener. "He'll kill me," MarySue had said. I was not going to let him strike again. Not without a struggle.

"I'm sorry," I said as calmly as I could while my heart was hammering. "We're closed for the day."

"Closed for the day or closed for good?" he asked.

I didn't know what to say. I laughed nervously. "Of course not," I said. "Dolce's is an institution. Part of the fabric of this neighborhood. The women of the city couldn't get along without us. We're here to stay."

"You think so? I don't think so. I think you'll be closed for good when I get through with you. You'll be sued for slander for starters."

"What?"

"You're Rita, aren't you?" Jim demanded.

A dozen different replies went through my mind.

No, I'm the cleaning lady. Or the temp. Or Dolce's niece.

But he didn't wait for my answer. "I know who you are." He pointed his finger at me. "You're the one who told the cops I killed my wife."

"No, no, of course not. You couldn't kill your wife. Why would you?"

Not surprisingly, he didn't answer. I didn't expect him to. I was just babbling, hoping to fill some time before I could escape.

He suddenly turned his back on me, barged into the hall and strode into the great room where he paced around a small antique chair that had belonged to Dolce's grandmother. I thought about making a break for it then and heading right out the front door. He looked dangerous and if he'd already killed MarySue, he wouldn't think twice about knocking me off too. But what chance would a cripple like me have with a determined murderer in pursuit? Curiosity got the better of me and I followed him. When he plopped into the antique chair, the legs creaked under his weight and I gasped. I thought *my* legs would collapse along with the chair legs, so I sat on a small tufted bench under the window, trying to catch my breath.

When I found my voice, I said, "Jim, you're upset. I don't blame you. MarySue has been gone for only a few days. I don't know who killed your wife. I certainly did not tell the police you killed your wife. I have no idea who did." *Unless it was you or Patti or some other customer who coveted her shoes.*

"Somebody told her it was me," he said grimly. "If it wasn't you, who was it? She came to my office and treated me like a common criminal. Do you know why?"

She? He must mean Detective Ramirez.

I shook my head. I was waiting to hear why.

"Insurance." He spat the word out like he could hardly get it out of his mouth fast enough. "They think I killed MarySue to collect the insurance on her. As if that would make up for my loss." He ran his hand through his close-cropped hair. "MarySue was the love of my life. Sure, we had our differences. Every married couple does. You know what I think? I think you killed her. Don't look so shocked. And don't think you'll get away with it. The police know everything. They know you came to my house that night to get the shoes back. Oh, yeah, she told me about that. She wouldn't give them to you, so you followed her to the park, didn't you? You waited your chance and you drugged her. Maybe you didn't mean to kill her. You just wanted to knock her out so you could take her shoes. You didn't need to take them. I would have paid you for them if you'd asked me. You didn't need to come after her like she was a common criminal. Now they're gone and they were all I had to remember her by." He buried his head in his hands and he started shaking all over. It even sounded like he was sobbing. Was he really upset or faking it for my benefit?

"But she said . . ."

"What?" he said, jumping up from his chair. "What did she say?"

She said you'd kill her. "I . . . I'm not sure," I stammered. "Something about being afraid of something. I can't remember."

"The only thing you need to remember is this: I'll get even with you, Rita. You can't pin my wife's murder on me and get away with it." He stood up and glared at me. "One more thing. You are not welcome at her funeral." Then he stomped out of the great room all the way to the front door, which he slammed behind him.

Suddenly the room was so quiet I could hear my heart pounding. What would happen next? Would Detective Ramirez come back to my house and arrest me based on Jim Jensen's crazy theories? Did Jim kill his wife or not? And if he didn't, why had he put the house up for sale and then taken it off the market? Also, if he didn't kill MarySue, who did?

All I had to remember her by. I grated my back teeth together. What crap. He had a closet full of clothes and shoes to remember MarySue by.

I heard my cab honk and I rushed out of the shop as fast as I could with my crutches and tote bag, locked the door behind me and collapsed in the backseat of the taxi.

As soon as I got home, I changed into a pair of jeans I had ripped and distressed myself with bleach, a piece of chalk and a penknife, and heated the *zama* for dinner. Fear and anxiety made me extra hungry, so even after that large lunch I was glad to have a ready-made green bean and chicken Romanian stew on hand. When I finished eating, I called Nick to thank him, but the receptionist at the gymnastics school said he was teaching a trampoline class, so I left a message. Then I put in a call to Detective Wall to tell him about Jim Jensen. I didn't want him to think I was a whiny crybaby afraid of my own shadow, but I did think he should know Jim had threatened me. "I'll get even with you," he'd said. And I believed him.

I got the detective's voice mail, so I left a brief message. I was just getting into bed in my organic knit pajamas that are as soft as an old T-shirt but more stylish, when Jack Wall called me back.

"Ms. Jewel," he said. "What's this about Jim Jensen?"

"It's probably nothing, but I thought you should know. He came to the shop after we'd closed today and said he'd had a visit from the police. He thought I told you he killed his wife. Naturally he was angry. He said he'd get even with me."

"I'm sorry about this," he said. "Detective Ramirez should have warned you he was on the warpath."

"Maybe she shouldn't have told him I'd fingered him. Or yes, she should have warned me. I was alone in the shop when he barged in. Maybe he's harmless, maybe not. All I can say is that I was scared." I certainly wouldn't mind if Detective Ramirez got in trouble for sending Jim Jensen on the warpath. At first I was willing to give her the benefit of a doubt, but I didn't think she deserved it. "Maybe your associate Ramirez wanted to scare me into confessing. Maybe she still thinks I killed MarySue."

"Of course not," Jack Wall assured me. "No one thinks that anymore. Except Jim Jensen."

"But why? What possible motive would I have? I barely knew her. Sure, I wanted her to pay Dolce for the shoes, but her being dead wasn't going to help matters. Another thing which I didn't have a chance to tell Jim Jensen is that I wasn't even there that night. Whoever killed her was at the Benefit. Do you have a guest list?"

"Yes, I do," he said. "It will take time, but we are questioning all the guests."

"Good," I said. "Although that's a lot of work and a waste of time if it was Jim all along. Any word on MarySue's life insurance as to who's the beneficiary?"

"As a matter of fact, we do have some information on that. Jim Jensen is the beneficiary. Don't jump to any conclusions," he cautioned. "Most married couples work it that way."

"But still, isn't that a good motive?" I asked eagerly. I'd love to see Jim behind bars and this whole mess put behind us.

"It could be," he said.

"How much will he get?" I asked.

"I'm afraid I can't disclose that information."

"Enough to hold onto his house, I assume."

"You are free to assume what you like, Rita," he said. At least he called me Rita as if we were friends. "Now tell me, do you still feel threatened? Do you want me to send over some police protection?"

I pictured a cop sitting in his marked car in front of my house, scaring all the neighbors.

"No, I'm okay." I hoped to get a little respect for bravery anyway. But who knew? Jack Wall was the type to keep his thoughts to himself.

"Next time Jim pays you a visit like that, give me a call right away. Or if you see anything suspicious. In the meantime, I have some pictures of Benefit guests you might know. I'd like your help in identifying them. I'll give you a call sometime this week."

I said good-bye and picked up my vampire book to soothe myself before turning out the light. The Gothic setting, the suspicious actions of the female vampire and her almost lifelike qualities were gripping but not soothing. I tossed and turned thinking about Detective Jack Wall. Then I got up and looked out my bedroom window. There on the street below a police car made its way slowly down the block,

pausing in front of my house before it drove on. A patrol car
sent to watch me? Or just a cop making his rounds? The
whole neighborhood was eerily quiet. I went back to bed
and pulled the covers over my head. But I couldn't sleep. I
felt empty inside even after a big bowl of *zama*. I needed
something to calm my nerves and my stomach. Something
all-American and non-Romanian. Unfortunately I'm not
much of a cook. But fortunately for me my next-door neighbor Mrs. Heldmyer had given me a jar of her homemade
pickles and I knew I had a loaf of whole-grain bread in the
freezer and a wedge of Vermont white sharp cheddar cheese
I'd picked up at Whole Foods. I wrapped up in a fleece robe,
went to the kitchen and made myself a grilled cheese sandwich with pickles in my countertop toaster oven. The combination of salty, sour pickles with the rich cheese and
crisply toasted bread was delicious. Warm inside and out, I
went back to bed and finally fell asleep.

The next few days were comparatively calm at the shop.
When I told Dolce about Jim Jensen threatening me, she
was horrified. She said we should hire a security guard, but
I decided if Jim didn't kill MarySue, then he was so overcome with grief that he was acting out his depression by
lashing out at me and probably felt remorseful by now. I'd
already told Detective Wall what I thought of Jim and his
rage. And Ramirez was apparently on his case. Although I
had a feeling she would prefer to implicate me and wouldn't
mind all that much if Jim attacked me either verbally or
physically. I knew I wasn't being fair. After all, Jim had just
lost his wife and wasn't himself. Anger is surely one of the
seven stages of grief. I wasn't sure what he was like before
the murder, but I wasn't all that fond of him now.

On Wednesday, I had my follow-up medical appointment.
The good news was that it seemed neither Nurse Chasseure

or Nurse Bijou were on duty at the hospital that day. They must still be working nights. Even better news was that Verity, the nurse practitioner who saw me, said my ankle was healing beautifully.

"Can I wear high heels by Sunday?" I asked, thinking of my date with Dr. Jonathan.

She shook her head. "Don't even think about it."

"Not even three inch?"

"Why? Big date?" she asked with a smile.

I nodded. But refrained from mentioning with whom.

"Not a good idea. Your ankle is still weak. I'd hate to see you take a tumble. Stick to flats. What about a simple Kenneth Cole in cracked leather?"

"Hmmm." I had to admit it was a fresh idea and not a bad one.

"Metallics are in this fall. When your ankle heals, you can pick up a pair of silver heels that are perfect for a fun night out or even work."

I felt a shiver go up my spine at the thought of the silver shoes and what they could lead to. I took a deep breath and continued. "The problem is, I don't have an outfit yet."

"What's the occasion?" she asked, turning from her computer screen where she was updating my file to study my work ensemble—a striped jacket, a spotted skirt and a flowered shirt. I could tell by her expression she was well aware that mixed prints were definitely in and similar-patterned outfits were out.

"Just a dinner date," I said offhandedly. I didn't want anyone at the clinic to find out I had a date with Dr. Jonathan. For all I knew, he was dating all the nurses at the hospital at the same time. Although if he was, why not take one of them to the café? "It's Sunday, so I don't want to go overboard and be overdressed."

"If I were you, I'd go with a filmy skirt. I don't know about you, but I'm so tired of stiff structured dresses."

"I couldn't agree more," I said. "Filmy it is. What do you think of the long look?"

"I like it, as long as you don't look like you just stepped out of *Little House on the Prairie*. You'd have to make it modern with bold jewelry and a narrow shirt or a casual stretchy top."

"And flats?" I had to be sure she was getting the same picture I was. "Are you sure?"

She stared at me for a long moment, then she nodded. "If it weren't for your sprain, I'd tell you to wear an ankle-strap sandal with . . . I don't know . . . maybe a peekaboo toe. That would be stunning. But I'm a nurse, not a fashion consultant," she said with a rueful smile.

"It's funny you should say that," I said. "I *am* a fashion consultant. I work at a boutique in Hayes Valley."

"It's not Dolce's, is it?"

Surprised, I asked, "Have you been there?"

"They have the most fabulous stuff. But it's so expensive. You probably get a big discount."

I nodded. "It's a great place to work. Usually," I added, thinking of MarySue stealing the silver shoes and my run-in with her husband.

"I love what you're wearing right now," she said. "It's so out there."

"Thank you." How often does a nurse notice what the patient is wearing? I noticed that under her white lab coat Verity was wearing a tunic and a pair of chic black leggings. I wanted to ask where she got them but thought that maybe it wasn't polite under the circumstances. What I did say was, "I love your braids. They're so Mary Kate." It was true. Her blond braids were wound tight at the crown and slightly loose at the side with tendrils to soften the look. "I wish I had long enough hair for braids."

"They're not real," she said. "They're extensions."

"I couldn't tell."

There was a knock on the door, and someone said her next patient was waiting in the next room.

"Good luck," she said as she left the room. "Stay off the ankle and I hope you have a great time Sunday."

I didn't mention that I couldn't stay off my ankle if I was going to a funeral that afternoon. Just mentioning a funeral seemed like a downer, and I didn't want to explain how and why and who died.

Dolce and I closed the shop at two and hung a sign in the window, "Closed for the Jensen Funeral." I didn't tell Dolce that Jim had warned me not to show up. What was he going to do when he saw me there? Toss me out? Dolce had enough to worry about without thinking about my confrontation with Jim.

She drove us in her rented Mercedes to the funeral parlor in the town of Colma, which advertises itself as the town with "fifteen hundred people above ground and one point million underground." It is truly the cemetery capital of California, maybe the whole world.

We were nervous about viewing MarySue in her open coffin, not knowing what she'd be wearing. Everyone would assume we'd dressed her, but we hadn't even been asked for our suggestions. That hurt. We should have been consulted. Under normal circumstances, we would have been. But these circumstances were definitely not normal.

"The coffin is stunning," Peter Butinski said when we ran into him just inside the viewing area. "It's a handmade mahogany box with a silk embroidered lining. Nothing but the best for MarySue as usual."

"I didn't know you knew her," Dolce said.

"You didn't? I know everyone in town and everyone knows me. Everyone who cares about footwear, that is."

"So is she wearing anything on her feet?" I asked.

Peter shook his head. "Not that I know of. I would hope I would know if she was. After all. You two will notice her outfit." He covered his mouth as if to hide a smile or a sneer. "I'm anxious to hear what you think of it."

"Who dressed her?" Dolce asked. "It wasn't us."

"You don't have to tell me," he said. "Who do you think did?"

"Was it Patti?" I guessed. "Or Jim?"

"I don't know," he said. "But it's too late now."

"Too late for what?" I asked Dolce in a sotto voce as we approached the coffin.

"Too late to change her clothes, I guess."

I couldn't remember ever seeing a dead person before, so I didn't know what to expect. What Dolce and I both expected was that she'd be wearing something from the shop. Or at least something suitable for a woman who cared deeply about fashion. Unless Jim was so angry with us and with his wife that he'd deliberately chosen something else.

Whoever picked out her outfit did so to shock us—and not just us. Dolce and I stood staring at the pin-striped suede and denim jacket she was wearing. Something you might wear to hang out with your BFF on Friday night, barhopping in the Mission. But not to your funeral. Since we could see only the top half of her body, we had no way of knowing what else she was wearing. Hopefully a pair of slouchy trousers with a low waistline, which would either offset the jacket or make a strong statement like "I'm dead and I'll wear whatever I want."

"Is it Tory Burch?" I muttered to Dolce.

"Or Agatha?" she asked.

I was just as eager as Dolce to identify the designer of her jacket. I stifled a desire to try to find the label under her collar. I have to say I was more than a little surprised to see something like this obviously one-of-a-kind item, but not disappointed. It was a bold choice, not what I would have chosen, but it wasn't my funeral. I could only hope it was what MarySue would have appreciated. After all, it was her last chance to make a splash. To show everyone she was a fashion original. To start a buzz before she was laid to rest.

On the whole she looked good. Her face was skillfully made up. Not overdone, just the right amount of foundation and blush. She was wearing a matte red lipstick, and her brows were artfully defined. Whoever was responsible should be congratulated. Her hair was swept into a soft, feminine updo, which had been gently and stylishly disheveled by someone's skillful fingers. Marsha's?

An ordinary person might have worn something in all-season wool jersey to her own funeral seeing as it was a transitional time between summer and fall. But MarySue had never been ordinary as much as Patti or Jim wanted her to be.

"Where did she get that jacket?" I whispered to Dolce.

"No idea," she muttered. "Why didn't she wear the Juicy Couture cashmere top she liked so much?" I could tell Dolce was upset that MarySue wasn't wearing one of the many outfits she'd bought at our boutique. Any of which would have been more appropriate than this jacket. "Or her black Alexander McQueen cape? Now that would have stood out from all the other bodies. It would have said, 'I'm not afraid to be myself. I can make a statement.'"

"Dead or alive," I murmured. "I was hoping to see her in something understated. Or what about the black Versace gown she bought for the Spring Gala?"

Dolce shook her head. "Not really funereal, Rita, but it would have been better than what she's wearing. Anything would. I just don't get it," she said sadly.

"It's because she didn't get to choose her clothes," I said out of the corner of my mouth. I just wondered who did. "I heard the Jackson family all wore Versace to Michael's funeral. Too bad the Jensens didn't coordinate their clothes that way. In honor of MarySue who would certainly have appreciated it." I surveyed the room. Jim Jensen was surrounded by friends. He looked properly serious. What did he think of the denim jacket? Was he the one who chose it as a rebuke to his wife for overspending on her wardrobe? I wouldn't put it past him. I only hoped he wouldn't explode with anger when he saw me. I planned to sit in the back row where I wouldn't be noticeable. "Maybe it was Patti," I suggested. Knowing that the two weren't close, I would suspect Patti of choosing something totally off the wall for her sister-in-law.

"Which reminds me, what happens to all MarySue's clothes?" I asked as we moved away from the open coffin toward the far wall.

"Good question. Wouldn't it be nice if Jim would donate them to a women's shelter?"

"I would suggest it if Jim didn't hate me," I said.

"Dolce," someone said, "how lovely to see you."

Dolce turned to greet a woman I didn't know, and I was left standing by myself. I took the opportunity to admire the banks of flowers which filled one side of the room. Huge bouquets like one with mixed roses and chrysanthemums all in yellow. Another was shaped like a heart made of red tulips. Tulips at this time of year? That must have cost a bundle. In the corner I saw the one Dolce had sent. It was small but lovely, made of peach-colored roses, pink carnations and gerbera daisies. Very simple but beautiful. I went over to smell the roses and read the card which said, "Deepest Sympathy to the Jensen family from Dolce and Rita." Dolce hadn't asked me to contribute so I was grateful to her for putting my name on it. The other cards had sentiments like—"MISSING YOU." "GODSPEED ON YOUR JOURNEY." "IN LOVING MEMORY."

Surveying the crowd I couldn't help thinking that the murderer was here. Isn't it true that most murders are committed by someone close to the victim, someone she knew very well? Of course, it could have been a random act of greed. Some stranger coveted her silver shoes and saw an opportunity to poison MarySue and seize them. But I didn't buy that theory. I'd bet my new black shearling ankle boots the killer was here in this room. I wasn't frightened. Who would kill again at his last victim's funeral? It just wasn't done. Not even in the movies or on HBO. I was just on edge, with a heightened sense of awareness of everyone and everything around me.

Every remark spoken by one of the mourners seemed amplified. No matter how banal or insensitive.

I heard someone say, "It was a blessing." As if MarySue had been suffering some fatal disease. Maybe she was because I overheard someone else say, "At least she's no longer suffering." People were going up to Jim and saying things like, "You should stay busy to take your mind off your loss," and "God never gives anyone more than he can handle." I moved away but not before I heard someone tell Jim, "I know just how you feel."

How did he feel? Angry? Yes. Relieved? Maybe. Nervous? Yes. Guilty? That depended on what he did besides yell at MarySue for her overspending.

I noticed Detective Wall was standing at the back of the room. I imagined he knew that axiom about killers finding their victims on familiar ground. How many husbands have murdered their unfaithful or nagging wives? How many children have murdered their critical, overbearing parents? Doesn't everyone know the story of Lizzie Borden who "gave her mother forty whacks and when she saw what she had done, she gave her father forty-one"?

I once read that killers often take a trophy from their victim. Like a pair of shoes. Which illustrates their need for self-magnification. I wanted to share these nuggets of insight with my favorite detective, but he'd warned me off, so I kept my distance. His loss. He'd have to find the murderer on his own.

I'd expected him to be wearing dark glasses to hide behind, but then he would have stood out and not in a good way. Instead he was wearing a conservative Calvin Klein single-breasted dark suit with plain-front trousers. With it a blue shirt with French cuffs and a striped old-school tie. He didn't look like a cop. Not today. Not ever really. He looked like he could be anybody, an old friend of Jim, or a cousin of MarySue. Anybody but the cop who was looking for MarySue's killer. I watched him watch everyone else. Trying to see who he was looking at.

Finally he looked straight at me. I took that as a sign not that I was a suspect, but that it was okay to go up and speak to him.

"I hope I'm not blowing your cover by speaking to you," I said, glancing around to be sure no one was near enough to hear me.

"You're actually giving me cover." He gave me a head-to-heels look, and I was glad I'd worn a black dress by a British designer with long sleeves and a jewel neckline. Just to be clear, it was the black dress that had the long sleeves and jewel neckline, not the British designer. It was flattering and still didn't shout "Look at me!" when the attention should rightfully be on the deceased. If I were somewhere besides a funeral and had two good ankles, I would have worn a pair of chunky heels and a leather jacket with it. Jack's gaze finally landed on my Paul Mayer black-lace ballet flats.

"Nice shoes," he said. Trust Jack to appreciate fine quality and styling.

"I can't wear anything with heels yet because of my accident. Thanks for noticing."

"I notice everything. It's my job."

"Then you already noticed the place is full of suspects. That's why you're here."

He didn't say anything. That was how I knew I was right. When I wasn't, he let me know. When the music started, it was a sign for everyone to take a seat. I went to the back row and looked around to see whether someone was actually playing the Chopin Piano Sonata or it was a recording. Jack came and sat next to me. I didn't see a piano, and I didn't see Dolce. Maybe she was sitting up in front with her friend.

Following the Chopin was the funeral march theme from Beethoven's Third Symphony. I must have looked surprised because Jack turned and whispered in my ear, "What's wrong? MarySue didn't like Beethoven?"

I shrugged. How would I know? But ask me about her taste in shoes and I could write a book. "What would you choose?" I asked under my breath.

"Some Dixieland jazz would be nice. And a parade through the streets."

I smiled at the image in my mind. Detective Jack Wall's coffin being carried through the streets of his beat by his parolees, with gangsters, pimps and drug addicts standing on the curb cheering or weeping as he passed by.

" 'When the Saints Go Marching In' . . . 'Didn't He Ramble' . . . 'Down By the Riverside' . . . You mean like those?"

He nodded. The recorded music continued. Mourners continued to file in.

"What about you?" Jack asked.

"I've always liked Barber's Adagio for Strings," I said, my eyes following the women who walked past in their little black dresses and the men in their dark suits. It was too bad someone didn't show some imagination. I didn't, but I didn't want to stand out. MarySue sure wanted to stand out. Had she had a premonition of her upcoming demise and ordered a jacket for this very occasion? Not likely.

"I think for me I'd choose something more upbeat," I said.

"What, like a barbershop quartet singing 'My Wild Irish Rose'?" he asked.

I pictured straw hats and bow ties, and I knew that wasn't really me. "I'm not Irish. So no quartet. I don't know. I just don't want my funeral to be a downer."

"Since you're planning ahead, you probably know what you'd wear," he said.

"To my funeral? Hmmm. Not really. I've never thought about it before."

"Neither did MarySue," he said soberly.

I nodded. She sure didn't. "Well, I might want to wear something different. Black is so obvious. What if I wore something sparkly, just to give everyone a lift? Put a smile on their faces? I'd want them to say, 'Isn't that just like Rita to wear sequins to her own funeral?' I'd want some festive earrings and a bracelet too. I'm actually more worried about drawing a crowd. I'm not MarySue. I'm new in town. What if no one comes?"

A woman sitting in front of us turned around to stare at

the latecomers straggling in. "I know one thing," I said softly. "You won't have to worry about attendance at your funeral. Cops always make a big deal when one of their own dies. Or is that only in the line of duty?"

He shrugged as if he didn't know.

"For a cop like you there will be a motorcycle parade, bagpipes playing taps, the whole thing," I said. "You don't get a choice."

"Maybe I'll die in my sleep, and I can skip the parade of escorts and the flyby," he said. "But I do want the jazz music."

"Live band?"

"Yeah, definitely. Saint Gabriel's Celestial Brass Band if they're not busy." He paused and squinted. "Who's the guy in the black sneakers and silk T-shirt?"

I didn't even need to look. "Peter Butinski."

"Why is he leaning over the coffin? Looks like he's crying."

"He's our shoe supplier."

"I'd like to have a talk with him."

"He'll freak out."

"I'm used to that."

"Don't tell me. It's part of your job."

"You know too much about me," he said wryly.

"One thing I know for sure. The guy is guilty of stealing our *Vogue* magazine and I want it back."

Finally the music stopped. A man in a nondenominational clerical collar stood and welcomed us. He gave a brief history of MarySue's life, her family, her background and her accomplishments, like being president of her neighborhood garden club. How fitting that she was killed in a park, I thought. Or was "ironic" the word I was looking for?

Next Jim stood and read a poem called "Life is Not a Destination, It's a Stopping Place on the Way to Heaven." I wasn't sure if he'd written it himself, but I hoped the sentiment was comforting to him and everyone else who missed MarySue. When he finished, he looked straight at me as if to dare me to accost him or deny that MarySue was in heaven. I didn't. I hoped I'd never see him again after today. Why should I? Unless he came by to pay for MarySue's shoes.

The next speaker said she was MarySue's sister, and she did bear a resemblance to our former customer. Being around the same size as her sister, maybe she'd inherit Mary-Sue's wardrobe. I hoped all those expensive clothes would get some use. Although I would have liked to see the home-less shelter get a donation of designer wear. Her sister read a poem called "Play Jolly Music at My Funeral." The poet wanted Dixieland music played—songs by Scott Joplin and Fats Waller.

I nudged Jack with my elbow and he nodded. He wasn't the only one who wanted happy music at his funeral. But did MarySue? I couldn't believe she really expected to die at such a young age. Was she thirty-five, forty? I didn't know and no one said.

For some reason the idea of playing happy music at a sad occasion made people tear up. Not me of course, but I could hear women sniffling and men blowing their noses into their monogrammed handkerchiefs. The final speaker was Har-lan, MarySue's brother and Patti's husband who rambled on about their idyllic childhood in the upscale East Bay town of Piedmont where the siblings spent happy summers taking golf and tennis lessons at their country club. When the cleric or emcee or whoever he was took over the microphone again, I assumed the ceremony was almost over. Well, the ceremony might have been over, but the excitement wasn't. Just then, the double doors behind us opened and a gust of wind blew through the room. I turned to see who had arrived so late he'd almost missed the funeral. It was a man in a fur hat and an orange robe holding a small brass bell in his hand. A hush fell over the room. Every eye was on the stranger. Some were thinking, isn't it too early in the season for fur? Others may have been wondering how he was connected to the Jensen family? Someone Jim knew through the airline he worked for? MarySue's yoga instructor? Jim's long-lost uncle? An old friend from a Sierra Club trip to the Himalayas the Jensens did years ago?

"Isn't that a shaman?" I whispered to Jack. I'd seen pictures of one once in a fashion magazine, what else? What was a shaman doing at MarySue's funeral?

Eight

The shaman—if he was indeed a shaman—rang his bell and began to dance his way to the front of the room. The cleric left his post in a big hurry and sat down to watch, whereas Jim stood up and stared, his mouth hanging open. Clearly this was no old friend or relation. As far as Jim knew, he was an unexpected guest. When the shaman reached the podium, he began to speak in a strange language. The only words we understood were "MarySue" and "death." So he was in the right place. No use pretending he'd gotten lost on his way to a Tibetan ceremony.

"Was MarySue a believer?" Jack asked me in an undertone.

"Not that I knew of," I whispered. "Jim doesn't look too happy about this, does he?"

Jack shook his head. Even from the back row I could see Jim's face was ashen and sweat was pouring from his forehead. He kept opening his mouth as if to speak, but no words came out. The only sound was the ringing of the shaman's bell.

As we all watched, Jim approached the shaman, reached out to touch him or take the bell, I have no idea. What I do know is that Jim clutched his chest and collapsed on the floor. After that there was pandemonium.

"Call 911," someone shouted. Others including Jack, raced up to surround Jim.

The funeral director in the black suit told everyone to leave the premises except for the immediate family. There was a rush for the doors, but I found Dolce.

"What happened?" I asked her as we walked slowly to the parking lot.

"My best guess?" she said. "A heart attack."

"He must have been overcome with grief or guilt or emotion," I said.

"Who was that strange man in the orange robe?" Dolce asked when we got into her car.

"My best guess? He's a shaman. A kind of holy man. A healer."

"What was he doing there? Obviously Jim didn't invite him."

"I think he came to escort MarySue to the afterlife," I said.

"Do you really believe that?" Dolce asked as she started the car and drove toward the exit. Before I could answer, an ambulance raced into the parking lot, sirens screaming. We watched the EMTs jump out and enter the building. Then we left. There was nothing more to be done.

"It's just possible," I said, following up on her question.

"I don't know what to believe," Dolce said.

"So no post-funeral celebration of MarySue's life today," I said as we drove past Portnoy's Tavern, the place Jim had planned to have the party. "I wonder if Jim will make it."

Dolce drove slowly down the street. "He looked awful," she said.

We drove in silence for a few minutes. My mind was spinning. Finally I said, "If the shaman is really a healer, why didn't he show up a little sooner like last week? If he cared about MarySue enough to come to her funeral and escort her to wherever she's going, why did he let her die in the Adirondack chair?"

"So if these shaman have certain powers, maybe he'll at least save Jim's life," she said.

"Maybe he will. I would have liked to ask him if he's the one who saved me when I fell into that oak tree. How else did I survive with just a sprained ankle and a minor concussion?"

Dolce looked at me as if I'd had another concussion because the thought of being rescued by a shaman was as alien to her as it would be to everyone at the funeral. I couldn't help hoping MarySue would have an escort to somewhere after what she did for me. Yes, she'd shoved me off the ladder, but then she'd taken me to the hospital— otherwise, I might be lying lifeless under her tree still today.

Later that week we heard Jim did indeed have a minor heart attack but he was "resting comfortably" as they say, in the hospital. Patti called Dolce to tell her that the shaman had paid Jim a hospital visit and assured him he'd live to see many more days. The holy man then confided he'd been invited to the funeral by MarySue's cousin Beth who had spent time at his ashram in Tibet. Patti agreed with Dolce that maybe Jim should have been told about the shaman ahead of time. Patti then assured Dolce the celebration of life at MarySue's favorite spot was still happening. Just as soon as Jim's doctors gave him the okay. In fact, the event along with the shaman's blessing had given Jim something to think about while in his hospital bed as well as an incentive to get well soon.

Around noon on Saturday when the crowd in the

boutique had thinned out a little, Dolce suggested we work on a new outfit for me. Our customers often took a shopping break at a café across the street where they could have a house-baked pastry, a lovely sandwich on seven-grain bread or homemade soup, all on the outdoor covered patio. Instead of us taking a lunch break, she and I went through the racks of late arrivals.

"We have to find something for your Sunday night date," she said.

"I was thinking of a filmy skirt," I told Dolce. "With a knit top." I didn't mention the idea came from my nurse practitioner.

"I like it," she said. "Relaxed elegance is what we're after." I was glad to see her so energetic and enthusiastic. Ever since MarySue's funeral, she'd not been herself. I wasn't sure if it was a lack of customers and sales or what. She spent more time in her office hunched over her computer, piles of bills on her desk, her brow furrowed. I was afraid to ask how bad the financial situation was.

She went to a rack of skirts and pulled out several for me to try. First was a bright floral print.

"It's vibrant and eye-catching," I said, blinking rapidly, "but . . ."

"A little too vibrant," she said, reading my mind like a true fashion consultant would. "Absolutely right." She immediately whisked the skirt back on the rack. Next up: a long skirt in creamy cognac. She held it up to my waist and stood staring at it before she snatched it away.

"Too utilitarian," she decided. I had to agree. Not just because she was my boss, but the skirt just didn't do anything for me. Finally we settled on a gray silk number with splashes of crimson handkerchief panels. I liked the way it swooshed around my calves. With a tight gray sleeveless sweater for balance against the gauzy skirt, I finally felt good about my selection. So did Dolce. She sat back on the padded bench in the middle of the room and looked me up and down.

"Ah, to be young again," she said. "I had a skirt like that once. I wore it to a wedding." She gazed off in the distance lost in her memory. What would I be doing at her age, I wondered. Would I be living alone above a shop somewhere, dressing others for parties and concerts I wasn't invited to? Would I stay home and worry about my customers not paying their bills? Or would I marry a doctor, a gymnast or a police detective, retire and join the ladies who lunch and shop? I was too goal oriented to while away my days that way. Maybe I could do volunteer work feeding the poor like Detective Wall did. Or maybe I'd have a few children. I'd send them to an alternate school where they'd learn cooperation instead of competition. They'd be artistic and imaginative instead of driven by money and financial success. Since living the good life in San Francisco can be expensive, maybe a jolt of ambition was not altogether a bad thing. I pictured myself dressing the little darlings up and taking them to brunch on Sunday to the Garden Court of the Palace Hotel where they'd behave perfectly and display good manners.

I was still daydreaming when Dolce jerked me back to the present where although I was well dressed, I was still relatively poor and definitely single. She reminded me I was not completely dressed for Sunday. Not yet. "All you need is a tailored blazer and you're good to go."

"I have a few of those," I said. Actually I had about ten in different colors and fabrics. "But what about shoes?"

"I guess you're not ready for a pair of sling backs." She looked at my bare feet and my still slightly swollen ankle.

"Or I have a low-heeled Chloé sandal that would be perfect with that skirt."

"Afraid not," I said sadly. "I can't wear any kind of heel yet, even a low one. Doctor's orders."

"I know!" she said and dashed off to the shoe department in the small alcove next to the accessories. She came back with a flat Alexandre Birman sandal. I knew how expensive they were, but Dolce told me not to worry. She could discount them seeing as they were from last spring's collection. They fit perfectly, and even though they were decidedly functional, they were stylish too.

"Now," Dolce said, "you'll need to have your hair done along with a pedicure and manicure. What about Harrington's sister Marsha? Isn't she a stylist at the Bella Noche in North Beach?"

"But it's Saturday, she'll be booked, won't she?" She'd also be expensive. Nervous about so many purchases, I was thinking of stopping at one of those discount places on my way home for a blow-dry.

"I'll give her a call. And don't worry about the cost. It's my present to you."

My eyes filled with grateful tears. "Dolce, how can I thank you?" I was truly touched but also worried. Sales were down, I knew that. Could Dolce really afford to be so generous? It worried me she hadn't had her car repaired or just bought a new one.

She brushed her hands together as if it was all in a day's work and she had no cares to keep her awake at night. "It's my pleasure," she said. "I couldn't be happier about these opportunities you're having if you were my own daughter. So let me indulge myself. It's what my great-aunt, Lauren, did for me when I was your age. I wish she could be here now." Dolce paused and looked around the shop. I swear she too had tears in her eyes. Would her great-aunt be pleased with what she'd done with her house? Or would she have wanted it kept completely the way she left it? What would she say if she knew her great niece was involved in a murder case? What would she say if she knew a customer had stiffed Dolce? Not to mention the loss of her car.

"Just remember all the details. Tell me everything. The food, the music, the atmosphere. The other diners. And your date of course. Now I'm going to get you an appointment with Marsha or someone."

It turned out she did get me an appointment with Harrington's sister. Why she was available on a busy Saturday afternoon I have no idea. I hoped it wasn't because she wasn't any good.

The salon was in trendy Noe Valley, not North Beach, and of course Dolce insisted I take a cab and take the rest of the day off. The minute I stepped inside Bella Noche, I felt a sense of peace and tranquility. It might have been the sand-colored hardwood floors and matching walls that made me feel like I was spending a day at the beach. Or maybe it was the New Age music coming from everywhere and nowhere. I didn't see Marsha at first. Her assistant gave me a cup of comforting herbal tea, then a stress-relieving scalp massage that left me as limp as a wet noodle.

I was so relaxed I forgot completely about MarySue, Jim Jensen or anyone connected with the murder. Even the dashing cop who might or might not still suspect me of having a hand in the homicide. When the color consultant came along and asked if I saw myself as a sleek redhead, a tousled brunette or a sun-streaked blond, I was thrown into confusion.

"Leave it to me," she said. So I did. Where was Marsha? I didn't need to worry. She came for the final round. Apparently she was at the highest level a stylist can be—she was only there to put the finishing touches: the cut and shaping and the final blow-dry.

"It's good to see you again," she said. "You are going to look fabulous when we get through with you."

Did that mean I was not at all fabulous before I came in? I wondered if she thought I was the biggest challenge she'd ever met. No, of course not. And yet the day I'd met her at the shop she did give me a certain look that bordered on pity. Or maybe it was just that she was dying to get her hands on me for the transformation. If so, I thought, go for it, Marsha. So far I'd been massaged, washed, dried, colored and now this. While she ran her hands through my hair, she called for a manicurist and pedicurist to work on my nails. I didn't remember asking for them, but apparently that's what Dolce ordered, so I sat back in the padded chair and let it all happen.

"I see you and your brother are both artistic," I said, watching Marsha work her magic on my newly streaked golden brown hair.

"That's right. He's my idol. If it weren't for him, I wouldn't be here. He paid for me to go to cosmetology school, then he got me an internship with Mr. Rene in Beverly Hills after my training with Vidal. He's always been my guardian angel. Fortunately for me, since our father wasn't around and our mother had to work two jobs. Harrington swore when he grew up he'd get me anything I wanted—clothes, jewelry, shoes, whatever. If he had to make it himself. Which he does. All I have to say is 'I like that dress,' or 'I love those shoes' and presto, he figures out a way to make them or somehow get them for me."

I wondered if one way to get a pair of shoes was to steal them. Not that Harrington seemed like a thief or anything. I just wondered. I wished I could forget the shoes for a few hours. But even now, having a luxury beauty treatment, the MarySue murder was on my mind.

"I suppose you had a lot of business right before that big benefit the other night," I said, still watching Marsha in the mirror.

"Oh yeah. Lots of women coming in at the last minute. It was a scene all right. We were open until seven. I was exhausted. I went home and collapsed."

So she wasn't at the Benefit. But was Harrington? "What about your brother?" I asked trying to sound like I was just making polite conversation. I hardly knew what polite conversation was anymore. Everything I said, every question I asked anyone was designed to elicit some information. Unfortunately it didn't always work out.

"He's amazing," she said proudly.

There you go. I didn't want to know how amazing he was, I wanted to know if he'd been at the park that night. The night MarySue was murdered for her shoes.

"Everyone says the shows he puts on at the high school are just as good as Broadway," I said.

"That's true," she said as she heated her curling iron for the final touches. "Especially the costumes and the sets. They're all his designs. All his work. Someday he will be directing plays on Broadway. I'm telling you, he's that good. He's wasted on that school. They don't appreciate him." With her curling iron in hand, she curled a few more strands around my face, then she stepped back and gave me a critical look from every angle.

"How do you like it?" Marsha asked, swiveling my chair around so I could get a full-front view of my new hairstyle. I gasped in surprise. I looked completely different. My hair was lighter, shorter, fuller and much more stylish. Did I look better? Marsha thought so. I hoped Dr. Jonathan would agree with her. When my nails were done, I thanked Marsha and gave her and the manicurist a healthy tip after I made sure her fee had been taken care of by Dolce.

She told me to have a good time wherever I was going. She said she'd come by the shop to look at the new collections on her day off next week. I was sure that meant she wouldn't be buying anything. Just like her brother, she was a window-shopper. Having heard about their background, I understood why. If I wasn't employed by Dolce, I'd probably be in their same boat wearing off-the-rack clothes. I shuddered at the thought.

When I got home with my new clothes in a shopping bag and my new hair, I wished I had somewhere to go. But I knew I had to rest my ankle for tomorrow. When Nick called and suggested coming by after his last yoga class with some cabbage rolls his aunt made for him, I couldn't say no. It was better than eating a bowl of cornflakes and feeling sorry for myself alone on a Saturday night.

Funny, only a few weeks ago I had expected to be home alone on a Saturday night. In fact, I was always alone on Saturday night and most every other night too. Now I'd gotten spoiled with three men in my life. I knew it wouldn't last, so I told myself to relax and enjoy it while I could. Who knew when Nick would be overbooked giving classes and Dr. Jonathan might fall for one of those nurses? *Not* Nurse Chasseure or Nurse Bijou, but someone else. It was almost worth having a sprained ankle, which was almost completely healed. I just hoped Nick wouldn't start in on my doctor and how he wasn't good enough to treat me. What would he say if he knew I had a date with him Sunday night?

Actually Nick wanted to talk about his classes instead of my doctor or me. He didn't say a word about my hair. Instead, he told me all about aerial skills, tumbling, conditioning and

break dancing until I was almost nodding off on the couch
while he heated the cabbage rolls. And he didn't say anything
about my joining his class. We ate in my living room so I
could keep my foot up on the coffee table.

"How do you like Aunt Meera's *galumpkis*?" he asked.
"She is famous for it, all the way back in Transylvania, they
talk about Meera's famous stuffed cabbage. The recipe is a
secret, so don't ask her."

I assured him I wouldn't. Besides who has time to make a
sauce, stuff a cabbage and then bake the whole thing for hours?
Not me. But I was very grateful to anyone who had that kind
of talent and time. Someday I'd learn to cook. I'd take classes
at the California Culinary Academy and throw little dinner
parties for my friends after shopping for fresh ingredients from
the Farmer's Market. Until then I would happily eat anything
someone brought me, like this ethnic Romanian dish.

"Delicious," I said, scooping up the sweet and sour
tomato sauce on the plate with my spoon.

"Not only delicious but good for you," Nick said. "Packed
with many vitamins. They say it can cure ulcers and it is
frugal too, which makes it a perfect food."

"Your aunt must be a wonderful cook. I would love to
have her recipe. Does she live around here?"

"In Marin County. When your foot is well, I will take
you on her tour."

"She gives tours of Marin County?"

"She gives vampire tours of San Francisco. She is Romanian after all and knows where they live. In the tunnels
under the city. Right here." He pointed at the floor of my
living room.

After minoring in Romanian in college, I shouldn't have
been surprised to hear his aunt believed vampires had taken
up residence beneath my house, but I was. "How . . . how

did she find out where they are?" I asked as if there were
nothing unusual about vampires being nearby.

"She's been studying vampires since a long, long time
ago. She is now one hundred and twenty-seven."

"Years old?" I couldn't help gasping.

He nodded, his mouth full of *galumpkis*, and poured me
another glass of Francusa, a soft, smooth Romanian wine
that complemented the cabbage rolls perfectly.

"And then she is a vampire herself," he said with a wink
while wiping the sauce off his mouth with his handkerchief.
"Which is how she says she knows many histories of San
Francisco. Famous people she knew like Mark Twain and
other forty-niners. It is all on her tour. Huntington Park,
Pacific Union Club hotels and cafés. You will see what a
good actress she is."

"I look forward to it," I said, sure that Nick didn't actually
believe his aunt was a vampire but just went along with it.
How I wished I could tell my Romanian professors about this
one-hundred-twenty-seven-year-old so-called vampire. After
I took the tour, I could send in her story to my alumni magazine along with a picture of the two of us on her tour. Of
course, no alums believed in vampires. But everyone loves a
good story. I'd take my camera and get some shots of the two
of us at historic spots where the vamps supposedly hung out.

When Nick refilled my glass, I protested, but he quoted
the old Romanian saying, "Three glasses of wine are just
enough. The first for your health. The second for your
delight. The third for a good rest."

He left before I had a third glass of wine, when I kept
yawning. I told him it must be the pain pills that made me
sleepy. Certainly not his vampire stories. He suggested a
trip to the Palace of the Legion of Honor to see the Impres-

sionist exhibit the next day, but I wanted to rest up and give myself a facial before my big date. So I said I had some e-mail to get caught up on. He promised to get us tickets for his aunt's tour in a week or two. Before he left he kissed me on both cheeks as they do in Romania, I suppose.

Nine

I pampered myself all day Sunday. First I washed my face with a gel cleanser, then I gave myself an exfoliating scrub, which left my face tingling. After that it was time to steam open my pores. I filled the bathroom sink with warm water and pressed a warm wet washcloth on my face three times. Next step—the mask. Some people make their own with glycerin, honey and oil, but I used a commercial hydrating clay mask. I had to keep it on for twenty minutes, so I went out to my back patio in a pair of old gym shorts and an extra-large T-shirt to sit on my deck chair and soak up some vitamin D on my pale legs. I slapped on my earphones, taking care not to disturb a single strand of hair, and listened to some tunes on my iPod to make the time pass.

I couldn't believe it when the sound of my front doorbell penetrated right through my earphones. I debated whether to ignore it and pretend I wasn't home. But maybe it was a special delivery package. Who cared if the delivery man saw me in my gray mask? I was sure he'd seen worse. And my hair still looked perfect. If he cared.

I rushed through the house to the front door so he wouldn't just leave a notice and drive his truck away with my package in it. But when I opened the front door, it was Detective Wall. I almost slammed the door in his face I was so startled and embarrassed. After a brief hesitation and a quick cover-up of a wry smile, he said he was sorry to bother me.

"It's no bother," I said stiffly so my face wouldn't crack. "It must be important for you to be working on a Sunday." I was more convinced than ever he was a workaholic either immersed in his police duties or his volunteer efforts.

"It is," he said. "I just received a series of photos from the newspaper taken at the Benefit. If you have a moment, I'd like to show them to you."

Realizing I didn't have a choice in the matter, I could only hope this would only take a moment. I glanced at my watch. I was afraid what might happen if the mask hardened on my face. I mean really hardened. I pictured myself trying to remove it with a sharp tool. Maybe having to call 911. How embarrassing that would be.

"This won't take long," he assured me. "I know you must have other things to do on your day off." I knew he was thinking, "like painting your face with gray sludge."

"Yes, I do." It was only weeks ago I couldn't say that. But my life had changed. I backed into my living room and sat on my usual couch, the same couch where the detectives had interrogated me previously. If Jack Wall could ignore the fact I was wearing a mask, then I could too. He handed me a manila envelope full of black-and-white eight-by-ten photos and sat down next to me.

"Take your time. See if there's anyone you recognize there."

I slid the pictures out on the table. "Actually I recognize several of these people. They're our customers."

I flipped through the pictures, naming names as I went. "Liz Forester in Gucci. Not my favorite design. Anita Halperin wearing a white trench over last year's gown. Not bad. Margot Fielding in an edgy design from Camelia Skaggs. Looks good in it, don't you think?"

He didn't answer. I felt his eyes on me. I sensed he was waiting to hear something more. He was waiting for me to say something he could wrap his inquisitive mind around. But I didn't know what. Until I came to the last picture. It was a woman in a black dress looking like any number of fashionistas we'd dressed who was holding a drink in her hand and talking to someone. Someone I knew quite well. Someone I had no idea was at the Benefit.

"Recognize her?" Jack Wall asked.

"That's my boss, Dolce."

"You sound surprised," he said.

"Not at all. Why should I be?"

"Because you didn't think she'd gone to the Benefit."

"Her social life is none of my business," I said stiffly.

"Uh huh."

I didn't like his tone.

"Why do you think she was there?" he asked.

"I couldn't say."

"Couldn't or wouldn't?" he asked. "You didn't know she was there, did you? I believe you assured me she doesn't do benefits. Yet here we have evidence she made an exception to her rule. Can you tell me why?"

"No," I snapped. What could I say? I couldn't believe she was there. Why would Dolce have gone to the Benefit without telling me? If she was there, why hadn't the detective found out sooner from another guest? And of course the big

question, why had she gone? She always said by the time
she'd dressed everyone else she had barely enough energy
to climb the stairs to her apartment and crash. Not to
mention the fact that the tickets were prohibitively expensive. I'd seen her the night of the Benefit before I left for
the Jensen house. She looked exhausted. The only reason I
could think of for her to leave the house was to retrieve the
shoes.

"Maybe I was wrong. Maybe it's someone who looks like
her," I suggested hopefully.

"I think it is her. I think your employer attended this
function for the sole reason of stealing back the shoes."

"It wouldn't be stealing," I insisted. I was so wrought up
by this accusation I felt my face mask crack. Now I'd have
to start my facial all over again when the detective left.
"Since MarySue hadn't paid for them in full, technically
they still belonged to Dolce. So if that is Dolce, either she
was just an innocent last-minute guest of one of our customers, or she'd gone there to get the shoes back. Either way,
what she did was no crime." Surely I didn't have to tell an
officer what was a crime and what wasn't.

"Murder is a crime," he said sternly.

"Dolce is not a murderer," I said firmly.

"You'll be glad to know she says the same about you."

"You asked her if I'd killed MarySue?" I felt a chill go
up my spine. I was incredulous that I was still a suspect.
After all we'd been through, the detective and I.

"You were at the Jensen house. You wanted the shoes.
It's not rocket science to assume that the shoes and the murder are connected."

"But I told you I was unconscious. You can ask my doctor."

"We have."

"What? You've questioned Dr. Rhodes?" Oh, fine, now he'd think he had a date with a homicidal maniac. My face was feeling hot. I began to worry. How much longer was this going on?

"He was extremely cooperative. He verified your story at least between certain hours."

"Then I'm no longer a suspect?"

"I would describe you as a person of interest."

"Which is why you're here, isn't it?"

"I'm here to encourage you to be more forthcoming. If you have information, I expect you to come forward with it."

"I do. I did. I told you about Jim Jensen threatening me, didn't I?"

"Have you seen him lately?" he asked.

"Not since the funeral. Have you?"

"Yes, I have. He's cooperating with our investigation, and he's recuperating at home. Still planning to have his big celebration for his wife."

"Really? I don't suppose I'm invited," I said. Invited or not, I was determined to go. How else could I continue to investigate this murder? I needed to see who else showed up, what they said, how they looked, how they acted and of course, what they wore. I couldn't tell Jack that. He thought I was a self-centered female who spent Sunday afternoons wearing a mud mask. But I would show him.

"Knowing you, I'm assuming you'll go anyway," he said.

I didn't say anything. I didn't want him to tell me not to. I was afraid that Jim would try to keep the time and date a secret, at least from me. But I was sure Dolce and I would find out and yes, we'd be there. She was just as determined as I was to get to the bottom of this crime. We needed to clear our names and the only way to do that was to catch the real killer. I'd bet anything, even my Manolo black alligator boots he or she would be there at the so-called celebration.

"Are you sure you haven't spoken to him since your encounter at your store?" Jack asked.

"Of course I'm sure. What did you think? That I'd harass him at his own home?" The look on Wall's face told me that's exactly what he thought. He thought I had no sympathy for Jim Jensen and he was partly right. "Meetings with Jim Jensen are hard to forget. Just ask his wife. No, you can't do that, can you?"

He didn't answer. Instead, he stood up, indicating the interview was over, at least I hoped so. My face felt like it was covered with cement. He thanked me for my time. "Sorry to bother you on a Sunday. When you are obviously in the midst of some sort of process."

"It's a facial mask," I explained tightly, even though I didn't owe him an explanation.

"I have a theory about people who wear masks," he said. "They usually have something to hide."

Despite my sore ankle, I stood and faced him. "I have a theory about people who work on Sundays. They should get a life."

A slight smile crossed his lips. Then he let himself out. After I watched his car disappear down the street, I breathed a sigh of relief. I rushed to the bathroom and peeled the old mask off using a stiff brush and started my facial all over again, taking care not to mess my hair. Gel cleanser, scrub, the whole bit until I'd washed away acres of dry skin and wrinkles. But I couldn't wash away the picture of Dolce with MarySue at the Benefit.

Dr. Rhodes, I mean Jonathan, came to pick me up at seven in a black Porsche 911 Carrera. "You look much better,"

he said after he'd taken in my filmy skirt, my classic blazer
and my clear, well-hydrated skin and the tendrils framing my
face. So it was all worth it. Just for that comment—*You look
much better.* "How's the ankle?"

I lifted my skirt to give him a good view of my foot, and
he bent down, tapped my anklebone and smiled his approval.
"I'm glad to see you're wearing flat shoes. Some women are
slaves to fashion when your health is what it's all about."

I smiled in total agreement, though I saw that Jonathan
was dressed in an outfit that could easily have appeared in
one of Dolce's magazines, with Jonathan himself as the
model. Instead of the white lab coat he was forced to wear
on the job, he'd gone completely in the other direction with
a black slim-cut shirt and a green and black striped tie. His
narrow pants were also black, as were his loafers. On anyone else it might have been too much, but with his tanned
skin and his surfer-dude sun-bleached hair, it was stunning.
I couldn't wait to tell Dolce every detail. I held my breath
expecting him to ask why a detective had asked him about
me. But he didn't. Maybe being in the ER, he was accus-
tomed to the police coming by to ask about his patients,
soliciting his opinion on cause and time of death or injury
and what weapon was used.

"Great place you've got here," he said, looking out my
back windows at the view of the Bay. "I'm trying to decide
where to locate. Telegraph Hill, the Marina, Pacific Heights,
or something out at the beach where I can catch a wave on
my days off. Right now I'm bunking with a buddy from med
school in a flat near the ballpark. In fact, I almost caught a
foul ball from our roof yesterday. Do you like baseball?"

Baseball? He wanted to discuss baseball instead of my
criminal activities? That was fine with me. So I said yes. I

didn't want to come across as being negative. For all I knew, he had season tickets to the San Francisco Giants and might be looking for someone to fill the seat next to him. Even though baseball was not part of my heritage, I was always open to new experiences. And tasty new food choices. I'd read in the newspaper the ballpark now offered Caribbean cha-cha bowls and tropical drinks as well as crab cocktails and grilled crab sandwiches. All that along with the traditional popcorn and hot dogs. I was willing to sit through a lot of baseball if it meant sitting next to Jonathan fortified with a cha-cha bowl or two. My mouth watered. I'd been so busy I hadn't eaten lunch and now I was weak with hunger. All the better to appreciate some French food.

"We didn't have a baseball team back in Columbus." At least I hoped we didn't or I'd look like an idiot.

"What about the Columbus Clippers?" he asked.

"The Clippers," I said, clapping my hands together. "What a season they've had, right?" I figured whether it was a good season or a bad one, it had to have been one or the other.

"Sometimes minor league ball can be just as exciting as the big show," he said.

"I couldn't agree more," I said as we walked out of the house. How did a doctor have time to surf, follow baseball and shop for the latest in men's fashions? I had to remember to read the sports section of the newspaper before my next date with Jonathan if there was one. With Nick I didn't have to bother. His sport was gymnastics and I wasn't expected to know anything about it. As for Detective Wall, all he wanted me to talk about was murder. No sports, just homicide.

I commented on Jonathan's car, and he said he'd always wanted a Carrera. "The Turbo is a little wider and a little lower, but I went with the nine-eleven."

"Good choice," I murmured as the engine purred.

Another good choice was Café Henri. I'd looked it up and read a review that said it was "an unpretentious neighborhood meeting place." What it didn't say was how terribly charming and French the restaurant was with its cozy banquettes for seating inside and its outdoor heated patio.

On a blackboard the specials were listed along with the standard onion soup gratinée, coq au vin in red wine sauce, croque monsieur and salade niçoise. A small sign advertised the Daniel Ortega Trio.

I wondered if Jonathan would take it upon himself to order for me as had Detective Wall. Was this the San Francisco way? Was I supposed to take the initiative and tell my date what I wanted? Or wait to be asked? Or just let them order for both of us?

What happened was our waiter suggested we order a leg of lamb with a robust Cote du Rhone wine. "It's been cooked for seven hours," he said. "Tender, succulent and delicious. And it comes with potatoes dauphinoise."

I should have eaten something before I came because I was now light-headed with hunger and anticipation. I slipped off my blazer, and when Jonathan asked me how I'd spent the day, I could hardly say I'd given myself two facials and had been interrogated once again by a detective because I was suspected of murder or at least of aiding and abetting a murderer. No matter what I'd done how could it compare with healing the sick and saving lives? I was sure he'd removed an appendix or two, delivered a baby and maybe even more—like admitting a vagrant with the DT's, discharging a malingerer, anesthetizing a pre-op, stitching up a knife wound . . . all while I was having a mud bath. Instead I said I'd spent some time in my garden hoping it sounded like I was the thoughtful, contemplative type who spends her Sundays in the fresh air gazing out through the trees toward the waters of the Bay and thinking deep thoughts about land preservation, the urban landscape and fighting toxic substances.

It was almost a relief when Jonathan brought up the subject of MarySue's demise. Otherwise the murder would have hung over our date like a dark cloud. "I probably shouldn't say anything," Jonathan said when the waiter brought our dinner salads. "But the police came to the hospital to ask about you." He leaned forward in case I wanted to confide in him that I was the high-society murderer. Maybe he wouldn't mind. Some people find homicide exciting and sexy. But that wasn't why he invited me here, was it?

"Really?" I said, feigning surprise. "Maybe it's because that was one of our customers at the boutique where I work who was murdered the same night I was brought in to the hospital."

"But what does that have to do with you?" he asked after he speared a stalk of white asparagus with his fork. "It was Saturday night. The place is full of victims. Gunshot wounds, hit-and-run, smoke inhalation from house fires, gang warfare. You name it, we've got it. Don't tell me the cops are blaming you for an unrelated homicide."

"Oh, no," I said lightly as if I wasn't worried about it. Nothing like being accused of murder to spoil a date with a doctor. "They're just asking everyone who was on the scene that night if they know anything."

"In any case, I assured them whatever it is they're investigating couldn't have anything to do with you," he said. "Although . . ."

I stiffened. Now what?

"It's nothing. Don't worry about it."

But I was worried.

"According to our records, I didn't see you until four in the morning," he said.

"Yes but I arrived at the hospital way before that. At least that's what the nurse said. She said I had to wait my turn in the hall because my injuries weren't as serious as some of the others, like the gunshot wounds you mentioned."

"Did you notice what time you actually did arrive?" he asked. "That would help."

"I was unconscious," I said. "So how could I? There must be a record on my chart."

"There should be, but sometimes on a Saturday night things fall through the cracks. Probably just a clerical error," he said. "I wouldn't worry about it if I were you. What possible reason would you have to kill someone?"

"Exactly," I said. I was glad that he knew nothing about the shoes. Even gladder he never asked about my fall from the ladder that had led to my concussion and sprained ankle.

He gave me a reassuring smile. He had a great smile. Dazzling white teeth offset by a tanned face. The kind of smile that made you warm inside. The kind of smile you couldn't help returning. I was able to forget MarySue and everyone connected to her demise once the food came. The lamb was every bit as tender and delicious as the waiter had said, and the creamy, cheesy potatoes were a perfect complement to it. The restaurant filled up, but the tables were placed in a way that everyone had a private dining experience. We continued to sip the wine and talk about how much we liked living in the City by the Bay—the cool climate, the stupendous views of the water, the hills and the stimulating people who lived here.

We ordered profiteroles for dessert and coffee. I excused myself to go to the ladies' room, which was just as awesome as I'd expected. The Zen atmosphere of calm and quiet, the designer fixtures, the music, the warm towels, it was all there. There were even original French paintings

on the wall. I was just about to leave the stall when someone else came in and I glanced over at the feet next to mine.
I almost fainted. The woman was wearing the very same
silver stilettos I'd last seen the day MarySue ripped them
out of my hand. I froze. I told myself I was hallucinating.
Or I'd had too much wine. My head was spinning. I tried to
speak, but my mouth was too dry. For one crazy moment I
thought MarySue had come back to life to haunt me. I bent
down for a better look and everything went black for a
moment.

I was so dizzy I had to sit down again. I knew if I had
another concussion I wouldn't have far to go to find a doctor. Or maybe it was a hangover from my last concussion.
Finally I stood and unlocked the door with trembling fingers. The woman in the shoes was standing at the sink.

I coughed. I choked. I reached out as if to grab her. She
breezed out of the bathroom so fast she left a trail of scent in
her wake. It was familiar, but I couldn't decide what it was.
There was a hint of musk, vanilla and spice. Was it Chanel?

I washed my hands and raced out of the bathroom. But
she was gone. Almost like the day MarySue rushed out of
the shop with the shoes in her hand. Just like then, I'd waited
too long once again. I walked slowly away from the rest-
rooms, looking right and left. What I couldn't do was crawl
on the floor to observe everyone's shoes. It was maddening
and frustrating. The shoe thief and presumed murderer was
right here in this restaurant. So it was a woman. Unless it
was a man who stole the shoes to give to a woman. Could
Jim Jensen have given them to his girlfriend? No one had
said he had a girlfriend, but maybe Detective Wall should
look into it. I circled the restaurant before I went back to our
table, but I didn't see anyone I knew or anyone who looked
like they were wearing silver shoes.

I took several deep breaths before I joined Jonathan at the table. I tried to act like nothing had happened, but Jonathan, being in the medical field, noticed.

"Are you all right?" he asked, looking at me closely.

"I'm fine. Just a little dizzy. I get that way sometimes ever since my accident. But I'm okay, really."

He put the back of his hand against my forehead. He frowned. "You may have a fever. Maybe we should leave."

"Oh, no, not now. Not before dessert." I knew the coffee and the pastry puffs filled with ice cream and smothered with chocolate sauce would help revive me. "Besides, we have to hear your friend play."

"If you're sure you feel up to it."

I nodded. What a thoughtful, considerate date he was. Just as thoughtful and considerate as he was at the hospital in his professional capacity. Besides wanting the wonderful evening to go on and on, I thought maybe I'd see the shoes walk by our table. And if I did? I'd pounce on the wearer and phone Detective Wall on the spot. I tried to pay attention to the trio of bass, trumpet and drums who played my favorites like "Two O'Clock Jump" and "Satin Doll," but all I could think about was the shoes. Fortunately Jonathan didn't seem to notice my wandering brain. When the trio took a break, he introduced me to Daniel, who, though his mother was South American, spoke English with a charming French accent.

It was like a dream, my being here with a handsome doctor, chatting with the musician and eating fabulous food. It was so dreamy that I almost forgot about the one negative. There was the possibility of a murderer in our midst. If she had known I was in that bathroom, the woman in the shoes might have killed me to keep me quiet. I shuddered at the thought.

After the music and an after-dinner drink, Jonathan took me home. He said he'd had a great time. I said I had too.

"I'd like to see you again," he said when he parked in front of my house. "But not for professional reasons."

"That would be great because I'm really fine," I assured him. "Completely healed except for a little soreness in my ankle." I felt fine except for the nagging feeling that I'd let the shoes slip through my fingers once again. How many times could this happen? I'd let MarySue get away with the shoes twice and now this. In every instance, I was younger and faster than my adversary, but not more motivated or I'd have the shoes in my hand by now.

"I'll check my schedule and see when my next day off is," Jonathan said. "There's so much to see and do in this town. Have you been to Alcatraz?"

I shook my head. Dolce told me she'd take me to the former prison on the island in the Bay, but so far we hadn't had a chance to go.

"I'll call you," he said. Then he leaned over, tilted my chin toward him and kissed me on the lips. I felt a shiver of pleasure up and down my spine. It was the perfect ending to a perfect evening. Except for one tiny detail.

I gave a full account to Dolce the next day except for that one detail. I debated who to tell first about the shoes. The detective or my boss. I hated for either one of them to know I'd failed to get them when I had the chance to grab them. Even worse, I missed a chance to find out who'd killed MarySue. I was sure the missing shoes were tied to her death. Whoever had the shoes had either killed her or knew who did.

The store was quiet that Monday morning, so I told Dolce I was going across the street to get us each a latte to go and I'd be right back.

Once outside I called Jack Wall and told him I'd seen the shoes at Café Henri last night.

"Where are they now?" he asked. He sounded tired. But was he tired of this case or just tired of working too hard?

"I don't know. I didn't act quickly enough. She got away."

"Any ideas? Any hunches? Any clue at all as to who it might have been?" he asked.

"I know who it wasn't. It wasn't Dolce. So you can cross her off your list."

"How do you know?" he asked. I could tell he didn't believe me. He thought I'd made up something to divert suspicion from my boss. "Because she wore perfume. Dolce never does. It was heavy, but not too heavy. A combination of musk and some other things. I've smelled it before, but I don't know where. But I'll know it if I ever smell it again."

"Isn't there some way you can pin it down a little better? This may be an important clue."

"I'll try, but I'm at work now. I can't just take off and go try on different scents."

"Never mind. I'll call Café Henri and ask for a list of their reservations for last night."

"That's a great idea," I said. It was interesting to know what you could find out with the power of the law behind you.

"I'm glad you think so," he said with a tinge of sarcasm. Detective Wall appeared to have a problem accepting praise, at least from me.

"You won't see my name on the list or anyone who came with a date unfortunately. But still . . ." I said.

I thought he might ask who my date was, but instead he said, "How was the food?"

"Fantastic," I said. "You should try it."

"I will. Once I get this case solved. Until then, it's deli sandwiches and the occasional business lunch."

I assumed he was referring to the lunch he'd taken me to. "I'm trying to help you," I said. In case he hadn't noticed.

"You'll have to try a little harder. You seem to get that close to the shoes. A little too close."

"I know, I know. Then they slip out of my grasp. But I'm getting closer. There's no way MarySue isn't really dead, is there? I mean, some people might think she was a vampire."

There was a choking sound on his end of the phone connection. "You're joking, right? You don't believe in vampires, do you?"

I was tempted to tell him about the vampire tour of the city, but he'd probably just laugh at me. You can't minor in Romanian as I did and not have a healthy respect for people who believed in the possible existence of vampires.

"Of course I don't believe in vampires," I assured him. "But many people do, and they're not all in Romania. What they believe is that you can't bury a vampire and expect her to stay buried unless you remove her heart. That's all I've got to say."

But before I hung up, I asked if he knew when the event was going to be, the one Jim was planning for MarySue.

"Forget it, Rita," he said. "It's only for close friends and family."

"I understand," I said. "And after our last meeting, I'd prefer not to see Jim Jensen," I said. "And if I did, I'd probably run the other way since he's convinced I'm the one who fingered him. My life would be much easier and safer if you'd catch the murderer."

"Your life? Try my life. This is my first high-profile murder case. The chief's job is on the line. Mine too for that matter. I'm going to solve it."

I was relieved when he finally hung up. I hoped he was right about solving it. It couldn't happen too soon to suit me. As for my not wanting to see Jim Jensen, I didn't, but that wouldn't stop me from attending this "close friends and family" party. I owed it to myself, to MarySue, to Dolce and to my adopted city to find out who murdered MarySue and took her silver shoes.

Ten

I bought two lattes and went back to work. It was a slow day, which was bad news for business and bad news for keeping one's mind off of murder. I couldn't stop thinking of that photo Jack had showed me. It couldn't have been Dolce. In the first place, why wouldn't she have told me she was there? "Because," said a little voice in my ear, "she didn't want anyone to know. If you don't know, you can't tell the police." But if she was really there, then other people saw her. Why not ask them? I almost called Jack Wall back to tell him my suggestion. Second, why would she go to the Benefit at all? The answer to that one was obvious. To retrieve the shoes. Still, I couldn't, wouldn't believe it.

I rearranged the jewelry and hung a Swarovski crystal necklace on a mannequin with a black rolled-neck cashmere sweater—the combination looked stunning. Even though the big social weekend was over, I pressed a few gowns and rehung them on a rack. I chatted with customers and actually

sold a scarf and a pair of gold hoop earrings. I wished I'd
called the restaurant myself for a list of the reservations, but
I knew Jack wouldn't want me to interfere.

I was almost glad to see Peter Butinski come in. That's
how bored I was. He had brought in more shoes. But he
didn't return the magazine he'd lifted from Dolce's desk.

"Have I got something for you," he said to me. "Five fall
shoes no girl can live without." He sat himself down in one
of Dolce's padded chairs as if he belonged there. "That
means you, Ms. Jewel."

"Not for me, Peter, but I want to see what you've got."
When had I not been interested in the latest fashion footwear?

He opened the boxes. He was right: a girl could do worse
than stocking up with his five selections—a kick-ass pair of
boots in gray suede, a wooden wedge heel that could go anywhere from dusk to dawn, an updated clog, an open-back
mule to wear now or later with tights, and a pump that looked
totally classic but, he explained, was actually waterproof.

"You may not know this," Peter said, "but the latest thing
for fall is wearing a pair of chic socks with your strappy heels."

"Socks, with strappy heels?" I was trying to visualize the
combination.

He nodded and reached into his canvas bag. "Like these
Falke over-the-knee socks in soft cotton. What do you
think?"

I ran my fingers over the ribbed socks. They were incred-
ibly soft and would look good with shorts and a pair of espadrilles.

"Fifty-five percent cotton, twenty-five percent virgin
wool."

"I love them," I confessed, "but . . ." I was losing sight
of my goal here, distracted as usual by something I just had

to have. I forced myself to focus on the problem at hand. I looked at the shoes he'd set on the table.

There was just one thing missing.

"No silver stilettos, Peter?"

I expected him to tell me he could get them if I wanted them. I didn't expect him to turn deathly pale, almost the color of gray suede.

"Wh . . . what do you mean?" he asked.

"I just wondered if you had anything like a pair of hand-made silver heels," I said as innocently as I could. "Not that I have any place to wear them like a society benefit or anything, but you never know. Always best to be prepared for any occasion, right?"

He hesitated for a moment, looking at me as if he thought I might know something I shouldn't. Then he recovered his poise. "I have ways of special ordering any shoe you want, my dear." Maybe he thought I might actually buy something from him. "Just let me know ahead of time. Now where's Dolce?"

"In her office."

"I'll leave the shoes then and the socks. I expect they'll fly off the shelf. Especially if you promote them. I'll make it worth your while." He looked at my feet. "What's your size?"

"Eight and a half," I said. I wondered what he had in mind. A discount on his shoes?

After he left, I went over our conversation in my mind. He knew something about MarySue's silver shoes, I could swear he did. But what?

The rest of the day dragged by. I didn't hear from Dr. Jonathan, Nick or the detective. I couldn't think of how to bring up the subject of the benefit with Dolce without sounding like I was accusing her of something. So I didn't. If Jack Wall thought it was her, let him do it. I just hoped he wouldn't. Dolce didn't need that kind of harassment.

The more I thought about it the more I was intrigued by the thought of MarySue returning as a vampire and going to dinner at Café Henri the same night I did. If only I was a true believer. If only I knew what perfume she wore. No, that was ridiculous. The woman whose shoes I'd seen at the restaurant was a living, breathing person, and I wanted to know who she was.

That night I couldn't face going straight home alone. I realized I was getting hooked on fun and excitement, if you can call looking for a murderer fun and exciting. With my ankle feeling almost normal, I decided to sign up for one of Nick's classes instead of resuming kung fu. It would give me something to do at night besides vegging out in front of my TV, and I didn't mind the fact that it would bring me into close attention with Nick.

At five o'clock I left Dolce's and took a bus to the Ocean View Gymnastics School on Vista Avenue. I wasn't sure if Nick would be there. If he was, I'd observe his class and see if he really was a good teacher. If he wasn't, I'd just sign up for one of his classes and take a chance. I didn't think he'd mind if I just dropped in. Hadn't he invited me to do just that? My action didn't count as chasing men, did it? If only Aunt Grace were around, I'd check with her to be sure.

Before I committed to anything, though, I'd take a look around the gym to see if there were students swinging from trapezes or gyrating to rock music or jumping on trampolines. If there were, I'd slip out unnoticed and find another activity for my empty evenings.

As it turned out, Nick was there, wearing shorts and a

"Romania the Land of Choice" T-shirt. He was just about to teach a tumbling class for children when he saw me at the front desk. "Rita, I am very glad to meet you again," Nick said. "You came to join the class, yes?"

"Wouldn't it be better if I joined one with adults?" I asked with a glance at the group of children waiting for him on the gym floor. I'd stand out like a sore thumb, being larger and less able to perform than everyone else.

"As you like, yes, if it makes you feel more comfortable."

"I'm afraid it would make me feel uncomfortable when I saw how well the children did and I didn't."

"Ah, yes, I understand. A beginning class is best for you, which meets on Wednesdays. How is that for you?"

"That would be fine. Is it okay if I watch this class this evening?" I asked, thinking I'd see what his technique was and if he was patient with the slow learners. I didn't need anyone else in my life criticizing me for making the wrong moves.

"Of course. Many parents will watch also. And afterward we can have a coffee between classes."

I told him it sounded good, then I took a seat on the risers with a good view of the class. The other adults there must be the parents he'd mentioned. While he had the kids doing warm-up exercises, I overheard them talking.

"Isn't he the best? Sasha just loves this class," one woman said to another.

"His accent is to die for, and those biceps. You can tell he's in good shape."

"Definitely eye candy," another mother said, her gaze focused on the gym instructor on the floor.

They were right. Nick was even better looking in shorts and a T-shirt than in his trench coat on the night I'd met him at the airport. And you couldn't say that about everyone.

Most people got worse looking the more clothes they removed. Which was why I was in the clothes and accessory business. I made women look better.

"I don't know any other Romanians," the first woman said. "Maybe they're all as hot as Nick Petrescu. My au pair has a major crush on him. He asked her out to some Romanian festival, and she's over the moon, completely gaga."

What? My Nick was going out with someone else? I told myself he had the right to date anyone and everyone he wanted to. As long as he didn't take her on the vampire tour too. After all, he was only one of the three men in my life. He was new in town and needed new friends just the way I did.

By the end of the class I hadn't made up my mind about taking a class, but I was glad I'd come. When Nick joined me, he had showered and changed into street clothes and still looked very attractive in a European way. He was totally different from the other two men in my life. One was a doctor who had the money to wine and dine me, one was more concerned that I was an accomplice in a murder, and then there was Nick, who just wanted me to meet his relatives and feed me.

Over coffee in the adjacent snack bar, Nick told me how glad he was I'd decided to take gymnastics. I was reluctant to make a commitment, so I said I'd have to check my schedule first before I signed up.

He asked if I was still interested in the vampire tour. "Don't worry," he said, "they do not go underground or to any stops that are seriously dangerous or frightening."

Not dangerous or frightening? Now I was worried it wasn't going to be authentic. "Of course I'm interested," I said. "I can't believe I never heard of it before."

"Aunt Meera doesn't advertise so much. She wants only

earnest students of history or her friends on her tour. Some do wear costumes, but only to get to the spirit, you understand. What is your liking, Friday or Saturday night? It begins at eight and ends at ten."

"Saturday would be fine," I said.

"I will tell my aunt. She is looking forward to your meeting her. I told her of how we met at the airport, of course. And how you dropped your shoes."

"She knows about the silver shoes?" I asked. By now I shouldn't be surprised. Everyone I knew had either seen the shoes, wanted the shoes, stolen the shoes, sold the shoes or worn the shoes. Maybe she was the one who took them. Maybe she was the one who was wearing them at the restaurant. If it was her, I was impressed at how fast a one-hundred-twenty-seven-year-old could dash through a restaurant.

"She knows about many things," he said.

"Because of her age," I said. "Do you know what kind of perfume she wears?"

"No," he said. "Why?"

"Oh, nothing."

"I am sorry to leave like this," Nick said, looking at his vintage Orex watch, "but I must attend schedule meeting. And after the meeting I have a, how do you say? A previous commitment."

Hmmm. Maybe the previous commitment was a date with the au pair. "Thanks for letting me observe," I said. "It was very interesting."

He stood and walked me to the door. "Until Saturday then. It will be so pleasant for me, and my aunt is the same. After the tour we will taste some Romanian food and drink together."

I stood at the bus stop feeling glad I'd made the effort to come out here and watch a class. I'd learned I wasn't the only woman in Nick's life. Which made me wonder what my competition was in Jack's life or my doctor's? So what should I do? Take a class from Nick? Return to kung fu? Do nothing? What I was sure of was that I was looking forward to the vampire tour. Even if I learned nothing about the lost shoes or came any closer to finding out who killed Mary-Sue, I would enjoy hearing more about the history of San Francisco and how vampires had supposedly participated in shaping the city. All that from a self-professed vampire guide who'd been around a long, long time. Maybe not one hundred years, but still quite a while. For once I'd like to go out and have a good time without thinking about MarySue, Jim Jensen, Peter Butinski or Harrington Harris. Nick knew nothing about MarySue Jensen and I was glad. I had hit a dead end trying to find out who'd killed her. I wanted to forget about her, her husband and her probable killer whoever he or she might be.

But I couldn't forget Harrington. The next day Dolce told me we'd been invited to see the dress rehearsal at the high school of *Bye Bye Birdie*, Harrington's play.

"Already? Didn't school just start this week?" I said.

"I can't keep track," Dolce said. "But apparently he's been rehearsing it all summer. He's certainly been talking about it all summer. No rest for the wicked, according to him. Even so, it's bound to be terrible. He said so himself. But he's invited all our customers. How would it look if we didn't go?"

"You're right," I said. "We're just one big happy family, aren't we?"

Dolce gave me an approving smile. I was glad she didn't think I was being sarcastic.

On Friday night Dolce said she'd take us to the play in her rental Range Rover, which was so unlike her. She explained she had to turn in the Mercedes and take the cheapest car in

the lot. Maybe she was afraid I'd bolt if she didn't make sure
I went with her. But first we went across the street from the
boutique to the upscale trendy bar, which was filled with Yup-
pies on a Friday night, what else? Dolce said she couldn't face
an amateur production without a drink first, and Aberration
was well-known for the mixologist behind the bar.

His reputation was well-deserved. I ordered a Galapagos
made with lemon and lime and even a splash of grapefruit
juice, and Dolce ordered a wanderlust, a kind of super mar-
tini with organic vodka.

"You should come here more often," Dolce told me, looking around at the crowd of young professionals. "Good place
to meet men."

I nodded. But what would I do with any more men?
"Actually I have another date tomorrow."

"With the doctor?" she asked.

"With Nick the gymnast. We're going on a vampire tour
of the city. It's led by his aunt. He says she claims to be a
vampire herself."

"Rita, you don't believe in vampires, do you?" she asked
with a frown.

"Of course not," I said. Why did everyone keep asking
me that? Not even Nick believed his aunt was for real. "But
I am interested in history. And since I minored in Romanian
in college I will be interested to hear what she has to say
about Vlad the Impaler who may or may not have been the
real Count Dracula."

When we got to the high school, I think both Dolce and
I wished we hadn't forfeited an evening of ordering drinks
and munching barbecued wonton, meatballs or shrimp cocktail at the bar to come see a bunch of high school kids jump
around on stage singing and dancing.

Just a glance around the little theatre told us the place

was full of the parents of the actors and a smattering of
Dolce's customers Harrington had conned into coming.
"What I won't do for my clients," Dolce murmured. Even
though I didn't need to remind her that Harrington was
hardly a good customer. Harrington met us in the lobby with
our tickets. For some reason he was dressed in seventies'
disco style—a bold-patterned polyester shirt that fit tightly
across his chest and a pair of wide-leg pants—even though
the play was set in the sixties. Close enough, I guessed. He
was greeting parents and friends alike as if he were the star
of the musical himself. He was the center of attention, glad-
handing the adults in the lobby as if he was Stephen Sond-
heim at the opening of *Sweeney Todd*.

His sister Marsha came up and studied my hair and my
outfit. I wasn't sure if she appreciated the combination of
my print dress and brown lace-up boots, which were a vintage tribute to the character of Elaine on *Seinfeld* who
always showed up in long floral skirts, blazers and granny
shoes with socks. Even if no one else realized what my fashion inspiration was on a given day, I was confident enough
to wear what I liked. Maybe I'd even be credited with bring-
ing back nineties TV-sitcom style.

"How was your date?" Marsha asked. Not a word about
my clothes. I refused to let it bother me.

"Wonderful. Thanks to you, I didn't have to worry about
my hair for a minute."

"Where did you go?"

"We had dinner at a little French place. Great food, and
a jazz trio played after dinner."

"Really? It wasn't Café Henri, was it?"

I stared at her. "Have you been there?" Had she seen the
woman in the silver shoes?

She nodded. "Sunday night. It was my birthday. You

should see what my brother gave me before we went to dinner. A pair of shoes to die for. He made them himself, but you'd never know. They look like they came from Italy or someplace. The man is a genius. Well, I'd better go get a seat up front. Harrington wants my take on his costumes. I know they'll be fabulous, but I'm taking notes for him." She waved a small notepad and left the lobby while I stood there staring with my mouth open.

Handmade shoes? I wondered. Would those shoes have been a pair of silver stilettos? And if so, did she really believe her brother made them? I knew he was clever, but really. Wasn't it more likely he stole them from MarySue and gave them to his sister? I should have paid attention to her perfume. I thought if I ever smelled that musky scent again, I'd know it. But now I wasn't so sure.

I almost followed Marsha into the theatre so I could sit behind her and get a whiff of her scent, if she was even wearing any. And then what? Ask her about the shoes? If she had been wearing the stolen silver stilettos, she'd never admit it. She was convinced her brother had made those shoes himself. Maybe he had. Maybe I was the one who was crazy. By the time I'd made up my mind to confront her, it was too late. As usual. This was the story of my life these days. When would I learn to act fast and decisively? When my ankle healed? Or never?

"Are you okay, Rita?" Dolce asked when she caught up with me. "You look like you've had a relapse. Maybe you're not quite recovered from your accident."

"Oh, no, I'm fine. But sometimes I do get a funny feeling." Like when I thought about a pair of missing silver shoes. Like when I thought about how they kept slipping away from me. Like when I kept missing opportunities to snatch them back. I rubbed my forehead and wondered how soon we could leave. The music was terrible and the dancing even worse. And don't get me started about the acting. Dolce suggested we go at intermission. If we could hold out that long. It occurred to me that it was actually convenient to have an injury like mine. I could blame it for just about anything, like inattention or fear of being arrested, fear of customers or their next of kin, fear of getting caught lying or looking guilty or fatigue or saying the wrong thing. I'd already used it as an excuse to avoid difficult questions. Yes, I could take the coward's way out and hang on to this injury for a while.

During the first act, which was definitely still a work in progress, I shifted restlessly in my seat. I looked around for Marsha in the front row, but I never saw her. Finally Dolce and I slipped away at the break. We'd made an appearance and that's what counted. I only hoped our customers noted that we supported the arts. I could still follow up on Marsha. All I had to do was make another hair appointment. She was expensive, and this time I'd have to pay for it myself, but if I could crack this mystery, it would be worth it.

Dolce drove me home, and I wrapped myself in a plush microfiber robe with matching slippers and sat alone in my living room with my foot up trying to put this shoe story together. If MarySue wore the shoes to the Benefit and turned up dead without shoes, how would Marsha have gotten them? Surely she wasn't even at the Benefit. If Dolce was at the Benefit as the photos suggested, she might have taken the shoes, which really belonged to her anyway. But why didn't she tell me? Because she killed MarySue?

If Jim Jensen killed his wife, then he possibly still had the shoes. Jim was holed up in his house while his heart healed. Which gave him a good excuse for hiding out. He was also angry, which may have brought about his heart attack if it wasn't caused by the arrival of the shaman. Then there was Patti French, who was also annoyed with her sister-in-law and had reasons to want to get rid of her. Did she? I kicked myself, only mentally of course, for not pursuing Marsha tonight. Why hadn't I just asked her, "Was that you in the bathroom wearing the silver shoes? And if so, what did you do with them?"

Saturday was a busy day at the shop, with lots of customers shopping for something to wear that night. What about me? Should I wear a costume as Nick had suggested others did on the vampire tour? Maybe just a black velvet dress, a cape and black boots. All of which I had in my closet. The important thing was the makeup. I'd powder my face white and wear lots of eye shadow.

Nick called me in the afternoon to make sure I was up to walking the streets of San Francisco. I assured him my ankle was feeling normal. He said he too would be wearing a black cape and he'd pick me up at seven thirty.

We parked in a lot on top of Nob Hill and joined his aunt and the group on the corner of Taylor and California Streets across the street from Grace Cathedral, the historic towering gothic church perched atop the hill.

Nick's aunt, Meera, said she was delighted to meet me after she'd heard so much about me. She spoke with a definite all-European accent, which could have been real . . . or not. She wore a flowing black dress and carried a battery-operated candelabra and led Nick, me and about ten others on a brisk walking tour of Nob Hill where the gold rush barons like Leland Stanford, James Flood and Mark Hopkins built their mansions in the nineteenth century.

"I've been here since 1857," Meera told us.

What? I was sure Nick said she was one hundred twenty-seven. But maybe even vampires lie about their age. Or maybe math was not her strong suit. I looked around the group, assembled in a circle in front of the Mark Hopkins Hotel, built on the site of the railroad magnate's mansion which was completed in 1878 after his death, but destroyed in the fire which followed the '06 earthquake. There I saw definite signs of amusement and even some plain disbelief on a few faces. Meera must get disbelievers on her tours all the time. She must be used to them. She certainly didn't look the least bit chagrined. In fact, she looked just about as charged up as the batteries on her candelabra.

Before anyone could question our tour leader, Meera continued. "I became a vampire in Romania, my home country and home to others more famous than myself—Vlad the Impaler and Count Dracula. The count was jealous of my power, and he's responsible for my becoming a vampress and for banishing me around the world to California. Of course, I was unwilling to go so far from home and family, but it turned out to be a good move for me. I arrived by ship in San Francisco, but at the time the action was all in the gold-fields, so it was overland for me to the mother lode country. Long story short, since the late nineties—that's the 1890s—I've lived under and on the streets of this great city. Until recently, when I moved to the suburbs. Of all the neighborhoods, Nob Hill, one of the original seven hills, is my favorite. When I retire, I intend to move back here." She waved her arm toward the houses nestled between high-rises. "It has the best views and the biggest mansions. I've seen a lot of history made here. Felt the aught-six earthquake. Escaped the fire. Saved a few lives. And met a lot of interesting people."

"But Count Dracula, he's not real is he? Isn't he just a character in a book?" a woman asked.

Meera shot her a stern look. "Romanians have many legends and stories, most based on true persons and facts. We have many counts, princes and kings. Only a Romanian knows for sure who is for real and who is not. It is not for me to spread rumors if I want to return to my country."

The questioner still looked dubious. I thought I'd better keep my mouth shut even if I had a few questions. That is if I wanted to stay on our guide's good side, not to mention the fact that I was the guest of her and her nephew.

"How does it feel to be so old?" someone asked. "Let's see, you must be . . ."

"One hundred twenty-seven," Meera said automatically as if she didn't realize she had her dates off. "I feel fine. Never better. My job allows me to talk about myself and my country and the history of this city every Friday and Saturday night. I know, some of you think vampires don't exist." Here she gave a pointed look toward the woman who'd had the audacity to question her. "They're only imaginary, mythical or literary, you may say. But here I am. A member of the undead, alive and in person."

She smiled and her sharp pointed teeth gleamed in the light from her candelabra.

"How do you feel about living forever?" someone else asked after Meera's remarks had settled in.

"It's great. How can I complain? As long as I have my health, I couldn't be happier. I get a front-row seat to history happening right before my eyes. I don't fear death or old age. What can be wrong with that?"

I thought I knew what Jack Wall would say. "Sure, she wears black, looks pale and has her teeth capped, but come on, give me a break. Don't you get it? She claims to have supernatural powers because she feels powerless. You don't have to be a psychotherapist to see what's going on here. She's a fraud, a phony and she's psycho."

I didn't let his unsaid words stop me from asking Meera a question.

"Do you ever get a chance to meet the recent undead, I mean those who have just crossed over?" I asked. I know it was crazy, but what was the harm in playing along with the woman? What if she knew something? Who was I to turn down any helpful information no matter who it came from? She looked confused. Maybe I wasn't phrasing it right. Maybe she didn't know who I meant. Maybe I should have waited until later to ask about a specific person, namely MarySue.

"We meet the new arrivals at orientation. So, yes, there's a meet-and-greet every few months. Is there someone special . . . ?" she asked eagerly. "Someone rich and famous perhaps?"

"Not really," I said. MarySue was richer than I was, but not rich enough to buy the kind of shoes she wanted. And famous? I'd have to say she was well-known in certain circles, but not really famous.

"She just died recently, and I have no reason to think she's a vampire. Except I saw someone wearing her shoes the other night and I thought maybe . . ." I waited hopefully. Not that Meera was really a vampire, but she might know something. It was worth a try.

"Of course you thought she'd returned. Which is quite possible especially if the mourners looked back as they left the grave site. Is that what happened?"

I shrugged. How did I know?

"That way the body could easily find her way back, you see."

I nodded, thought I really didn't see.

"But I have to tell you the undead often come back in a different form than when they were alive," Meera said. "And they usually wouldn't be wearing the same shoes."

I felt foolish for asking. Now everyone would think I was gullible enough to believe.

The next question was from a guy standing on the edge of the crowd. I wasn't even sure he was with the tour.

"Do you drink blood?" he asked.

"Good question. Most vampires do not actually drink blood," Meera said patiently. "We enjoy real food, mostly red meat but leafy green vegetables also."

"Do you only come out at night?" a woman asked.

"Vampires typically have night jobs," Meera said. "We find it difficult to adjust to daytime schedules. So we work as night watchmen, security guards, nurses, air-traffic controllers or funeral directors. Things like that."

When she finished the tour of the hotels, the men's club and a private residence, Meera thanked us for our attention. Then she handed out discount cards for the Transylvania Café to everyone. She told Nick she'd meet us there.

"Are they still open?" I asked Nick as he drove west on California Street.

"Of course. Romanians dine stylishly late. It's their custom. You will find others from the tour there. The chef is an old friend of Meera's."

"By old do you mean more than one hundred twenty-seven?"

He chuckled. "I don't believe Chef Ramon is as old as my aunt, but I am sometimes wrong about such matters. In any case, the food is authentic and they stay open for those who work late."

"Like security guards and funeral directors?"

"Perhaps," he said.

The food in the tiny restaurant out in a residential neighborhood called the Sunset was served family style. I didn't see any of my fellow tourists there, but there were other eaters who looked like they might be Romanian. Of course I was famished by that time, and the *sarmalute*, cabbage stuffed with rice, meat and herbs, was delicious. There were bowls of pickled vegetables on the table and a carafe of dark red wine. For dessert the chef brought out a cake called *cozonoc*, that Nick told me was often served at Christmas or Easter.

Meera sat next to Nick and spoke Romanian to him from time to time. Then she leaned over and told me she was so happy to have her favorite nephew here in the United States where there was more opportunity for jobs.

"He's a very good teacher," I said. "I observed his class recently."

"And you yourself will be taking gymnastics, Nick tells me," she said. "Many women have signed up for classes at the gym since my nephew arrived. He is not only a gifted teacher, but a very attractive man, in case you didn't notice."

"Yes, I did," I said politely. "And I'm definitely interested in a class. As soon as my ankle is completely healed and I have a go-ahead from my doctor." I wanted to have an out in case I decided I wanted to go back to kung fu.

Before we left the restaurant, I asked Meera what was the difference between *galumpkis* and *sarmalute*. She sighed, then she thought for a long moment before she said she couldn't explain it, you had to eat some of both and it was best to be Romanian to understand and she was exhausted from her tour. So I just snapped a picture of her even though she ducked her head and said, "I'm not photo-genic. I take terrible pictures." I thanked Nick for a wonderful evening and I meant it.

Sure enough, later when I'd kicked off my shoes and wiped the white makeup off my face, I checked the play-back icon on my Nikon and saw I'd taken some great shots of the park, the hotel and the restaurant, but Nick's aunt's image was nowhere to be seen. There was just a blur where she was sitting at the table. I sat at my kitchen table staring off into space. There was no such thing as vampires, but anyone who believed in them would tell me it is impossible to take their pictures and capture them on film. A blur just mean I'd jostled my camera, that's all.

Eleven

The next week was a downer at Dolce's. I knew I should ask Dolce if and why she was at the Benefit before Jack Wall zoomed in on her and took her down to the station, wherever that was, for questioning, but I hated to bring up the subject. So I kept putting it off. With the Benefit over and other parties fading from the schedule, there weren't many customers. Nick didn't call. Maybe he was disappointed I didn't sign up for his class. Or maybe he had gotten involved with that au pair or one of his many adult female students. Dr. Jonathan didn't call. Maybe he was on call or he'd hooked up with an attractive, warm and caring nurse. I didn't hear from Detective Wall either. Maybe he'd solved the case on his own and didn't need me anymore. If so, the least he could do was to let me know. But the silence out there was deafening.

On Tuesday I was sick of trying to act busy when I had

nothing to do, so I suggested we have a fashion show. Dolce perked up a little, then she frowned. She was worried about the lack of customers and sales, I could tell. "But we can't afford to hire models. Even if we did, who would come to see the show?"

"Your best customers will be the models. They'll love it," I said. "Everyone wants to be a model. And when they wear something for the show, they'll want to buy it."

"You think so?" she asked. "You really think so?"

I nodded emphatically. "As for who will come to see the show . . . their friends and their husbands. We'll serve drinks and finger food. We'll clear out the great room and set up folding chairs. The women can dress in the alcove. I'll make up a sign-up sheet."

Dolce seemed happy to have me organize the event, and I was glad to have something to do. We picked a date, five o'clock on Friday night. I went into her office, flipped through her file and started calling the customers. By the next day the place was full of wannabe models trying on clothes for the fashion show. Dolce told me I was a genius.

"Let's see how much they actually buy," I said in an undertone, "before we go out and celebrate."

When Patti French came out of one of the dressing rooms wearing a silk trench coat, a canvas jacket and silk pants all in the same shade, she asked me what I thought.

"Gorgeous," I said. "The best way to mix and match neutrals is to combine different fabrics and textures."

"That's what I thought," she said, running her hand over the smooth silk of her rolled-up pants.

"With your height you could have been a model," I said. It was true. She had the slim figure and the cheekbones to pull it off. "And your hair looks fabulous."

She ran her hand over her sixties beehive. "You like it? Harrington's sister did it for me. She assured me I wouldn't look too retro."

"Not at all," I assured her. "It's more textured than earlier versions. Very much in the now."

"My hair is so fine she had to use a ton of a thickening hairspray," Patti said.

"Whatever works," I said. "Marsha really knows what she's doing. I wonder if she'd like to model. She's short, but that's okay. She has great taste." Maybe I could get her to wear the shoes her brother made for her. I'd love to get a closer look at them without her suspecting that I suspected her or her brother of anything. When I got back to the office, I called and left a message telling her to come by the shop if she was interested in being in our show.

Claire Timkin, the schoolteacher, was thrilled to be a model. She said she'd invite all the moms of her current students now that school had started. I said the more the merrier even though I wasn't sure those women were our target audience, but maybe they had more money than Claire. I suggested she model some designer denim, but she wanted a fresh, feminine look.

"Prints are fun," I said, pulling a Missoni dress off a hook for her to try. "I'll find you some jewelry to complement the look." I brought her some bangles for her upper arms, which were nicely toned thanks to the hours she spent doing bicep curls or maybe just lifting books off the shelves.

She said she loved the dress I showed her and asked what kind of a discount we would give her if she bought it. I told her to ask Dolce. I knew how hard it was to be poor in the midst of wealth, but somehow Claire had found a way to dress like a millionaire on a teacher's salary. On a whim I asked, "Were you at the Benefit, Claire? What did you wear?"

"I was there, and I wore a blue silk and jersey dress Dolce sold me last year. Long sleeved. Maybe you remember it? Timeless, she told me at the time. Of course, I would have loved something new, but you know how it is . . ." She shrugged. Yes, I knew how it was.

"Anyway it was a fabulous happening event," Claire said. "I'm sorry you weren't there. The clothes, the shoes, the gardens. It was the last time I saw MarySue," she said, blinking rapidly as if she was going to cry. Had they been friends?

"How did she seem?" I asked, zipping her dress for her.

"Just the same. Full of life." Claire shook her head. "I wish I'd known she was going to die. I would have said something to her."

"Like what?" I asked. I really wondered.

"Well, I would have told her how much I admired her style. I was always envious of her. A big house, a successful husband and all the clothes and shoes she ever wanted."

I wondered how many other women envied MarySue with no idea she was in financial trouble.

"Who else but MarySue had the confidence to wear a plain black dress with silver shoes? I don't know how much they cost. Probably a fortune. You know what they say, if you have to ask, you probably can't afford them. Anyway she looked great. If you have to die, you should look your best, don't you think?"

"I do," I said thinking of her funeral. "Definitely. I suppose she was there with Jim?"

"I guess so. I know he was there. Everyone was there, even Dolce."

I wasn't sure I'd heard her right. "Dolce? Are you sure?"

So she was there. How many people had seen her? And how many people had she seen?

"Oh, yes it was her. But I only saw her for a minute. She was going toward the garden. I was surprised, you know?"

"You mean because she hardly ever goes to these things," I said.

She nodded and went to look around the shop for another fashion show outfit.

Now I was really worried. First the newspaper photo and now Claire, who would have no reason to lie about seeing Dolce. What about Claire? Did she covet those silver shoes enough to kill MarySue to get them? She loved clothes, and she didn't have the kind of money the other customers had.

By the end of the day we had ten customer-models lined up, each with two complete outfits to wear on our faux runway in our shop. Not every model would buy a complete outfit, not everyone would buy anything they wore, but it was worth a try, I told Dolce before she closed up that evening. And even if we didn't sell to our models, we had the audience watching, admiring, clapping and hopefully buying. Each of our models would invite all their friends and relatives.

We were hanging up the outfits with the matching names taped to the dresses, pants and tops when Marsha came in.

"I got your message," she said. "I hope I'm not too late. I'd love to be in your fashion show."

"Great," I said. Dolce told her to take her time and choose a couple of ensembles for the show. When she picked a pair of sleek black pants and a striped shirt to go with them, Dolce took one look and found her a pair of black spike-heeled sandals that looked stunning with her outfit.

"You're short so you can wear these heels," Dolce said. To add to the look, I gave her a pair of dark sunglasses and some silver jewelry.

"I love it," Dolce told her. "No one else has the look you do."

I agreed. With her pale blond hair and deliberate dark roots and dark nail polish, Marsha would stand out. It didn't hurt that she was so short; in fact, she'd stand out because she was different.

For her next outfit we had her try on a short black skirt and a white silk tailored blouse with a suit jacket over it. The whole thing was so tailored yet so sexy with Marsha's bare legs Dolce and I just stood there looking at her.

"You don't think it's too . . ." Marsha said, giving herself a critical look in the full-length mirror.

"It's perfect," I said.

"Terrific," Dolce added. "Wait, I've got some black leather clogs."

"Or I could wear a pair of silver sandals my brother made for me."

Dolce and I exchanged a knowing look.

"Why not?" Dolce said.

"That sounds good," I said trying not to jump up and down with excitement. Since it was her idea I didn't even have to suggest it. But why would she want to wear them unless they were just copies and not the real thing? Were we barking up the wrong tree?

Before she left, she gave us a stack of her business cards. "In case anyone wants a special hairstyle for the fashion show," she said. We promised to hand them out for her. After she left, neither Dolce nor I said anything for several minutes.

Finally, Dolce broke the silence. "You don't think . . ." she said.

I shook my head. "It couldn't be them."

And that's all we said. But I'm sure both our minds were spinning and wondering. Had her brother really made her a pair of silver shoes? Or . . . We were both exhausted but pleased with our work and determined to put anything negative out of our minds.

"Rita, you should be in the show too," Dolce said before I left. "You'd make just as good a model as any of the customers."

"But I don't have a posse to bring in any sales the way the others do," I said. Still, I couldn't deny I longed to strut the faux runway in some dazzling outfit.

"I insist," Dolce said. "You have a perfect model's body, tall and just curvy enough to look good in anything you wear."

I blushed at the compliment. "Well," I said, "I would love to do it if you're sure."

All of a sudden Dolce got her second wind. She'd looked so tired a few minutes ago, I thought she was ready to call it a day. Now she was springing from rack to rack from room to room to find something perfect for me. Maybe it was just a coping mechanism. Or it was just Dolce being Dolce. Give her a challenge, like dressing me, and she was a real fireball. It was a treat to see her in action. Both of us realized how awful it was to imagine Harrington's sister as a shoe thief or murderess.

Dolce's actions put me in mind of the day of the Benefit. She had looked totally worn out when I left her to go to the Jensens' to retrieve the shoes. And yet I had two ways of proving she'd gone to the Benefit. The photos and Claire's account.

Sooner or later I was going to have to confront her. But how could I when she was being the proverbial fairy godmother, outfitting me as if I were Cinderella.

I stood in front of the full-length mirror studying myself in an Etro patterned V-neck dress. It was a figure-hugging cut in dark gray and beige with a pencil skirt that was so in this fall season. I did a three-sixty turn and gave myself a critical look. Did I really have a model's body? I wanted to think so, but Dolce was known to always say the right thing to her customers. No matter what you bought or didn't buy at Dolce's, you left feeling good about yourself. Unless you were MarySue or Jim Jensen, of course. Their behavior had stretched Dolce's goodwill to the breaking point.

"It's noble, dressy and simply chic," Dolce said with a proud smile. After all, she'd picked the dress way back in spring when she'd ordered her fall merchandise. "I've been waiting for the right person to come along for that dress. All you need is a pair of black booties or some peep toes."

I chose the booties, and Dolce was determined to find me another outfit. "Every one of our models should have two turns on the runway, and that includes you," she said. "Something different this time, don't you think?"

What could I say? I went into the tiny dressing room and slipped out of the Etro. When she opened the door, she handed me four pieces in matching burnt orange. There was a sweater, a leather jacket, tight leather pants and leather boots that covered the knees. I have to say, I was dubious. There was a certain equestrienne look to the outfit that wasn't really me. As if I were ready to compete at the Derby. But as usual Dolce knew best. When I came out, she gasped at the total effect of all that burnt orange.

"Too much?" I asked anxiously.

"Oh, no," she said. "It's rich and warm and sumptuous and so right for fall. Simply gorgeous. No need for jewelry or a scarf," she added.

I changed back into my work clothes—a pair of white

linen pants and a silver diamond-quilted jacket—which I thought were fine that morning but now seemed dull by comparison.

The question of whether Dolce was at the Benefit sat heavily on my mind. I walked to the front door, paused and turned around. I went back to Dolce's office and knocked on the door.

"Rita, I thought you'd gone," she said when she opened the door.

I took a deep breath. "Dolce, a funny thing happened today. Claire Timkin said she saw you at the Benefit." I didn't mention I'd also seen a photo of her at the Benefit. Why bring in the police if I didn't have to?

"Really? I didn't see her."

"Then you were there."

"Only briefly. I just had to try to get the shoes back."

"But you didn't," I said, hoping she'd confirm it.

She shook her head. "I was either too late or too early. I made a quick tour around the garden, said hello to a customer or two, but I never saw MarySue. Dead or alive."

I didn't ask why she hadn't mentioned this before. She had her reasons, and one of them probably was she didn't want to be questioned by the police. But now Detective Wall had proof she was there, and he was going to ask her about it. I told myself it was none of my business. I was satisfied with Dolce's explanation, and I hoped the police would be too.

I said good night and left.

I was too enervated to go home. And there were too many more questions I needed answers to. One was, who put the shoe box in my garbage? Another was, who took me to the hospital that night? MarySue? Jim Jensen? The gardeners? A stranger?

I decided to take the bus to San Francisco General Hospital and ask the after-hours staff in the Admissions Department. The same personnel who'd admitted me that fateful night as well as MarySue. Surely they didn't just allow anyone to dump a body on the doorstep without getting an ID. I didn't know why I hadn't thought of tracking them down before. Maybe because I had other things on my mind. Like murder. Also, I wasn't able to do much but keep my foot elevated. Now that I was mobile again, I could tie up some loose ends that were bothering me.

The big old brick hospital was a hotbed of activity, even on a weekday evening. Doctors rushing through the halls clutching patients' charts. Friends and relatives pacing the floor as they waited for news of their loved ones. Children crying. Ambulance sirens in the distance. I could just imagine what it had been like on the Saturday night I was brought in. I was lucky I'd gotten seen at all, let alone by the amazing Dr. Jonathan Rhodes. I stopped at the information desk hoping I wouldn't see Nurse Chasseure or Nurse Bijou but hoping I might see Dr. Rhodes. When I got redirected to Admissions, a stiff and formal nurse clad in a stiff and formal white uniform checked her records.

"Here it is, under 'Involuntary Admissions.'"

"That's right. I was unconscious. What I want to know is who brought me here."

"I can't say," she said glaring at me.

I thought of asking "Can't or won't?" but I didn't. I'm not that kind of person. So I stood there staring at her, waiting to hear something. Anything.

"It says here 'depressed and suicidal,'" she said finally.

"What? Who said that? About me?" I asked incredulously. Surely it wasn't Dr. Rhodes.

"The party who brought you in said you jumped from a

second-floor window. I'm surprised you were treated at all. We don't take psychiatric patients without a referral." She picked up a file folder and starting looking through it as if she was done with me. If she thought that she had another think coming.

"I'm not crazy," I insisted. "And I assure you I didn't jump. I fell off a ladder. It was an accident." I leaned forward trying to read from my chart that was on her desk. Without looking up she moved it toward her and away from me and then shot a hostile look at me.

"We can't be too careful," she said. "Just the other night one of our nurses was assaulted in the psych ward."

"I'm sorry to hear it," I said. I wouldn't have been surprised to hear she was the one assaulted. I was tired of trying to explain I was not mentally ill. "All I want to know is who brought me here so I can thank them. If it weren't for this good Samaritan I'd still be lying under an oak tree in Pacific Heights."

The Admissions clerk looked like she wished I was still there.

When I realized she wasn't going to tell me anything, I asked her where the cafeteria was. She directed me to the stairway down the hall. I wasn't quite ready to give up yet, but I knew I needed some fortification to keep up my strength. Surely the cafeteria would have the kind of hearty food to keep the night nurses and emergency staff going.

I went through the cafeteria line and chose the personal-size vegetarian pizza—even though I had to wait ten minutes, it was worth it. I ordered a Caesar salad too and watched the man behind the counter toss it with grated Parmesan cheese. Whatever the Admissions Department lacked, the hospital made up for in this cafeteria.

I'd just set my tray on a table in the bustling cafeteria

when I saw my doctor across the room. He looked just as gorgeous in his white lab coat and his surfer blond hair as the last time I'd seen him. My heart pounded with excitement. What should I do?

I stifled the urge to shout his name. I didn't even know if I should wave. What would he think? That I was some kind of stalker who'd come here to spy on him? What would Aunt Grace think if she knew? But I had a good excuse. In fact, I'd hardly thought of the possibility of running into him when I decided to come here this evening. But now that I had, I couldn't let this opportunity pass me by.

I waved discreetly and when he saw me, he smiled broadly and walked toward me. Even if I didn't get any information from this hospital visit, that smile made it all worthwhile.

"Rita," he said, putting his tray down on my table. "What are you doing here? Not another fall from a ladder, I hope."

"No, no, I'm fine."

"Are you sure? Let me see your ankle." He bent down, I stretched my leg out and he eyeballed my ankle. "Looks good. I'm glad to see you're wearing sensible shoes. Two-tone brogues. Italian, aren't they?"

"Testoni," I said.

He raised his eyebrows to indicate his appreciation for my good taste. I was glad to find someone who noticed. Not that I wore them just to get attention. They were not only super stylish, they even felt comfy.

"I came to see if I could find out who brought me to the hospital that Saturday night. Since I was unconscious when I arrived, I don't know how I got here. I owe someone a huge thank-you."

He sat down, and I saw he had a huge plate of beef stew

with mashed potatoes and a large helping of mixed vegetables. Being an ER doctor must require a lot of fuel to get through the night. He glanced at my pizza, and I offered him a piece. He took me up on it and then asked, "Any luck in finding the mysterious stranger?"

I shook my head. "The Admissions lady insisted I was a psychiatric patient and said she couldn't give out any information on who'd brought me in."

"That's ridiculous," Jonathan said in between bites of my pizza. "There's nothing wrong with your mind. Her bark is worse than her bite. But the rules are there to protect the innocent. It's called the Good Samaritan Law. There's no requirement that someone who steps in to help in an emergency situation give his or her name. That way people are more likely to volunteer their help if they know they can't be accused of malpractice or interference. I'm sorry about that."

"It was worth a try," I said while I ate my salad. "But I understand completely."

"I wish I could stay and talk," he said. "But I'm on duty in fifteen minutes. It's good to see you. I'm glad you stopped by."

I wanted to protest that I hadn't stopped by to see him, but he already knew that.

"I was going to call you," he said. "I have Sunday off again. I know I sound like a tourist, but I want to go to Alcatraz. Are you available Sunday afternoon if I can get tickets?"

"I'm dying to see the prison," I said. "I hear the tours are fascinating. And the boat trip to the island would be fun." I pictured us out on the deck watching the sea life, the waves, the sun, and enjoying the breeze off the ocean. I'd wear

layers of fall clothes like a silky top, a cashmere sweater
and my new super-skinny jeans advertised for the discrim-
inating but not fussy modern woman. If that wasn't me,
what was?

By wearing layers, I could be comfortable on the boat
and peel them off once I got to the island. Jonathan would
no doubt be wearing designer jeans, Top-Siders for the boat
deck with a sweater tied around his shoulders. He looked
good in whatever he wore, so no problem there.

"It's a date then," he said. "I'll pick you up at two, and
we'll get a bite to eat after the tour somewhere on the Bay.
How does that sound?"

I told him it sounded just fine. I couldn't believe how my
"California the Beautiful" calendar would be filled up. The
fashion show on Friday and now this.

"See you Sunday," he said. After he'd finished off my
pizza and his beef stew, he left for work.

I felt upbeat when I left the hospital. I'd eaten my salad
and half a pizza and snagged a date with the best-looking
doctor at San Francisco General and maybe the whole state
of California. I had come to a dead end on the trail of the
person who'd dropped me off, but I wasn't ready to quit. I
couldn't help thinking that whoever brought me to this hospital was connected to the Jensen house or neighborhood.
So I hopped on a bus and went up to Pacific Heights. I
wished I'd bought a Fast Pass. It would have saved me a lot
of money on bus rides, but who knew I'd be dashing around
the city this way. I shouldn't complain. It was cheaper than
taking a cab or having a car. And I was just happy to have
my ankle functional again.

When I got off the bus, I had to walk a few blocks to the
Jensen house. I remembered that Detective Wall had told

me Jim was recuperating at home, which encouraged me to walk right up through his well-landscaped front yard and ring the bell. I felt a chill go up my spine remembering the last time I was here, when MarySue tried to kill me or at least slow me down. I desperately wanted to go to that memorial party for MarySue, so if Jim came to the door I'd apologize for any slight I'd given. I'd tell him I never meant to imply he was guilty. I'd say I hoped there were no hard feelings.

If Jim answered the door, I'd say, "Hi, I'm Rita from the boutique," as if I had nothing to hide. No reason not to drop by. "Hope you're feeling better," I'd add. I just didn't want to hear him accuse me of murdering his wife again.

The longer I stood there, the more chickenhearted I became. Maybe I ought to take off. What if he saw me and had a relapse and blamed it on me? I glanced up at the third-floor windows where I'd thought I'd first seen MarySue. Something moved. Someone or just a curtain? I leaned against the pillar on the front porch for support. I could just imagine Jim coming downstairs to confront me with accusations. I didn't mind the yelling as much as I'd mind if he tried to kill me the way he'd killed his wife. All I wanted to know was, did he bring me to the hospital that night? Or was it MarySue?

I looked around. No car in the driveway. But I did see the gardeners' truck down the street. Had they brought me to the hospital? It wouldn't hurt to ask. All I wanted to do was thank them and fill in a blank in my memory bank. They wouldn't be offended if I approached them, would they? I had to try.

I was walking down the street toward the house with the truck in the driveway when my cell phone rang. It was Jonathan.

"Rita, I just talked to the Admissions Department. The man on duty that night remembered you."

"Really? And did he remember who brought me in?"

"He said she didn't leave a name."

"She? It was definitely a she?"

"He said she was wearing a black dress."

"And shoes? What kind of shoes?" I held my breath.

"Silver shoes. He said he'd never seen silver shoes before so they stuck in his mind. When he asked for your name or her name, she left. He remembered that because it was so unusual. He called after her, but she was gone."

"Oh, my God," I said.

"Does that help?" he asked.

"Yes. I mean, I think so. It had to be MarySue, the woman who was murdered that night. The one who was brought into the hospital later, after I got there. So she was there twice that night. Once alive, the other time dead. Thanks, Jonathan."

"You're welcome. Gotta run now. They're paging me."

I put my phone into my Michael Kors zip-top designer satchel and kept walking past the truck, past the mansions with the city's most hoity-toity addresses. I was so caught up with the idea that the same person who'd tried to kill me had turned around and taken me to the hospital that I scarcely noticed the stately Victorians with elaborate wooden gables and towers and the house that looked like a French Baroque chateau. I was walking past some of the most elaborate symbols of the city's colorful past and all I could think of was how glad I was to be alive. I didn't even care if I never lived in a mansion built by a tycoon with a view of the Golden Gate Bridge. I was alive. The only way I could think of to thank my rescuer, MarySue Jensen, was to find her killer. I owed it to her. I glanced back for a last look at her house before I turned the corner.

"Don't worry," I said softly. "I'll avenge your death. I'll catch your killer. It's the least I can do for you."

I glanced at the garden truck to see a man who was lifting a fifty-pound bag of fertilizer stop and stare at me. Hadn't he ever heard anyone talking to herself before?

Twelve

When I got home, I called Jack Wall and told him about the fashion show. "I suggest you come by," I said. "Besides all the possible suspects under one roof, there's a chance the silver shoes will be there too."

"The stolen silver shoes?"

"I don't know. I can't be sure, but there's a good chance. I'm not saying the wearer is the murderer or even a thief, but—"

"Never mind speculating or accusing anyone," he said. "That's my job."

"I thought you'd be glad I alerted you," I said stiffly. "And I was wondering if you had identified the fingerprints on the shoe box you found in my garbage can," I said.

"So far they don't match any known criminal in our system."

Exasperated, I said, "Of course they don't. They belong to any one of a short list of people who wanted those shoes. Society women who are not in your database because they haven't committed any previous crimes. Not until now. Which I will be happy to provide you with."

"The list or the shoes?"

"I don't have the shoes," I said through clenched teeth. Sometimes I wondered why I went out of my way to help the police.

"Do you admit you want the shoes?" he said. "Would you turn them down if they appeared in a box in your garbage can?"

"Yes, I would. I am not the silver-shoe type. But I repeat: they did not appear in my garbage. That was the box, but not the shoes."

"Who is?"

"Who is what?" I asked.

"The silver-shoe type."

"I'll make the list for you," I said. That was the kind of job I loved. Matching customers with the right styles. That's what I was good at. Dolce thought so anyway.

"You do that," he said.

Sometimes I thought he was only humoring me. That he didn't really find my information very helpful. I considered telling him about MarySue and the hospital, but I didn't like being humored. Besides, what would he do if he knew how I got to the hospital? I'd done everything I could to help the police except bring the murderer into the station with a full confession. And where did it get me? Nowhere. It got me only lectures on how not to help the police do their job even though they weren't doing a very good job of it. That was it. If Jack Wall didn't find out anything at our fashion show, I would have to avenge the murder on my own as I'd promised MarySue or her ghost. I couldn't wash my hands of this murder even if I wanted to. I was stuck. I just hoped I found the killer before he struck again. I also hoped he or she wouldn't strike at me. If I kept my detective work under the radar I shouldn't have anything to worry about.

The upcoming fashion show kept Dolce and me busy all week. The so-called models were all agog. They tried on their clothes, and they tried on each others' clothes. They practiced walking and turning and smiling or alternately looking snobby. They went on crash diets to look even thinner than they were.

On Friday morning, I suggested to Dolce that she make an introduction for the show and talk a little about "How to Transition Your Summer Wardrobe into Fall."

"What a good idea," she said. "So timely."

"And such a good way to encourage more sales after the show."

She patted me on the back. "Which we could really use," she said. I didn't like the way the worry lines were carved in her forehead. Ever since the MarySue incident, business had fallen off. To cheer her up, I told her she looked like a walking advertisement for the shop in sequined pants and a navy satin vintage Victorian-era top.

As for me, I'd decided to start out funky with a pair of high-top multicolored sneakers and an Italian cotton voile print dress by the Italian designer Marni. It was from her fall collection, and I'd admired it since Dolce got it in earlier.

"I love the dress on you. I know you've already got your two outfits, but those sneakers have so much attitude," Dolce said. "You have to wear them. They say 'girls just wanna have fun,' don't you think?"

"Which reminds me," I said, "is Peter coming tonight?"

"You know him. Wouldn't miss an opportunity to pitch his shoes," Dolce said.

"He won't be happy I'm not wearing any of his shoes," I said.

"You can always use your ankle as an excuse," Dolce suggested.

When all the models arrived around five, we were hungry, so we ordered takeout and sat around the great room in our street clothes munching on food delivered from Dolce's favorite Chicago-style eatery down the street. I was sure no real models would ever indulge in hot dogs and Polish sausage sandwiches on poppy-seed buns loaded with peppers, tomatoes, pickle relish, onions and dill pickle spears. They'd probably have a bottle of water and a cracker and call it dinner, but then, we weren't professionals.

Every one of us chowed down as if we hadn't eaten all week—which some of us hadn't—though the aftereffect was that we all had to spray our mouths with an advanced formula breath freshener in Dolce's powder room.

The last one to arrive just as we were getting dressed was Marsha. She said she'd had some last-minute clients. By that time we had all the chairs set up and were just putting on our makeup. Marsha very kindly offered to do comb-outs for anyone who wanted one.

"I'll sign up," I said. "I know what a genius you are."

"Tousled beach waves are really gone," she explained with a critical look at my hair as she heated her flat iron in Dolce's office. "It's fine to embrace your natural waves for summer, but not now that it's fall. Straight hair is in, the silkier and shinier the better."

My hair wasn't nearly as silky or shiny as she would have liked, but what could I do? At least she didn't suggest a retro beehive. Instead, she told me to increase my intake of Vitamin E. "You should eat more brown rice, nuts and wheat germ, which will help get your hair healthy."

I was glad she hadn't witnessed the Polish sausage sandwich I'd just eaten. I vowed that tomorrow I'd go on a Vitamin E diet. I bent over so she could iron my hair on a towel on Dolce's desk. I couldn't help notice she'd brought a cloth bag with her shoes in it. I could hardly restrain myself I wanted to look at them so badly.

"So those are the shoes your brother made?" I asked as she smoothed my hair with practiced fingers.

"Right. You won't believe how fabulous they are."

I wouldn't believe he'd made them either, and neither would the police, I thought.

"He'll be here, won't he?" I asked.

"Wouldn't miss it," she said. "You know Harrington."

I wondered if I did know Harrington. I knew he'd do anything for his sister. But would he steal for her? Kill for her? Whatever he did, I was sure she didn't know about it. How could she if she'd brought the shoes to wear tonight.

When I came out of her office, Dolce gasped in surprise at my straight, flattened hair. Everyone said it matched my funky outfit perfectly. Marsha did some of the others as well and by seven o'clock, all of us—Patti, Claire, Patricia, Dolce, two other customers, Lisa and Allison, and I—were ready to go.

Dolce greeted everyone at the front door. The rest of us were in the accessory alcove peeking around the corner. I was afraid enough people wouldn't come, but the place filled up. I saw Peter Butinksi looking ridiculous as usual in his plastic shoes and his thinning hair dyed a startling shade of brown. I saw Patti's husband and Harrington, and at least twenty or thirty others, men and women alike. I had a warm feeling of satisfaction all over about my idea of the fashion show. It was working. It was really working. Now if only some of these voyeurs would turn into buyers.

Dolce gave a great talk about transitioning your summer wardrobe into fall. She suggested scarves and held up a few from a local designer. She wrapped a lightweight cashmere scarf with ruffled edges around her neck and knotted it over one shoulder. "Why not try a scarf like this over a tank top with a pair of designer denims?" she asked.

I could see women nodding their agreement.

"This time of year can be tricky," she explained. "It's fall but it feels like summer. Some days are warm, but the September fashion magazines"—she held up a recent *Vogue*—"tell us it's fall. It's no wonder we're all in a kind of clothing confusion."

There was a smattering of light laughter. Dolce was a natural at this. If anyone could encourage loads of sales, it was Dolce.

"The best way to transition from one season to the next is with accessories," she said. "Fortunately our shop has everything you need, and if we don't, we can get it for you. If there's one thought I want you to take away with you today, it's scarves and pashminas. Wear them outdoors and indoors. Over tanks and tees and a light jacket for cooler days. And now what you've been waiting for, our fall collection worn by our very own models."

Dolce perched on a stool at the side of our makeshift stage and narrated like a pro. She introduced us and told what we were wearing. When it was my turn, I strutted the way I'd seen the real models do. I was glad I was wearing my high-tops even though my ankle felt almost normal. The shoes gave me confidence I wouldn't trip or fall. Until I saw Detective Wall. Then I stumbled but caught myself before I fell. I don't know why I was so surprised. I'd told him to come tonight. In the excitement of being a model, I'd forgotten about him.

He was standing at the back of the room in a shawl-collared Henley and straight-fit cords. No uniform for him, of course. He could have been anybody. Somebody's brother, boyfriend or husband. But he wasn't. He was looking right at me with narrowed eyes as if I was under suspicion. And just as I was about to make my turn the way Dolce told me, head held high and hips swiveling, the front door opened and Jim Jensen walked in, looking fit and completely healthy. Several people turned to see who it was, but most of the others didn't even notice he was wearing a pair of J. Crew classic-fit wool pants and suede Macalister shoes. He looked normal tonight, his cheeks a ruddy color and no scowl on his face. Was he finished healing? Had he been given an okay from his doctor to resume activities? Or had he dragged himself out of bed to confront me once again? Or was he finished blaming me for his wife's death?

I looked at Dolce, she looked at me. She must have been surprised to see him, but she never lost her poise. Did she know he was coming? I didn't think so.

I went back to the accessory room to change into my V-neck dress with booties.

"Isn't this fun?" Patti said to me as she zipped the skirt she was wearing. "MarySue would have loved it if she'd lived. She always wanted to be a model. She blamed Jim for standing in her way. He said there was only room for one professional in their family."

"I'm glad he was able to come tonight," I said. "After what he's been through." I wondered if Jim felt threatened by MarySue even though she wasn't a model and she didn't have a job as far as I knew.

"I knew he'd want to be here, so I told him he had to get an okay from his doctor first. I'd left a message for him about the show. I thought it would do him good to get out for a change and not stay home taking his medicine and doing his exercises. He's had too much time to think. It was getting him down."

"He's looking good," I said. "It must not have been a serious heart attack."

"I believe it was more of a warning than a real attack," she said. "So now he's busy planning MarySue's memorial celebration. You and Dolce have to come. We're having the party at Portnoy's Tavern across from the cemetery. You know the place. It's been there forever. A real San Francisco icon and one of MarySue's favorite spots. Death doesn't have to be horrible, you know. She wouldn't want us to go on grieving forever."

Three weeks is hardly forever, I thought. But whatever. I knew death didn't have to be horrible especially if you didn't get along with the deceased.

"It will be a chance to remember MarySue's life," Patti said. "We'll serve her favorite drinks, a little food, say nice things about her, play her favorite songs and talk about the good times. Well, I'd better get my shoes on. I'm next." She peeked around the corner. "Don't tell me that's Detective Wall back there? Looking hot as usual. I didn't know he was into fashion."

"Oh, yes, definitely," I said. I was sure Detective Wall was here undercover and wanted to remain that way while he observed the guests. I had to agree he was hot looking. Not only that, he had money and good taste in clothes. If only he didn't have a suspicious nature and an attitude problem.

I took a seat off to the side of our makeshift runway to watch the others model their clothes. I was so anxious about seeing Marsha in those shoes, I gripped the edge of my chair.

When she came out of Dolce's office, she was wearing a

tangerine strapless chiffon gown with an empire shirred bodice I'd never seen before. Where had that come from? Not our shop. I looked over at Dolce, whose eyes were fastened on the dress as if she'd never seen it before. But it was the shoes I couldn't stop staring at. Oh my God, the shoes. I could have sworn . . . The shoes were the exact copy if not the exact shoes that MarySue had ordered, I'd carried across country and MarySue had worn to the Benefit. Were they the same shoes I'd seen at the restaurant?

Were they or weren't they? I blinked rapidly and kept my eyes glued to her feet as Marsha walked slowly around the room, a coy smile on her face. Because she knew she looked great? Or because she knew her brother made the shoes, which looked fantastic with the orange dress? Or were those *the* shoes that had cost a fortune? How many people in that room knew the history of the shoes?

I tore my eyes from Marsha and studied the audience's reaction. Peter Butinksi had leapt out of his chair and was standing, staring at her shoes. Detective Wall held a tiny camera in his hand, no doubt getting evidence, but of what? Dolce's mouth was hanging wide open. Jim Jensen looked pale. A man in the back row gave an admiring whistle. Her husband? Her boyfriend? Or was it Harrington? Marsha did look sensational, her blond hair, the tangerine dress and the silver shoes. She might not have been the most stylish, in fact her dress was almost bridesmaidy, but she made the rest of us look pale and anemic by comparison.

Marsha had just finished her pivot and was headed back to our makeshift dressing room when Detective Wall walked up and stood in front of the room.

"San Francisco PD," he said, holding his badge up. "Sorry to interrupt, but there is a pair of shoes I need as stolen evidence in an unsolved murder case."

The tension in the great room was so thick you could cut it with a knife. Some people gasped, others murmured something like, "Oh, no."

The fashion show stopped dead. Detective Wall followed Marsha, who never broke her stride. What poise, I thought. I wished I could see her face. Would she be resigned? Would she be nervous? Did she know she was wearing stolen shoes?

The next thing I heard was Harrington shouting at Jack Wall. "Just a damn minute," he yelled as he followed his sister and the detective out of the room. "Those are my shoes. I made those shoes. You can't take those shoes. They're hers."

Thank heavens for Dolce. She calmed the crowd. She explained that this act was all part of the fashion show. That the clothes and the shoes we were wearing were all worthy of being stolen but of course they weren't. They were all available through Dolce's exclusive women's wear. Did anyone believe her? I couldn't tell. The important thing was they all sat down and acted like they did. And the show went on. Without Jim Jensen. The next time I looked around the room, he was gone. Why? A recurrence of his "warning"? Would he make it home or had he collapsed on the front steps? I looked out the window but he wasn't there.

I was shaking, and I was sure the other models were too, but we couldn't let Dolce down. I had to make three appearances in three complete outfits. But not Marsha. She had disappeared. Was she thinking that she couldn't outdo her first entrance? Jack was gone too. Had he taken her away to be questioned? And what about her brother?

I glanced at Dolce. She shrugged. I wanted to go back to her office where I suspected some kind of scene was playing out between Jack, Marsha and Harrington. But we all stuck to our parts in the charade. We owed it to Dolce and the other guests.

After the show was over, the audience clapped enthusi-
astically. Then we models changed into our street clothes,
which, by the way, were not too shabby, and served wine
and tiny little cheese puffs from the caterer down the street.
Of course the guests must have been curious. Surely they
didn't all swallow Dolce's story that the scene was a setup.
But no one said anything.

I caught Dolce coming out of her office with a glass of
wine in her hand.

"They're gone," she muttered.

"But where?" I asked with a glance over my shoulder to be
sure we were alone. There were only a few people left in the
great room. Everyone else had had a drink, a bite to eat and
left. My fellow models had gone home with their families.

"How should I know?" Dolce said.

"What about the shoes?" I asked.

"That's what I'm talking about. The shoes. The shoes are
gone. So is Jim. Along with Marsha, her brother and the
police."

"You don't think Detective Wall arrested any of them,
do you?" I asked.

"You tell me," she said. "Were they the same shoes?"

"I . . . I can't be sure."

"But you saw them. You picked them up in Florida. You
brought them here. You saw MarySue before she went to
the Benefit. They must have looked different from the copies. They had to look one-of-a-kind expensive." Dolce was
staring at me, her face inches from mine.

"But you were at the Benefit. You saw the shoes too," I
said. "Didn't you?"

She avoided my gaze. She looked at my necklace and
studied the collar of my dress. Wasn't that a dead giveaway
of someone lying? Now I was getting worried. My beloved

boss was acting so strange I wondered if I really knew her at all.

"I think I told you I never saw MarySue, by the time I got to the Benefit, it was late and she wasn't anywhere to be found. I blame myself. If I'd gone earlier, if I'd found her first, taken the shoes back, she might still be alive."

"You mean by the time you arrived she was already . . ."

"Dead? I don't know. I have no idea what time she was murdered and I don't want to know. I keep imagining her in the Adirondack chair with her legs stretched out, barefoot."

"So you've never . . ." I said.

"Never saw the shoes. No. Never saw her. I only know about where she was found from listening to the news. I never saw the so-called copies of the shoes either. All I've seen is the picture of them in the magazine. You, Rita, you're the only one who's been involved in both pairs of shoes—the real ones and the copies. So which was Marsha wearing tonight?" She grasped my wrist and held me tight. So tight I couldn't breathe. I started to panic. She was desperate for answers. I was just desperate. After a whole evening of being charming, Dolce was finally cracking. Her eyes were blood-shot, her lower lip trembling, her grip tightened. My fingers were numb.

"I don't know," I said as calmly as I could. "This is the second time I've seen Marsha in those shoes. The first time I was sure those were the ones. But now . . ." I shook my head and jerked my arm away from Dolce. I was a fashion-ista. I studied clothes, jewelry, shoes and accessories for fun and for my livelihood. I was proud of my knowledge of the latest trends. But when it counted, when someone's life was at stake, it seemed I couldn't tell the difference between fake shoes and real ones. My self-confidence was crumbling. I had to get out of there and put some space between me and my boss and those damn shoes.

"What's wrong, Rita?" Dolce said, picking up on my fast-fading composure. "Is it your ankle?"

"It does feel a little weak," I said, rubbing my anklebone. Not to mention my wrist. "I'd better go home and ice it. It was a wonderful show. The interruption just made it more exciting. I venture to say everyone who was here tonight will be talking about it for some time to come."

"Talk is cheap, Rita. Let's hope they do more than talk." She took a deep breath and made a visible effort to bring herself under control. When she finally spoke her voice shook only slightly. "You know," she said, "that's what I love about you. You always put a positive spin on everything."

She didn't say, "Even murder," but that's what she was thinking. As for the detective, what was he thinking, I wondered as I rode home in the cab Dolce called for me. In the past she'd always paid the driver before I left, but not tonight. Tonight I had to pay myself. Was she really hurting for money? Or just hurting? I'd never seen her lose her cool like that.

I also wondered if it was possible Dolce had seen Mary-Sue without her shoes. If so, why hadn't she mentioned it to me before? Was I really the only one in the world who'd seen both pairs of shoes? If so, it was too bad I couldn't tell the difference between them. Was that a testimony to the skill of Harrington Harris?

When I got home, I put in a call to Detective Wall. How could I not? I had to know what happened. Didn't I deserve to know what had happened? After all I'd been through. Of course he didn't answer, so I left a message asking for a follow-up. I hoped he wouldn't give me the official line about how this was none of my business.

He didn't call me back that night, and I had to go to work

the next day. After the fashion show, it seemed the energy had been sucked out of the shop. The customers who'd been there last night were nowhere to be seen. I didn't blame them. If I hadn't had to work, I'd be home too, sipping lemonade on my patio and watching the sailboats bobbing in the Bay. And getting lost in a vampire novel, which was my favorite way of forgetting my troubles, which were minor compared to being bitten by a vampire and turning into one. Although Nick's aunt seemed to do all right posing as a vampire. She had a good job and seemed to lead an interesting life.

By the end of the day I'd refreshed all the outfits we'd worn in the fashion show the night before and hung them back on hangers. I didn't notice any uptick in sales thanks to the fashion show; in fact, there was a decided slump, but you never know what the future might bring. I still hadn't heard from Jack Wall, and Dolce hadn't heard from Harrington or Patricia even though she'd tried repeatedly to call them. We speculated that they were both locked up or they were out on bail or it was a big mistake and Jack Wall apologized profusely and gave them complimentary tickets to the Policeman's Ball.

"Any plans for tonight?" Dolce asked me as I got ready to leave at five. Since there was no one in the shop but us, I knew she wouldn't ask me to stay late, and I didn't see how I could face another minute pretending all was well.

"No, actually not. I have a date to go to Alcatraz tomorrow with Dr. Jonathan. But tonight it's just me and some reruns of *The Young Doctors* I TiVo-ed."

She nodded as if she felt terrible that someone my age would have to spend Saturday night watching a dated Australian soap opera where the sexy doctors flirt and cure patients at the same time. Maybe she thought I hoped it would give me an insight into the life of sexy Dr. Jonathan Rhodes.

As for Dolce, she'd acted more or less normal today, but I was sure she was just as tired as she looked. "What about you?" I asked.

"I'm going to do a little bookkeeping in my office. I've had to let our accountant go. No reason I can't handle it myself. It's not like we're taking in thousands every day."

I frowned. "Business is down, isn't it?" I asked.

She nodded sadly. "Don't worry about it," she told me. "We'll pull out of it. On second thought, I might just go to bed and not get up until Monday. I'll have the Sunday papers delivered along with Chinese food from the Grand Palace."

"Good for you," I said. "You deserve to be pampered after what you've been through."

"What we've all been through," she said with a weak smile. "I wish I'd never seen those silver shoes."

Puzzled, I said, "But you didn't."

"I mean I wish I'd never heard of them. Never ordered them, never sent you to pick them up."

"If I hadn't, MarySue would be alive today," I mused.

"Are you sure she isn't?" Dolce said, her gaze somewhere far away. "There are times when I feel her presence, hear her voice saying, 'I have to have those shoes.' "

As for me, I could almost hear Dolce's voice saying she'd get the shoes back . . . "If I have to hunt her down." Is that what she did? Is that why she went to the Benefit?

"Get some rest," I told her, and then I hurried down the front steps without a backward glance. I had planned on going straight home to rest and recuperate, but an evening at home suddenly seemed dull and boring.

I walked down the street. The bars were filling up with people my age. The restaurants had lines waiting outside. I could stop in for a drink or dinner. But the usual activities of swinging singles, like flirting and hooking up, didn't hold much attraction. Then I remembered Detective Wall said he served dinner to the homeless at Saint Anthony's Dining Room on Saturday nights.

I could have taken the bus, but when a cab pulled up in front of a popular hangout and some of the beautiful people got out, I got in and gave the name of the famous church in the Tenderloin, one of San Francisco's worst neighborhoods. I'd avoided the area since I arrived in town thanks to Dolce's warnings that it was full of drug dealers, addicts, prostitutes and other lowlifes, but it was time to step out of my comfort zone and see how people who didn't wear Gucci, Pucci or Ralph Lauren lived.

Thirteen

Saint Anthony's was more than a church. It was a school, a job training center, a nursery, a homeless shelter, a health care facility and a cafeteria. I saw the line for the cafeteria snaking around the block the minute I got out of the cab. I went to a side entrance and told a woman at the door I was there to volunteer.

"Are you with the Sons of Norway Lodge contingent?"

"Are they serving dinner?" I asked.

She gave me a funny look as if to say, "You don't look the least bit Nordic, and if you didn't know they were serving dinner, then you probably aren't with them."

"I mean I wasn't sure if it was lunch or dinner. Actually I'm volunteering with the police department."

She studied a list in her hand.

"Detective Jack Wall," I said. "He should be here."

"Is he expecting you?" she asked.

"He always needs help," I said. That much was true.

Whether I could help him or he could help me remained to be seen. "In any case, I'm a whiz at scooping mashed potatoes." Surely mashed potatoes would be on the menu, wouldn't they? At least I hoped so.

"Okay," she said finally. "Pick up your apron in the closet and your hairnet."

"Got it," I said and hurried by before she could stop me. By following another woman, I found the closet and an apron and a hairnet. Now all I needed was to find Detective Wall. To say that he was surprised to see me behind the steam table was putting it mildly. Still he was not one to display his emotions, so he just nodded when I squeezed in between him and a large burly fellow whose name tag said "Tim" and who seemed to be in charge of mixed vegetables.

"Are you new?" Tim asked with a friendly smile.

"First time tonight," I said, tying my apron around my waist. "I hope I won't spill anything."

"What are you doing here?" Jack Wall muttered under his breath. "What's in it for you?"

"Why does anyone volunteer? I came to help out. Is that so hard to believe? That I'd do something useful besides dress rich women. I could ask you the same thing. Is this part of your job?" I took a tray and heaped a pile of potatoes on it. I smiled at the woman across the counter, and she thanked me.

"I like to keep an eye on my parolees," he said under his breath.

"Point them out. I'll give them an extra scoop," I said.

"I thought I told you not to meddle in official business."

"I'm not. I'm simply . . ."

"You're not simply anything."

I bit my lip. How could I answer that? "Sorry," I muttered. "I've been trying to get in touch with you."

"Not now," he said.

I wanted to show him I was not only patient but also sincere about doing a good job, whether selling women's clothes and accessories or feeding the hungry, so I paid attention to the potatoes and I even went back to the kitchen to refill the tray when we ran out. Everyone in the kitchen was friendly, and the customers, if you could call them that, were so grateful I considered signing up for a weekly slot. I asked myself if it had anything to do with the proximity of the sexy cop working next to me, but I couldn't be sure of my motives. Not until this Jensen case was over. Then maybe I'd be able to think clearly and I'd have no reason to see Jack Wall unless one of us wanted to make an effort and admit it had nothing to do with either of our jobs.

"You can't be surprised I want to talk to you," I said when there was a brief break in the line of people waiting for food.

"I'm not surprised at anything you do," he said. "And I can't promise to tell you anything you want to know."

"But you don't even know what I want to know," I protested.

"I can guess," he said with a sideways glance in my direction.

"How long is this shift?" I asked the nice man on the other side, who was much more outgoing and friendly both to me and to the eaters.

"Hour and a half," he said. "First timer?"

I smiled and nodded. "But not the last. It's a great place, and the food looks good."

"It is. You see people coming back for seconds."

"Is that allowed?" I asked.

"It is when I'm serving beef stroganoff," he said with a smile. "Some of us are going out for burgers afterward. Care to join us?"

I glanced over at Jack, who frowned, and I told Tim I had other plans tonight. At least I hoped I did. If Jack bailed on me, I'd be seriously annoyed. Okay, he didn't want to tell me anything, but he couldn't just walk out of my fashion show with three customers and not tell me what happened.

After our shift ended at seven o'clock, my ankle hurt as well as both of my feet. I dropped my apron and hairnet in a bin in the dressing room and rushed out to catch Jack before he escaped without me. For a moment I thought he'd run off, but when I looked around, I saw him standing on the sidewalk checking his watch. I had no doubt he was giving me a certain allotted time to show up and then he was out of there. Maybe he had a date. How would I know? He wasn't the type to talk about his social life, if he had one.

"Thanks for waiting," I said breathlessly. "Aren't you hungry after working so hard? I'm starving. Can I buy you dinner? I owe you." Taking cabs and buying dinner for a man. It was like I was rolling in money when my boss was worried about the financial state of her store. Maybe she wouldn't be able to afford to pay me much longer. Maybe I should be worried too. I would worry later, I told myself, just like Scarlett O'Hara.

"You think you can bribe me?" he asked as we walked down the street, passing an occasional homeless person pushing a grocery cart loaded with his belongings.

"It's worth a try," I said. "All I want is a little information." I remembered reading about a Vietnamese restaurant in the area that had gotten some rave reviews online.

"Do you like Vietnamese food?" I asked.

He looked surprised. "Do you?"

"I don't know. I've never had any."

"If you like Angkor Wat, I think you'll like Little Saigon too. It's very good."

So he remembered I'd ordered Cambodian. "I pretty much like all kinds of food. And serving food to others makes me hungry."

"What doesn't?" he asked.

I frowned. "What does that mean?"

"Nothing," he said. "I had lunch with you two weeks ago, and I have to say it's rare to find a woman with a healthy appetite. So many are on diets. You never know."

"I'll take that as a compliment," I said. "You could have said 'big appetite' instead of healthy. Unless you think I should be on a diet. I know one thing, I'm glad I'm not a professional model who has to squeeze into size twos. I was raised in the Midwest. Where I come from, there are lots of steak houses and German restaurants. So when someone took me out for Cambodian food when I first got here, I was hooked. It was so different, so exotic, I was blown away."

"Prepare to be blown away again tonight," he said. "If you're serious about Vietnamese food, tonight you'll have to try the green papaya salad and the lettuce wraps. And of course the *pho*."

I didn't mention how I was looking forward to being blown away by whatever he agreed to tell me about the present case at hand. I was just grateful we'd gotten this far.

After we were seated in the restaurant with the purple walls covered with black and white photographs of Vietnam, I let Jack order since he'd been there before. Just like he'd done at lunch that day. He also ordered a large bottle of Samuel Smith's Nut Brown Ale, which he said went well

with the food. Even though this was my idea, he quickly
took over. What else did I expect from a former dot-com
millionaire turned city cop?

The lovely slender young waitress greeted Jack warmly
and took our order.

"Do you come here often?" I asked.

"It's a high-crime area," he said. "So I'm around a lot.
Eating here is one of the perks of my job."

"Like wearing designer clothes is for me. Or shoes."

He poured beer into my glass and set the bottle down.
"Let's get it out of the way. You want to know what happened to the silver shoes."

"Of course. I not only want to talk about them, I want to
see them. I think I have the right. Who else knows as much
as I do about those shoes? I brought the shoes from Florida.
It was me MarySue snatched them from. I'm the one she
tried to kill. Oh, by the way, I found out it was MarySue
who took me to the hospital that night."

He looked surprised. "How do you know that?"

"I, uh, an inside source." I didn't want to get my doctor in
trouble.

"I thought they weren't allowed to divulge that information. You must have pulled strings." I thought I detected a
hint of respect in his voice, or maybe that was anger that
someone at the hospital had broken the rules. If by chance
it was respect, maybe I could capitalize on it to get him to
share information with me.

"The Admissions people didn't want to talk, believe me,"
I said, not admitting that Dr. Jonathan had helped me.

"I believe you."

"If I could see the shoes you confiscated, I might be able
to tell if they were MarySue's or the ones Harrington made
for his sister," I said.

"You think so?" he asked raising an eyebrow.

"I know something about footwear," I said modestly. "I could try."

When the waitress brought the imperial rolls stuffed with seafood, pork and vegetables, I watched Jack dip his in *nuoc mam* sauce and wrap it in a lettuce leaf with shredded carrot and noodles. Then I copied what he did and got a mouthful of crunchy rice paper wrapped around spicy ground pork, crab and vegetables.

"Delicious," I said. "So do we have a deal? I help you ID the shoes and you forget my boss is a possible suspect."

He shook his head, but he was smiling ruefully at my naïveté. "I don't make deals, Rita."

"Oh, sure you do. I read the papers. I watch TV. I know what goes on in big-city crime scenes."

"If your boss is innocent, she has nothing to worry about," he said.

I hesitated only a second while I considered the possibility that she wasn't innocent. "She isn't worried, I am. Because I'm the one who's responsible for the shoes." Dolce was very worried, more about money than anything, but that was none of his business. I paused while the waitress brought steaming bowls of the beef noodle soup they called *pho*. I watched Jack add bean sprouts, mint leaves, fresh basil and a large dash of hoisin sauce. Then I did the same. "All I'm asking is, what happened after the fashion show?"

"I can't tell you that," he said.

"Okay, I understand you have rules to follow, so I'll tell you what I think happened." I could only hope his reaction would reveal how close I came to guessing the actual scenario. He shrugged as if I could do whatever I wanted, he wouldn't stop me, but he wasn't going to help me either. I

leaned forward across the table and looked him in the eye.
"You mistook the silver shoes Marsha wore for the real
thing. I'm guessing you made a mistake, which you found
out when Harrington told you how he'd made the shoes, and
I bet he could prove it by showing you, oh I don't know,
stitches or holes or marks on the shoes or maybe his initials
carved on the soles. After all, he is an artiste. So you let the
suspects go, and you kept the shoes as evidence or as a guide
for when you find the real thing. So you don't really need
me to tell you those are copies. But where are the real shoes?
That's the question, isn't it? Does the person who killed
MarySue still have the shoes? Because why kill her if you
can't keep the shoes? That's what I want to know. Isn't that
what you want to know too?"

He didn't say anything. He asked for a pot of tea, and we
drank it with small dishes of coconut ice cream called *che*.

After a long silence that wasn't really uncomfortable con-
sidering I didn't expect him to answer me, I said, "There's
something else I'd like to know and that's, who put that shoe
box in my garbage?"

"Sorry," Jack said. "No luck on that. Anything else I can
help you with?"

As if he would. His job was to keep me in the dark. And
my job was to keep bugging him and keep investigating on
my own.

"Actually there is something that's been bothering me.
It's the fortune I got with my Cambodian food the other day.
It's not really a fortune, it's a puzzle." I reached into my
purse and pulled out the small crumpled printed message.
" 'You cannot step in the same river twice without getting
your feet twice as wet.' Well?"

He didn't miss a beat. He said, "It's obvious what it

means. You should forget this investigation. Not only have you stepped in the same river twice, you've stepped in it too many times and you're in danger of getting very wet. Maybe even dangerously wet."

"As in drowning?" I asked with a little trickle of fear across my scalp. I wrapped my hands around my teacup to warm them.

"That's right," he said sternly.

Detective Wall drove me home in his BMW convertible he'd parked in an underground garage. "Are you sure you're not nervous about staying here alone?" he asked when he pulled up in front of my house.

"Should I be?"

"Just keep out of this investigation. That's my advice to you. The more distance between the shoes and yourself the better."

"Whoever put the shoe box in my garbage knows where I live. I wish I knew who that was. Can I assume you've ruled out Harrington and his sister as possible suspects?"

"Let me put it this way: you have nothing to fear from them except the possibility of imitation designer shoes and clothes."

"I appreciate your warning me, but I can't rest until I locate the real shoes."

"Rita, forget the shoes."

"Okay," I said. Why not let him and everyone think I had given up? That's what a normal person would do. Forget the shoes, MarySue and her murder. "What about MarySue's celebration of life next week?" I asked.

"If I were you, I'd stay home," he said. "With a big crowd like that your absence wouldn't be noticed."

"But it's a party," I protested. "Aren't you going?"

"Of course," he said.

"I'm going to go," I said. "I have to. If I don't, it would be admitting that I'm afraid of seeing Jim Jensen, which I am, but I don't want him to know that. He wouldn't dare accuse me of murdering his wife again at his own wife's party, would he?"

"I doubt it," Jack said. I was hoping he'd say something more forceful like, "He'd better not, or I'll arrest him," but he didn't.

"I'm sure Dolce will close the shop for the afternoon so we can go. Everyone who is anyone will be there."

"I can't stop you," he said. "I can only warn you."

"Here's a warning you might laugh at but don't say I didn't warn you. There is a theory that MarySue may have been bitten by a vampire, which would explain why you can't find her attacker." I paused, expecting him to burst into uncontrollable laughter, but he didn't.

"Go on," he said.

"In which case according to legend she won't stay buried long. Unless of course she's buried in such a way she can't find her way out of the grave."

"And what way would that be?" he asked.

Of course he was humoring me. No way did he believe in vampires. Neither did I. But what harm did it do to speculate? We'd both be singing a different tune if MarySue magically reappeared.

"No point in looking for her killer when she is undead and has been all along."

"Please, Rita, spare me the folklore," he said.

"I can't help it," I said. "You and I don't believe in vampires, but some people do. Those people say that one way is to bury the body facedown, then the corpse is confused and can't find her way out of her coffin. Another way would be to—"

"That's enough," he said. "Let me know if you learn anything important."

I assured him I would even though his definition of "important" was different from mine. After another pointless warning to forget about MarySue's murder, he walked me to my door and waited until I'd bolted it. After he drove away I went to my closet to look for something to wear to the memorial. I pulled out a black crepe Alberto di Feretti dress with a sleek silhouette and stitch-detailed paneling that Dolce had given me. I took a sleek clutch out of my drawer and slipped on a Lanvin bracelet. If I were going out for cocktails to the Top of the Mark I'd wear sky-high ankle boots, but this was a celebration of life at a neighborhood tavern and I wasn't allowed to wear sky-high heels anyway. Not yet.

I knew that at MarySue's memorial party as well as everywhere I went, I represented Dolce and our shop and I owed it to her to look my best. So what about shoes? I sat down on a bench and tried on a pair of flat ankle boots with my dress, but they were too casual. Next, strappy sandals in glossy patent with a pair of opaque tights. Better but not perfect. Maybe glossy wasn't subdued enough for this occasion, although MarySue would have appreciated them. I kept the tights and tried a pair of black suede peep toes. Yes. My ankle was still a little weak, but I couldn't baby it forever.

When I got up the next morning, the air was crisp and the sun was shining. Seeing as I hadn't been to kung fu for weeks, I decided I needed some exercise, so I joined a group of people practicing tai chi in Golden Gate Park. My kung fu instructor had recommended it to us because he had a reciprocal arrangement with the instructor. I'd observed them previously, and I was impressed by their fluid, seemingly effortless movements. Just my kind of exercise, I thought. I just hoped Nick didn't walk by and ask me why I didn't take his class instead of that one.

I didn't want to hurt his feelings, but sometimes it's nice to exercise anonymously. Before the MarySue shoe episode, I did everything anonymously; now it seemed as though every time I left the house, I ran into someone I knew. Just in case I did, I was wearing a pair of stretch leggings that were comfortable as well as stylish with a high-performance racer-back tank and a black training jacket. On my feet were a pair of MBT sneakers, which as everyone who exercises seriously knows can activate neglected muscles and tone and shape the entire body. MBT stands for Masai Barefoot Technology, of course. Since the Masai tribes are the best runners in the world, I had no doubt their shoes would help me run faster if I needed to.

When I arrived at the meadow where the tai chi instructor held his class, he smiled and beckoned to me to take a place in the front row, but I stuck to the back so I could watch the others and copy their movements. I quickly found it was harder than I'd thought it would be to achieve that fluid movement I'd admired. I knew it involved deep breathing and mental focus, but today I was happy just to be waving my arms around slowly and inhaling the fresh air, and feeling proud of myself for making the effort while other fashionistas were still in bed. The focus would come later, I hoped. I wanted to focus just enough to forget the scene that had almost torpedoed Dolce's fashion show.

After the class I felt refreshed and invigorated, so I wandered around the park, into the area called Chain of Lakes, enjoying the feeling of being away from the hustle and bustle of cars and tourists and screaming children flying kites or kicking balls in the field. I walked around the misty lake, drinking in the atmosphere and hearing the wind in the trees.

As fate would have it, there was a food, art and music festival going on in the concourse, so I stopped for a Korean taco stuffed with seasoned rice, *kalbi* short ribs and kimchee salsa folded into Japanese and Korean toasted seaweeds. It was so good I would have ordered another, but I had to get back and get ready for my date with Jonathan. I hadn't even decided what to wear yet.

Layers. That was all I could think of. I started with my new skinny jeans, tossing my old boyfriend jeans aside. They were so torn up and dated I could barely believe I was ever tempted to buy them.

Next, shoes. Knee-high boots or loafers with argyle socks? The boots looked great with the jeans tucked in, but since I'd be with Dr. Jonathan, I decided to be sensible and go with the loafers. I chose a silky top and a black hooded cashmere sweater over it. Slim fitting and luxurious, it felt soft and warm. That way I'd be comfortable on the boat and on shore and in the prison and wherever we went afterward.

When Jonathan picked me up, he gave me an approving look right down to my loafers. I would have looked even better if I'd had Marsha do my hair, but I ironed it myself and it looked pretty sleek, I thought.

He told me last night had been busy at the ER.

"Like most every Saturday night, I imagine," I said. "I'm fortunate I came through with only minor injuries. So just another typical Saturday night in the ER."

"That's right. Gunshot wounds, overdoses, car crashes, you name it, we've got it."

"But no society women poisoned by their husbands."

"Not that I noticed," he said with one of his dazzling smiles as if I'd been joking. I was, but only partly.

"One of the nurses told me you specialize in sports medicine."

"I did a rotation in sports medicine. It was interesting. Saw a lot of tendonitis, arthritis, bursitis and some fractures. But to me the ER is more exciting."

"All those gunshot wounds."

"And accidents like yours. You never told me how you landed in a tree that night the woman in the silver shoes brought you in. Or is that none of my business?"

"It's a long story. Maybe later," I said. Or maybe never. I just didn't want to talk about it now. I wanted to hop on a boat and set sail for an island. Which we did. We stood at the railing and the wind whipped my sleek shiny hair around, but I didn't care. I was on a date with a gorgeous doctor far from the society scene where everyone knew more than they wanted to about everyone else. I should never have gone to Marsha to have my hair done. I needed to break away from the Dolce crowd. Like today.

"I took a tai chi class today," I said. "Have you ever done it?"

"No, but I've read the literature, and I hear from patients that it helps with chronic pain and stress reduction. I'm interested in all kinds of alternative medicine. Acupuncture, herbs, meditation, I'm open to anything that works."

"I'm glad to hear you say that. Although I can't complain about the traditional medicine you treated me with. I feel fine."

"You look fine too," he said with an appreciative gleam in his blue eyes.

I felt a flutter in the pit of my stomach. It could have been a twinge of seasickness, but it was more likely the proximity of the gorgeous and brilliant doctor I was with. Who would have thought a few weeks ago I'd be on a boat in the Bay admiring a spectacular view of the city with a man who was not only a skillful, highly trained ER physician, but also a sexy straight guy with fashion sense. I sighed happily as the white buildings in the city receded in the distance and we approached the island. All my worries about Dolce, the shop and the murder faded along with the city we'd left behind.

Our group was met at the landing by a guide who gave us a brief history of Alcatraz. He told us the island had a grim past but a bright future. He instructed us to "imagine yourself on a cold and windy morning. You are a prisoner headed for your final destination, Alcatraz, where no one has knowingly ever escaped from." He paused to be sure he had our attention. He had mine, that was for sure. "It is a cold and foggy morning. Heavy steel shackles bind your ankles and wrists. You are shivering from the cold and the fear of incarceration." I wasn't a prisoner, but I was shivering anyway. "Your fellow prisoners on the "Rock," as it's called, are the most hardened criminals in the American prison system. Their crimes range from kidnapping to espionage, bank robbery and murder." He paused and switched gears to a more pleasant subject—the history of the island. "It was used as a fort during the Civil War times to protect the San Francisco Bay and Harbor. After that it was a prison known as "the Rock" that housed some of the high-profile criminals of the day like Machine Gun Kelly, Al Capone and the Birdman of Alcatraz.

He listed the various escape attempts and said it wasn't surprising that no one succeeded given the cold water, the waves and the high level of security.

"What about the sharks?" someone asked.

"No man-eating sharks in this water," the guide answered.

"The water isn't that cold," Jonathan told me as we walked up the path to the prison gate. "Jack LaLanne swam it, and some triathletes make it every year, but the prisoners weren't in very good shape."

"A terrible diet and no exercise. Was that the problem?"

Jonathan nodded, and I vowed to reset my exercise program. Not that I was afraid of being incarcerated. I just wished the police would catch MarySue's murderer before he struck again. Whoever he or she was, they wouldn't be housed at Alcatraz. It was closed as a prison in the sixties. Whoever killed MarySue would have it easy compared to those times. "Nowadays prisoners can take classes," the guide told us, "and work on-site jobs where they can earn money and play sports to keep in shape."

They were probably in better shape than I was, I thought. I was determined to get serious about exercising. Tai chi was too tame, kung fu too strenuous. I turned for one last look at the city in the distance. Our tour boat was on its way back to pick up another group. What if they didn't make it back for some reason? An earthquake, a tidal wave, or the boat ran out of gas? We'd be stuck on the island. For how long? What would we do? It would get cold at night and we had no food. At least the prisoners had shelter even if they were in solitary confinement.

Jonathan saw me shiver, and he put his jacket over my shoulders. I gave him a grateful smile.

"When we get a chance to look around the prison, we can actually go into the little dark cells in the place they call 'the hole,' " he said.

"The hole?" I repeated. Now I was shivering despite the

warmth of his jacket. I almost wished we hadn't come here. There were so many other interesting places to visit on a Sunday afternoon, like the Palace of Fine Arts, that relic from the Pan Pacific Exposition of 1915 or the zoo or . . . I didn't think this prison tour would freak me out if I weren't up to my knees in the MarySue murder case. I knew prisons weren't like Alcatraz anymore, but I still didn't want to go to one for any length of time.

But determined to be a good sport with a positive attitude, I said, "How cool. I can hardly wait."

A guide in a green uniform stepped forward to take over from the one who came on the boat with us. "Welcome home. Welcome to Alcatraz," she said with a smile. "That's the way the prisoners were greeted. We try to keep things as authentic for you as possible."

"Excuse me." A woman in the back of the crowd had raised her hand when the guide stopped. "Have there been any vampires incarcerated here?"

There was a smattering of light laughter, and the guide said not as far as she knew. I turned to see who'd asked the question, and there was Nick's aunt, Meera, in her usual black outfit with black boots and a shawl over her shoulders.

I turned quickly, hoping she hadn't seen me. That's all I needed was for Meera to say hello and for Jonathan to think I hung out with vampire wannabes. Fortunately, at that moment we were all given earphones for the audio tour, which featured actual guards and prisoners speaking about their experiences. Now was the time we could proceed at our own pace, and hopefully I could avoid running into Meera.

The narration was so good I got caught up listening to

the voices of real people and was startled when Jonathan nudged me. I took off my earpiece.

"Have you noticed, there's a woman who keeps staring at you," he said.

"Oh no," I muttered. But he was right. Meera in her flowing black dress had her gaze fixed on me. She smiled and waved to me, and I had to say hello, though I hoped Jonathan would resume the tour without me. Imagine trying to explain the presence of a one-hundred-twenty-seven-year-old vampire to your doctor.

"It's good to see you again," she said. "So we are both history buffs. Who is your handsome friend?" she asked, standing on tiptoe for a glimpse of Jonathan, who'd stopped to read an account of the Native American occupation of the island in the sixties.

I could just imagine her telling Nick that I had been seen with a man at Alcatraz. Would he care? Probably not. He was meeting plenty of admiring women at his gym, along with their au pairs. Even though I appreciated his friendship and the soup he brought me, I wasn't ready to settle down with anyone.

I should have known someday there would be a clash of at least two of my several lives, and it happened there at the prison. Jonathan came up to tell me he'd found Al Capone's cell, and I had to introduce him to Meera. I could tell she was just dying to meet him by the way she was staring at him and batting her extra-long eyelashes. If only she didn't say anything about being a you-know-what.

We chatted briefly about the prison and the prisoners, and I was just about to break away when Meera mentioned her old friend Al Capone. "I'm the one who picked him up when he was released from prison in 1939. They got him on tax evasion, you know. How ironic."

"How very interesting," I said. "Well, we have to be moving along."

"Wait," Jonathan said to her before I could take a step toward the solitary cells. "Did you say you knew Al Capone?" I could tell by his puzzled expression he was trying to figure out how that could be.

"Oh yes, we go way back, the Capones and I. I didn't always live in San Francisco, you know. I spent a few years in Chicago in the twenties. What a time that was." She shook her head with a nostalgic smile. "But originally I am from Eastern Europe, and I know something about prisons. This place is a palace compared to some I've been to in my country."

I sent Jonathan a silent message. Please don't ask why or where she's been imprisoned. Or how old she is or how she got here or how I know her.

"Do you know what happened to the missing and presumed drowned inmates who tried to swim their way to freedom?" she asked, putting her icy fingers on my shoulder. "I do."

Before she could say they'd turned into vampires and were haunting the island, I said we were behind schedule and had to catch up. "Nice to see you, Meera," I said and took Jonathan's arm to nudge him along.

"Who was that?" he asked when we'd turned the corner to face the solitary cells.

"Just a friend of a friend. She leads tours of Nob Hill, which is how I met her."

"How old is she?" he asked, looking puzzled.

Good question. I couldn't say she was one hundred twenty-seven or he'd think I was crazy or naïve or both, so I just said I wasn't sure but she looked younger than she was.

Just to get the complete Alcatraz experience, I had to go

into one of the solitary cells; even though I didn't really want to, I also didn't want Jonathan to think I was neurotic. But when I pulled the door shut, I had a panic attack. Especially when Meera came by and looked in at me like she was the warden and I was Public Enemy Number One.

"Why haven't you called my nephew?" she asked, pressing her face against the narrow bars. "He is all alone, far from home. He needs a friend." Her voice echoed off the concrete walls.

"I will," I said, my heart pounding erratically. "Definitely. It's just that I've been busy at work." Where was Jonathan? Where was the tour guide? Where were the other visitors?

I looked through the bars at Meera. Her eyes were like deep black holes. Her face suddenly looked as old as she said she was. I knew she wasn't really a vampire, but up close and personal, I could see the resemblance between her and the pictures of Vlad the Impaler. The same sharp cheekbones, the hooked nose, the same dark eyes and the same pointed chin. I decided there were worse things than being charged with murder. One of those things was being trapped by a crazy woman in an old prison.

I was breathing hard, she was leering at me. I wasn't locked in, but suddenly I wished I was. A moment later our tour guide came around the corner. Meera disappeared down the hall in the other direction.

"The last ferry leaves in one half hour," she said. "You don't want to be stuck here overnight."

Not with a weirdo on the loose, I thought. The guide smiled, but I didn't. My face felt frozen. Before I could say, "Wait for me," he'd hurried on by on his way to round up the rest of the tour group. I pushed on the cell door. It wouldn't budge. Where was everyone? Even Meera had gone. I tried to scream, but my throat was clogged and I couldn't speak. I was a prisoner inside a solitary cell even though I had done nothing wrong. I'd be here at least overnight and God only knew how long until someone found me.

Fourteen

================================

I took several deep calming breaths and told myself Jonathan wouldn't leave without me. But I couldn't hear a sound. No voices, nothing but the voices in my head from the prisoners and their guards who were all dead and gone. Is this how they felt when visiting hours were over? Or were there no visiting hours? I'd forgotten to ask. If I got out of here alive, there were a lot of questions I'd ask.

I'd ask Jim Jensen if he killed his wife. I'd tell him she said he would if he found out about the shoes. So, did he? I'd ask everyone I knew what the fortune meant—"You cannot step in the same river twice without getting your feet twice as wet."

Did that message have something to do with MarySue's death? Or was it meant for me especially?

Another question I'd ask everyone involved in the Mary-Sue affair was, "Did you put the shoe box in my garbage? And if so, why?"

After about two minutes I gathered up all my strength and pushed against the cell door. It swung open, and I almost laughed with relief. I hadn't been locked in at all. My rabid imagination was running away with me. I ran down the corridor and out the front door into the fresh air where Jonathan was waiting for me.

"There you are," he said. "I was asking everyone if they'd seen you."

"I was getting the complete prison experience," I said breathlessly. "I'm glad I don't have to stay here."

As we boarded the last ferry, I looked around but didn't see Meera. Was she still on the island by choice? I didn't know and I didn't care.

Jonathan and I stood outside on the deck as shadows fell across the city. He put his arm around my shoulders, and I was grateful for the warmth of the arm and his jacket, which I was still wearing.

He said he'd made reservations at the Cliff House, and I almost swooned. The place was historic. Perched on the cliffs above Ocean Beach, it was once a bathhouse but now housed one of the most famous and expensive restaurants in the city. We had a table at the floor-to-ceiling windows. It was still light enough to see the seals on the rocks below and hear the waves crashing. I couldn't believe little me from Columbus, Ohio, was here watching the sun set over the Pacific with one of the city's most eligible bachelors—or maybe *the* most eligible.

We ordered baby spinach salad with citrus and candied pecans, then crab cakes and filet mignon with truffled potatoes. We seemed to have the exact same taste in food and maybe lots of other things, like fashion. And what a relief to be with a man who didn't constantly tell me to butt out of his business. Jonathan seemed to enjoy talking about his job and didn't mind when I chimed in and asked questions. My kind of man.

He picked up the menu and read the back cover. "There's been a cliff house at this location since 1863," he said. I didn't bother to do the math, but I wondered, if Meera were here with us, would she tell us she'd been around then? She'd probably have some interesting stories to share of how she met the Stanfords, the Crockers and the Hearsts, who would drive their carriages out to the beach for horse racing and kite flying. Sometimes the life of an ageless, undead vampire pretender sounded downright glamorous. I just didn't want to hear about it or even worse, hear her threaten me. Isn't that what she'd done in the prison? Or was I being too sensitive?

I forced myself to stop thinking about Meera or my other obsession, which was the murder of MarySue. When Jonathan brought me home, I told him it was the most perfect day I'd had since I'd arrived over six months ago. Of course it would have been more perfect without Meera, but I put her face out of my mind.

Jonathan said he'd had a great time too. I felt I had to reciprocate after he'd spent a fortune on me, so I said I'd invite him over for brunch on my patio where I had a not-so-shabby view of the Bay. I decided I'd worry about what a non-cook like myself would serve later. And I didn't say anything about MarySue's upcoming memorial. Surely he wouldn't want to attend. He couldn't possibly attend the funeral of every patient he'd lost. I wouldn't go either if I didn't have an interest in studying the crowd to see who looked sad, who looked relieved and who got hysterical.

I said good night to Jonathan and told him I'd see him soon. Then I checked my messages. There was one from Detective

Jack Wall asking me to come down to the station to identify
the silver shoes Marsha had worn at the fashion show. "If it
isn't too much trouble."

He sounded slightly sarcastic, but with him you never
knew. In any case I was eager to ID the shoes. I knew it was
wrong to make up my mind too early, but I just knew they
weren't the shoes I'd brought back from Florida.

The next day I phoned Dolce to tell her I'd be late because
I was heading for the police station to ID the silver shoes.
She seemed nervous, but I didn't know why. Money problems? Was she going to ask me to cut back on my hours? Was
she going to close the shop? I couldn't bear to think about it.

I dressed carefully in an easy-fitting double-breasted
jacket, high-waisted fluid harem pants and my brogues. Then
I took the bus, transferring once, to the small station in the
same neighborhood where I'd volunteered at the church and
I'd eaten Vietnamese food with Jack. No wonder he knew
his way around, where to eat and where to volunteer. This
was his beat. One not many others would want, but definitely
where the action was if that's what you were interested in.

He was sitting at a desk behind a glass partition, which
I assumed was bulletproof. He stood and gave me a long
look as if he couldn't remember who I was or why I was
there. Or maybe he was just trying to decide if I was wearing Tahari or Jil Sander, both known for exceptional pant-
suits. Finally he pressed a buzzer that allowed me to walk
in. He thanked me for coming. I said I was always glad to
help the police. He didn't mention my hiding behind a mask,
and I didn't say anything about his lack of a social life. We
went into a small room lined with files and boxes. He took
a box from a shelf and lifted the lid. There they were, a pair
of silver stilettos gleaming in the rays of the overhead light.

For a moment I wasn't sure. Were they or weren't they? What was wrong with me? Had I lost my keen sense of real versus fake?

"Can I touch them?"

He held out a pair of rubber gloves. I put them on. Then I picked up the shoes one at a time and looked at them, ran my fingers over the leather and tapped the heels lightly with my knuckles. All the while Jack was watching me. What he thought, I had no idea. Maybe he thought I was faking it. That I didn't know anything. But I did. My confidence was returning. I knew my shoes and I knew I knew them.

"Well," he said after I'd done the same with both shoes and put them back in their box.

"Fake," I said.

"How can you be sure?" he said.

I picked up a shoe and held it up to the light. "A slanted, easily breakable heel, faux leather, and studs instead of diamonds," I said.

"Can anyone tell the difference?" he asked. "Or just you?"

I didn't want to brag, but I had to be honest. "No, they can't and even if they can, it may be worth it to buy the fake for forty-six dollars if the real thing is over a thousand or many thousands."

He whistled softly.

"I don't mean to put down Harrington's work," I said. "If he made these. It can't be easy to make a pair of shoes. Marsha looked stunning in them, didn't you think?"

He shrugged. "I'm not big on orange dresses and silver shoes."

"Tangerine," I corrected. "I still don't understand where that dress came from. It was not Dolce's. So now what? Will you give the shoes back to Marsha?"

"I will, but I'd like to find the originals," he said.

"Because they will lead you to the killer, am I right?" I held my breath. If he was true to form, he wouldn't tell me anything.

Instead of answering my question, he asked, "If you wanted to buy a pair of knockoffs, where would you look?"

"Online. There are dozens of outlets."

"Would you ever buy a knockoff?" he asked, leaning back in his chair and flipping a pen from one hand to the other.

"I have. Some designers don't mind. They take knock-offs as a compliment. If they make beautiful shoes or dresses or whatever. They're confident that the copies just don't compare. Like those shoes." I glanced at Marsha's silver shoes. "They don't have the same feel or the same texture, and they certainly can't fit as well as the originals. But other designers hate being copied. They want to see us have a fashion copyright law like they have for books, music, films or art. They feel ripped off by the counterfeiters. As for Harrington making one copy for his sister or a costume for his play, I hardly think anyone could complain about that."

"You convinced me," Jack said. "I'll give her back her shoes."

"And the real shoes, the ones I brought from Miami, the ones MarySue was wearing?" I asked.

"Your guess is as good as mine," he said.

I didn't believe that for a minute. I believed he had a very good guess who had them and where they were, but he didn't have enough evidence to pounce or get a search warrant. It was maddening.

"Are you sure MarySue was wearing the shoes at the Benefit?" he asked. "You weren't there, were you?"

I wondered if he was trying to trick me into confessing

that I was actually at the Benefit and I'd killed MarySue to get the shoes back.

"No, I wasn't there," I said. "I can't be sure about the shoes, but why would MarySue steal them and then not wear them? It doesn't make sense. Everyone who was there says she was wearing silver shoes. There are only two pairs, Harrington's and the real ones. Unless there are more knockoffs out there we don't know about." I suddenly had a horrible vision of boatloads of silver stilettos being unloaded from faraway countries where little children worked for pennies a day. I buried my head in my hands.

I heard Jack scrape his chair across the floor. When I looked up, he was standing. He was obviously tired of talking about and hearing about these shoes, and who could blame him? He must have other problems, other cases on his desk.

"Well," I said, "I have to go to work. Perhaps I'll see you at the memorial Jim is hosting at MarySue's favorite hot spot." I wanted him to know I had no intention of staying away.

He looked like he wanted to warn me, but after a moment, he said, "I'll be there," and he walked out to the front door with me.

....

Portnoy's Tavern was supposed to be closed to anyone who wasn't with the Jensen funeral. I'd never been there before, and I had to give Jim credit or whoever planned it for booking a historic saloon across the street from the cemetery. Of course, they'd chosen it because it was MarySue's favorite hangout. I just hoped I could continue to avoid running into Jim in case he still held a grudge.

The other person I would have liked to avoid was Nick's aunt, Meera. But there she was standing at the bar. "What's she doing here?" I muttered. "I thought this was a private party."

"Who?" Dolce said, handing me a pisco punch.

"Meera, the one-hundred-year-old-plus so-called vampire who is Nick's aunt."

"Maybe she hangs out at cemeteries just in case—"

"In case she locates another undead vampire on their way back to earth? Right." I took a sip of my punch hoping I wouldn't have to speak to her. "Delicious," I said. Out of the corner of my eye I could see the woman approaching.

"I see you've found me in my home away from home," she said, greeting me with air kisses as if we were old friends. "Good choice," she said, either referring to my glass or the tavern itself. "I've been coming here for ages. The place is almost as old as I am," she said with a twinkle in her eye. Knowing her, I was sure this was either a hint for Dolce to ask how old she was or an attempt to bring the conversation around to the topic of her vampire status. I nudged Dolce to keep quiet so I wouldn't have to hear her story again.

"You know," she continued, "I've been coming here since the days of the Barbary Coast, speakeasies, Prohibition. You name it, I've seen it all." She turned to Dolce. "Who's your friend?"

"Dolce is my boss. Dolce, this is Nick's aunt, Meera."

"You're both in style," she said, giving us each a once-over. I had the distinct feeling she didn't approve of our choices of funeral attire. "In style" but not stylish enough? Not funereal enough? "How interesting. Call me old-fashioned, but I think once you've found your style you should stick to it even if times change, do you agree?"

It was obvious what era she'd chosen. She was wearing a bonnet, a cape and a long full skirt. I'd hardly ever seen Dolce at a loss for words, especially when the subject was fashion, but at that moment she just stood there staring at Meera, a vision in a turn-of-the-century costume who could have stepped out of a museum. For all I knew, she had.

"Where do you get your clothes?" Dolce said at last.

"I have them made for me," Meera said, smoothing her bouffant skirt with her hand, "by my tailor. And I don't mean my friend Mr. Levi Strauss."

"You knew the man who made the first blue jeans?" I asked. I should have known since Meera had been telling us she'd been around for a long time.

"Of course," she said, twirling her parasol. "In those days San Francisco was a small city. We all knew each other. Mark Hopkins, Collis Huntington, Leland Stanford, James Flood and myself. I don't know if you know this, but Strauss came to California from Bavaria to open a branch of the family dry goods business. He had the most charming accent." She smiled dreamily and Dolce shot me a look that said, "Can you believe this woman?"

"When he got here he planned to make tents and wagon covers out of canvas for the forty-niners. He knew there was money to be made in the support services. But nobody wanted his tents. I felt terrible for him. He told me he was thinking of going back to Bavaria, but I convinced him to stay. I suggested he try something new like making sturdy pants for the miners."

"So you were responsible for his success. It was your idea he should make Levi's?" I asked politely. I knew I sounded skeptical. I was. She didn't mind. She must be used to it.

She nodded. "But not out of canvas. Too stiff. Too hard to work with. I suggested he use a kind of denim with copper rivets." She twisted her gold ring around her finger. What could we say? There was no one around to contradict her. Everyone from that era was dead. I began to see the benefits of being a vampire and living forever. I wanted to pin her down about her age and the discrepancy in her stories. How could she have hung out with the miners and the early movers and shakers if she was really only 128? But now was not the time to do it. Maybe that time was never.

"I don't think I've seen you here before," Meera said to me.

I wanted to say, "I don't think I've seen you since Alcatraz," but I pretended I'd forgotten all about our last meeting when she tried to lock me in the cell.

"I've never been here before," I said. "We're here for a . . . gathering . . . One of our customers, uh, recently died unexpectedly. We're here to celebrate her life."

"It must be Mrs. Jensen," Meera said. "I heard about her. What did she die of?"

"Actually, she was poisoned at a society function."

"A murder?" Meera's eyes lit up. "How exciting. Who did it?"

Out of the corner of my eye I saw a few people I recognized from the funeral just arriving at the historic tavern. Dolce drifted away from me and toward them. Probably had had enough of Meera. For some reason I hung around. Wasn't it possible Meera knew something I wanted to know, like who might have killed MarySue?

"No one knows," I said. "But it seems to be connected to a pair of expensive shoes she was wearing at the time."

"Killed for a pair of shoes!" Meera said. "They must have been some shoes."

"They were silver stilettos."

"I say forget the shoes and look for the next of kin," Meera said, peering over her spectacles to observe the crowd gathering at the bar. "Is that her husband over there?"

I followed her glance to where Jim was playing the host by serving drinks.

"That's Jim," I said. "But why would he want to kill his wife?" Of course I knew the answer to that one. He was furious with her for ordering the shoes and spending so much money. He could collect on her life insurance, and he might even have planned to return the shoes and get the deposit money back.

"I know nothing about this case, but I have been witness to many a murder over the years. President Harding died right here in San Francisco."

"Really? When was that?" I asked.

"I'm not sure, twenty-two or three, I think. Poisoned. Just like your friend MarySue. Some suspected his wife Florence, but in that case it was not a matter of cherchez la femme. No, there's the difference. If I were the officials, I would definitely go after the husband here. Jim is his name? He looks guilty to me."

I thought about the life insurance, and I had to admit that she had something there. But I didn't want to give her the satisfaction of thinking she'd solved in minutes a crime the police hadn't been able to solve in weeks.

As if she'd read my mind, she said, "I will have to have a word with the police. I've been helpful to them in the past you know. Ah, there is that handsome policeman now."

I turned to see Jack standing in the doorway. Now how did Meera know who he was? No uniform. He blended in with the other mourners who were filling the bar now. How Meera intended to help Jack solve this crime, I didn't know. I watched as she walked across the room, her lace-up boots clacking against the floorboards. She sidled up to Jack and began an animated conversation. I had no doubt she'd let him know exactly what she thought she knew. I was glad because Jack wouldn't have believed me if he didn't have this chance to interact with her himself.

Dolce found me and handed me a fresh drink. "I thought you could use one after getting rid of that nutcase."

"So you didn't buy her story?" I asked.

"Hardly," she said. "It's a story, that's all."

"I know," I said. "If she really wants us to believe she was around for the gold rush, then she's got to confess to being at least one hundred seventy, doesn't she?"

Dolce frowned. "Rita, I'm worried about you. There's no such thing as vampires. The woman is a con artist."

"I know," I assured her. "It's just—"

"You've been working too hard trying to help the police. Forget the murder. It's not your problem."

"I can't forget it," I protested. "Not when I'm a suspect." Or *you* are a suspect, I wanted to say, but I didn't. I didn't want Dolce as worried or involved as I was.

"Who suspects you?" she asked me.

I pointed across the room to where Meera and Jack were still talking. "Jack, the cop on the case, thinks I know more than I'm letting on. I had a motive—to get the shoes back. I thought I had an alibi, but no one clocked me in at the hospital when I arrived. Someone saw a woman who could have been MarySue drop me off, but it's all so murky," I said, shaking my head. "I'm going to find the ladies' room," I said. I had to freshen up before more people arrived. I headed toward the rear of the bar where I saw a sign in several languages.

I'd just turned the corner down a dim hallway toward the restroom when I heard footsteps behind me. When I turned around, I saw Jim Jensen looming over me.

"There you are," he said. "You have a lot of guts coming to my party."

"Who me?" I said. Maybe he'd mistaken me for someone else in the dark.

"Yes, you, Rita Jewel. You're responsible for MarySue's death."

"I wasn't even there that night. I was in the hospital."

"I don't care if you were in the morgue. You are an enabler. You knew MarySue had a compulsive shopping addiction."

"No, no, I didn't," I protested. I wondered if Dolce knew.

"And you did nothing. Worse than nothing. You encouraged her to buy more stuff. Her closet was overflowing. Her credit card was maxed out until I cut it in half. I signed her up for a twelve-step program, but she wouldn't go. She went shopping instead. Mumbled something about 'retail therapy.'"

"I swear I didn't know," I said, backing up until I hit the wall.

"You went to Miami to buy those shoes for her, don't deny it."

"Yes, but I thought—"

"You didn't think. All you cared about was your commission on a pair of shoes. You might not have put the poison in the champagne, but you are responsible for my wife's death just the same. You brought the shoes for her, and someone wanted the shoes so bad he killed her to get them."

By then I was shaking, my arms were covered with goose bumps. I didn't know what to say except something like *How do you know it was a he*? I was more convinced than ever that Jim had killed MarySue himself and he was looking for someone to take the blame. It wasn't going to be me. I took a deep breath.

"Jim," I said as calmly as I could, "I'm sorry for your loss. You're obviously on step one in the seven stages of grief. It's stressful and exhausting, but it's natural. Everyone has to go through it. You aren't alone and you're not yourself."

"How do you know I'm not myself?" he demanded.

"I, uh, I just know. I know you have to work through it. There's no skipping over even one step. Believe me, I had no idea MarySue had a shopping problem. I mean, our store is full of shoppers who buy clothes and accessories day after day. MarySue wasn't any different than they are."

"She was sick," he shouted. "She needed help. Don't you see the difference?"

I shook my head and backed slowly down the hall away from Jim the way you're supposed to when faced with a grizzly bear. I was afraid he'd have another heart attack. This time it wouldn't be a warning, it would be for real and I'd be to blame. I thought he'd follow me, but he didn't.

When Jack saw me reappear in the bar a few minutes later, he raised his eyebrows. He pointed to a small table, and I went there, sat down and put my head in my hands. My legs were shaking, and the room was spinning around. When I heard someone approach, I looked up thinking it had to be Jack and I could tell him what had happened. I knew I was in danger of repeating myself, but I was more sure than ever Jim had killed his wife. Seven stages of grief? That surely didn't apply to the murderer, did it? I'd made that up. I'd just been trying to humor Jim, playing along with him, because if he knew that I'd discovered the truth, he'd kill me too.

But it wasn't Jack who joined me at the table. It was Patti, MarySue's sister-in-law. "I heard Jim yelling at you," she said, putting her multiringed hand over mine. "He's not supposed to get upset."

"I don't know what I said to upset him," I said.

"It's not your fault, it's mine," she said.

I frowned. "What is?"

"It's my fault MarySue saw the picture of the shoes in *Vogue*. I showed them to her, then she had to have them for the Benefit. One way or another." She shook her head slowly. "I should have known Jim would be livid. She was compulsive that way. It drove him crazy."

"I can imagine," I muttered. It made him so crazy he killed his wife. I wondered how sorry Patti was that her sister-in-law was out of her life. She didn't mention her husband, MarySue's brother. I hadn't seen him today. Was he grieving at all, or not so much? "The silver shoes were in *Vogue* magazine?" I asked to be sure I heard right. If they were in *Vogue*, why hadn't I seen them? Because Peter lifted Dolce's copy from her office while I was on the phone. The next time I saw him, I was going to ask for it back.

"It's sad, isn't it?" Patti asked.

"Yes," I said, though I wasn't sure what was sad. MarySue's murder? The shoes stolen? MarySue's shopping addiction?

"I mean that anyone would buy a pair of shoes right out of *Slumdog Millionaire*," Patti said. "But that's what happened. If you believe the story in *Vogue*. You and I know where those shoes came from."

We do? Yes, I knew they came from a small exclusive shop in Miami. What did that have to do with a movie about a TV quiz show in India where a kid from the slums wins a million dollars?

"The question is, where did they go?" I asked. "Were they stolen or . . . She didn't . . . she wasn't buried in them, was she?"

Patti's blue eyes widened. "Oh, my God, I never thought of that. All that money buried in the ground. I've been assuming that Jim returned the shoes after she died, because he needed the money. He was furious with her for buying them. But he's been so worked up over it there's no telling what he might have done with them. I wouldn't be surprised if he'd thrown them in the Bay."

"He didn't return them to Dolce's," I said. I didn't mention the fact that MarySue hadn't paid in full for the shoes. I knew it was wrong to speak ill of the dead. For all I knew, Patti had taken the shoes herself and was putting up a good front of innocence. Did she kill her sister-in-law or was it Jim? I stared at her, wondering if she could possibly have done it. I just couldn't picture it. Although she had a motive and the opportunity. I shifted my gaze to the crowd at the bar. A minute ago I was sure it was Jim who'd killed MarySue, now I was wavering. I had a feeling that the murderer was here today, but where? And who?

"Let me know if you hear anything," Patti said, standing up. I had to admit she looked great if a tad inappropriate in her little black cocktail dress and huge black hat. Dressed as she was, she could have been on her way to tea at the Ritz-Carlton. Her long legs were covered with leather boots with zippers and buckles, what else? And she hadn't spared the jewelry.

I agreed, but I wondered what she meant by "if you hear anything."

I signaled to Dolce, and she came to my table with another drink in her hand. "This one's an appletini, so it's really good for you. You know what they say about an apple a day," she said just before draining her glass. "Are you ready to go?"

I nodded. "I had no idea these affairs were so stressful. There's just one thing. Could we stop by the cemetery on our way home?"

Dolce gave me a funny look. Then she shrugged. "Sure."

"I just want to see where she's buried." I didn't dare tell Dolce what I feared because it was so irrational. The rational part of me knew that MarySue could not have been bitten by a vampire that night at the Benefit because there was no such thing as a vampire. But the irrational part also knew enough about vampire legends to know that if vampires existed and even if they'd buried MarySue facedown, she'd find a way to get out of her grave. Not that I wanted to see her or that she'd want to see me. I didn't know what I'd do if I saw her. Probably run the other way.

On our way out of the tavern, we had to stop and speak to some of our customers, so it was a good thing we'd put in an appearance for the sake of Dolce's business. When we finally got to the parking lot, I offered to drive since I'd had less to drink than Dolce. I just got in to the driver's seat when Jack came walking across the parking lot toward our car.

"Leaving so soon?" he asked when I rolled down my window.

"I don't do well at social functions," I confessed.

"You seemed disturbed. What happened?" he asked.

"Just the usual. Nothing new. Jim Jensen accused me of killing his wife. That's all. What about you? Did you learn anything?"

"Maybe. So you're off?"

Dolce leaned over toward the window. "We're going to the cemetery."

I nudged her. If she hadn't had three drinks, she wouldn't have blabbed.

"Really," he said, giving me a curious look. "So you don't do well at social functions, but you do better at cemeteries. I have to say I'm surprised."

"Just to pay our respects without a big crowd around," I explained. He didn't look convinced. I wanted to see the spot where MarySue was buried. That's all.

"So did you get a chance to talk to Peter?" I asked.

"The shoe guy? Yes. He's an odd one. He seemed nervous."

"That's the effect you have on people. Or didn't you tell him you were a cop?"

"I told him. He told me MarySue was a good customer with superior taste."

"I think the word he was looking for was 'expensive' taste. I wonder if Jim knows how good a customer she was of Peter's. If he does, he should be threatening Peter and not me. What did I do besides pick up the shoes in Miami?"

Jack didn't answer. He just stood there looking thoughtful, then he said good-bye and we drove off.

The cemetery was deserted. I was having second thoughts before I even got to the gate and asked the guard where MarySue was buried. Dolce obviously thought I was insane to come here when it was so depressing. But to her credit she didn't say a word. Maybe the effect of the final appletini. She just thanked me for driving, leaned back in the passenger seat and closed her eyes.

I parked and left Dolce in the car. I just wanted to look at her grave. I wanted to know if she was wearing the silver shoes. But I would never know that.

The sod was still fresh on her grave, the stone was polished and engraved with her name and the dates of her birth and death. I stood there alone for a long moment staring at the ground. Nothing moved. Nothing happened. Of course it didn't.

"I'm sorry, MarySue," I said quietly. "I never should have gone to your house that night. Thank you for taking me to the hospital if that was you. I appreciate it. If you hadn't . . . On the other hand, you're the one who shoved me off the ladder. But let's let bygones be bygones. I just wish I knew who killed you. But I'll find out, I promise I will."

I sighed and went back to the car feeling more than a little foolish for talking to a dead person. How ridiculous was that?

Fifteen

::::::::::::::::::::::::::::::::

The next day Dolce was, not surprisingly, hungover and down in the dumps, and I was more determined than ever to solve this mystery before Jack did. I didn't know why. He was the cop, I was the sales assistant and fashion consultant. But I was sick and tired of being accused of killing Mary-Sue, and the only way to stop it was to find the real killer myself. I borrowed Dolce's car to go to every bookstore in town on my lunch hour. I was looking for the recent issue of *Vogue*, but they were sold out. "It's not unusual," one clerk told me. "We don't order that many and it's the giant fall issue, 'biggest in twenty years,'" she said. Even though my lunch hour was over and I still hadn't eaten anything, I went to the main library.

There it was at the far end of the periodical section between the *US Weekly* and the *Western Horse Review*. I snatched it up and sat down at a large table where I could spread it out. I flipped the pages madly past articles on "How to Make Menswear Look Chic," "110 Best Beauty Buys" and "Must-Have Messenger Bags." I knew I was late. I knew I was leaving Dolce in the lurch with her postparty headache, but I just couldn't resist perusing the article on the new fall boots. I lusted after a pair of lace-up suede and leather high-tops, and I wondered if Dolce would want to put in an order. But where was the article I was looking for?

Frustrated, I went back to the table of contents, and there it was on page ninety-one: "Third World Shoe Scam! Don't Get Taken In!" My heart was pounding, my fingers stuck to the pages. Eighty, eighty-five, ninety . . . ninety-two. What? Where was ninety-one? Gone, that's where. It had been ripped out. I could see the jagged edges.

I sat there staring at the place where the article should have been. I was in shock. As close to collapse, coma or even sudden death as I'd ever been.

I had to have that article. If someone wanted it badly enough to rip it out, it must be important. I went outside and called Dolce. "I haven't found what I'm looking for. Can you handle everything for another hour?" I hated to impose on her good nature, especially when she wasn't feeling quite right, but I couldn't stop now. I had to find that article, even if I had to drive all over California. There must be a copy somewhere.

"Of course," she said. "It's not very busy. In fact, the only person who's been in is Peter, and he's not a customer."

"What did he want?"

"He wanted to speak to you, but I told you you were out looking for a magazine."

"What? Oh, I wish you hadn't."

"Why? He wants to help you. He asked me which one you wanted because he keeps all his old copies."

I sucked in a short breath. I didn't want anyone to know

I was looking for this article. Peter Butinksi was probably a harmless bore, but who knew how many people he'd be talking to during his travels from boutique to boutique.

I got back into Dolce's car and headed across the Golden Gate Bridge toward Marin County. Whoever had bought up all the magazines in the city and tore out the article in the library probably hadn't gotten to Marin yet, or had they?

I stepped on the gas, and instead of admiring one of the world's most beautiful bridges or the sparkling blue waters of the Bay or the view of the skyscrapers on the city's skyline in my rearview mirror, I stared straight ahead, my teeth clenched so tight my jaw hurt. I was determined not to return until I had that magazine in my hands.

The first town I came to I turned off and hit the chain bookstore in the large shopping center. I smiled at the security guard at the entrance, glad to see the books and magazines were well protected. You wouldn't get away with ripping out a page here or walking out with a magazine you didn't pay for.

There they were, racks of magazines. And there in the last rack was the very issue I was looking for. On the cover was a famous movie star wearing a leopard print bustier. I reached for the magazine. I had it in my grasp when someone grabbed it and pulled it out of my hand. I yanked it back. Then I looked up and almost lost my grip. It was Peter Butinski in his tweed jacket with the leather elbow patches, ill-fitting pants and leather sandals. I was dying to tell Dolce.

"Peter," I gasped. "What are you doing here?"

"The same thing you are," he said. "Buying a magazine."

"This one's mine," I said and used both hands to hang on to the magazine. *My* magazine.

"I don't think so," he said, ripping it out of my hands with a forceful jerk.

That made me so angry I felt a surge of superhuman strength. "Give it back," I shouted.

"What's going on here?" someone said. I turned and saw the clerk standing at the edge of the rack, his mouth open in astonishment as if he'd never seen two customers fight over a magazine before.

"He's got my magazine," I said, and I lunged for it. I got hold of it by the corner, but Peter pulled so hard I heard a ripping sound as the magazine tore apart. I stumbled backward into another rack of magazines and landed on my butt.

"Security," the clerk shouted, obviously worried about the crazies in the store.

Peter was not waiting for any security guard to escort him out. Not without the magazine—or half the magazine. He bolted for the back door of the store, and I just sat there on the floor surrounded by magazines. I was panting and holding my half of the *Vogue* tightly in my hand. But was page nine-one in my hand or in Peter's? And would I be arrested for dismembering a magazine? Not if I paid for it, which I planned to do. But first things first.

I staggered to my feet and explained as calmly as I could to the security guard that I wanted to buy that magazine and I was sorry I caused a disturbance. I said I'd be glad to pick up all the fallen magazines and of course pay for the one in my hand, which was really only half a magazine. I observed that the other man wanted the magazine too, which must have been obvious. If he hadn't done anything wrong, then why did he flee? Where had he gone? Actually I didn't care as long as I had the article I'd come for.

I couldn't wait another minute. While standing there, I started flipping through the pages again, this time ignoring all the tempting lists, like "Ten Best Beauty Tips" and "Naughty Sex Questions." I'd get to them later.

I was almost up to page ninety-one when the store manager appeared and surveyed the damage. One bookcase on the floor and magazines everywhere. He asked for my name and phone number. I closed the magazine and told him I'd be glad to pay for any damaged magazines, but that it wasn't my fault. He looked dubious.

Instead of standing there another minute and subjecting myself to questions and accusations, I decided to leave as quickly and gracefully as I could. It turned out they charged me for the *Vogue* and that was all. Finally alone in Dolce's car, I found the page.

There they were, a large color photograph of the silver shoes, the same silver shoes I'd transported across country. The same silver shoes ripped from my grasp by MarySue Jensen. The same silver shoes MarySue had worn to the Benefit. The same silver shoes that had caused her murder. But who did it? Who killed her? Who stole her shoes?

I scanned the article under the heading "Third World Shoe Scam!" Then I read the questions: "Are you guilty of causing child labor? Are you wearing shoes made by children who earn pennies a day in poor countries? Do you contribute to a *Slumdog Millionaire*'s millions by buying shoes like these? Do you care about poor children, or do you care more about high fashion?" They mentioned the price of the shoes and I gasped.

Oh my God, what was I going to do? When I heard a loud rapping on my window, I looked up to see Peter's face pressed against the glass. His mouth was open and he was shouting at me. "You think you're a super salesman. Well, you're nothing compared to me."

I rolled down my window a crack and glared at him.

"I'm the one who knows how to sell shoes. Who do you think got MarySue to buy the stilettos?"

"Patti," I said. "Not you." I knew he wouldn't let anyone top him in the sales department.

"Hah. Did Patti tell you that? She's nothing compared to me. I was born to sell. I could sell snow to Eskimos. Or stilettos to socialites like MarySue. All it took was one look at the shoes. I showed them to her. I told her to order them."

"I thought it was Harrington," I said.

"That second-rate drama queen? Maybe he did but I'm the one she turned to for fashion tips. Now give me that magazine." He knew I had the article he wanted. I pushed the key in the ignition and tore out of that parking lot, leaving him standing there waving his arms in the air. I headed for the bridge hoping he wouldn't follow me and cause an accident. I was shaking all over. My fingers gripped the steering wheel so tightly they were stiff. I might need help removing them so I could get out of the car.

When I got to Dolce's, I parked in the no-parking zone in front of the shop because I didn't have the strength to look for a legal space on a side street. I took the half magazine and ran up the front steps to the shop.

Dolce was with a customer. I could feel her eyes on me as I rushed past her to her office. In a few minutes she joined me.

"Where have you been?" she asked. "You look like you've seen a ghost."

"Worse than a ghost. I've seen Peter Butinski," I said. "But I've got the magazine." I held it up. She sat down at her desk and squinted. "What magazine?"

"The magazine with the article about the silver shoes. The one Patti showed MarySue, or Peter or Harrington or maybe all three showed them to her. Which made MarySue fall in love with the shoes,"

Dolce donned her bifocals and was scanning the page I

gave her. "But it says if you buy these shoes you're contributing to child labor."

"I know," I said. "Maybe MarySue didn't read that far. Maybe she just saw the picture."

"Then what?" Dolce said. "She ordered them from us. I ordered them from the atelier, you picked them up. If that's how it happened, we're all guilty."

I shook my head. How could we be guilty for ordering a pair of shoes? "Talk about guilty. Peter Butinski is more involved than we thought. He even bragged about it to me. Said he's the one who told MarySue about the shoes, not Patti and not Harrington. This was right after he tried to get the magazine before I did."

"Maybe I shouldn't have told him you were out shopping when he dropped in," Dolce said. "But I thought he was harmless."

"Maybe he is, maybe he isn't," I said. "So that's why he was out looking for magazines, hoping to beat me to the punch. I suspect he has destroyed all the other copies in the city just so no one would know where the shoes came from or his name would be mud. No self-respecting socialite would ever buy from him again knowing he was a slumdog shoe seller."

"But she didn't buy them from him, she bought them from me," Dolce said.

"According to him, he's the one who talked her into them. I'm guessing he gets a commission on every pair. No matter who sells them, there's probably enough profit to go around. If you believe this article."

"I feel terrible," Dolce said. "All those poor children slaving away. What can we do about it besides never order from them again?"

"Right now I'm going to call Peter and offer him a deal.

I won't tell anyone what he's done if he'll give us back the shoes and promise never to exploit the children ever again."

"But you don't know if he has the shoes."

"I have to make him think I do know." I tried to sound like I knew what I was doing, but I only had a vague idea.

"I don't like it," Dolce said, leaning forward across her desk. "He could be dangerous. He might be the one who killed MarySue."

"I can't believe he's a murderer. Of all people, Peter Butinski?" Then I pictured his face contorted with fury in the parking lot. "But I'll take precautions. I'll get Peter to meet me here, then I'll get Detective Wall to stand by."

"I'll be here too," Dolce said. "Hiding in the dressing room."

I smiled. Dolce was the perfect boss. I wouldn't be alone.

I left a message on Peter's phone. "Sorry about today," I said. "I guess we both got carried away. We know you have MarySue's silver shoes. Dolce and I want them back. We're prepared to make a deal with you because we're out a considerable amount of money. Bring the shoes to the shop tonight after five and we will keep this whole affair to ourselves. We don't care how you got the shoes. We don't care where you buy your shoes or sell them. After all, you have to make a living too." I paused. Was I laying it on too thick? Or not thick enough? What motive would he have for handing over the shoes? What if he didn't have them? I didn't want to mention murder. I didn't know what else to say, so I hung up.

Dolce stared at me as if she was surprised by my courage—or was she surprised I'd changed my story or surprised I expected Peter to appear with the shoes and hand them over?

"Even if he doesn't have them, I think he'll show up just to tell us he doesn't have them, don't you?" I asked.

She nodded, but I wasn't sure she was convinced. Then

I called Jack and left a message. I sure hoped he'd get it and be prepared. For what? To arrest Peter? To protect us from Peter? To stand around and be bored when Peter didn't show up?

The hours dragged by. Dolce said we needed to keep up our strength, so she ordered lunch to be delivered from a take-out place around the corner, two Californians—turkey with avocado and jack cheese and two high-energy smoothies. You'd think I would have been too nervous to eat, but tension always makes me extra hungry and I was famished. As soon as the delivery guy arrived, we went to her office and ate our sandwiches and drank our smoothies. I stared at my cell phone wishing I'd hear from my favorite law-and-order man. I thought I could handle Peter by myself, especially with Dolce as backup, but I wanted Jack around just in case.

I kept an eye on the clock while waiting on customers. Amazing how many women are surprised by the arrival of fall and suddenly have nothing to wear. For a badly needed diversion, I threw myself into making suggestions like "Let's try mixing your neutrals, camel with gray, brown layered with a black sweater," and "How about some massive heels with those pants?" Or "Nothing says fall like a chunky sweater." Thank heavens for those women with expensive taste and lots of money or I wouldn't have a job and Dolce wouldn't be able to keep her doors open. Which reminded me that Dolce still looked worried these days even when we weren't concerned there was a murderer in our midst. If money was a problem, would she ask me to take a salary cut? Work half-time? Close the shop on Mondays?

I pushed these problems aside and kept one ear open to hear the phone ringing. But Jack didn't call. I had my cell phone tucked in the pocket of my gamine five-pocket skinny trousers that channeled Audrey Hepburn. I liked the combination of the pants with my white cable-knit sweater, which had been a bargain.

But still no call from Jack. I left another message. I reminded myself he had other crimes to solve. Now that MarySue was buried (hopefully facedown), everyone including the police seemed to have forgotten about her. But not me. If I didn't find out who did it, at least I had hopes of getting her shoes back. I told myself that's what she would have wanted. But honestly I bet she would have wanted to be buried with them on. Maybe she was and all this was for nothing.

At five minutes to five there was a knock on the door. I waved to Dolce, who raced to the dressing room and closed the door behind her. But when I went to the door, it was Maureen Boyle, a good customer who wanted something to wear to a poetry reading that night. I took a deep breath to calm down. No need to freak out in front of a regular customer. Besides, who knew if Peter would really show up? For a casual poetry reading at a local café I suggested jean leggings, a military vest, a drawstring cardigan and some suede engineer boots with low heels. To my surprise she looked around the shop, noticed we were alone, and confessed she'd been buying her shoes at the Glass Slipper, but when she tried to return a pair of espadrilles, they wouldn't take them back.

"Our policy is not like that," I said. "You can always return anything you bought here. No statute of limitations. Dolce insists on customer satisfaction. That's the only way to do business, she says."

Maureen nodded. "I'll never make that mistake again," she said, then she bought the whole outfit. Every little bit helps, I thought. I glanced at the dressing room, wondering if Dolce would pop out and give me a high five, but she didn't. I hoped she hadn't fallen asleep in there.

I walked to the door with Maureen, told her to have a great time. Then I looked up and down the street. No one there except the usual neighborhood residents and tourists. I didn't know whether to be relieved or disappointed that Peter wasn't coming. Had I misjudged him? Was he simply a blowhard who hadn't really done anything even slightly illegal? Had I overestimated my persuasiveness? Hadn't I made it clear what was at stake?

And by the way, where was Jack? I was beginning to have a letdown after all that adrenaline. I locked the front door and went back inside. I was about to see what happened to Dolce when my phone rang.

"Are you alone?"

I bit my lip. "Yes, Peter, where are you?" I wanted to say, "Have you got the shoes?" but I thought it was best to get him in the shop first.

"I'm outside. Open the door."

I skidded across the floor, the soles of my Gucci sandals slipping out from under me. There he was, looking more ridiculous than ever, which had a way of calming me down. How could I be afraid of anyone wearing a tweed jacket, a white shirt and a string tie? Also the fact that he was carrying a shopping bag was encouraging. The shoes. It had to be the shoes.

"Here they are," he said, thrusting the bag at me.

I grabbed it. I wasn't going to let these shoes get away from me again. The shoes were wrapped in tissue paper just as they had been when I picked them up in Florida. I took them out and examined them carefully while he stood there staring at me. I didn't care who made them, these shoes were gorgeous. No wonder MarySue had wanted them. No wonder he wanted them.

"Okay, cough it up," he said.

"I don't understand," I said.

"There's nothing to understand. I brought you the shoes, you give me the money."

"What money?"

He laughed a mirthless laugh. "We all know how much they're worth. You read the article. Hand over the money."

"Peter, the deal is that you give me the shoes and I keep quiet about where I got them. We don't have that kind of money."

"What kind do you have?" he asked.

I laughed nervously. "Oh, you know just the day's receipts."

"Fine," he said. "Hand them over."

"You're kidding right? You wouldn't steal Dolce's hard-earned money from her, would you?"

"Why wouldn't I? She's got a big house here and I've got jack squat. Hand it over."

He looked so wild-eyed and crazy I decided to play along for now. "How about I write you a check on Dolce's account?"

"As long as it's got a lot of zeros."

"Sure," I said, turning toward the office. I figured Jack would be along any minute and I could stall. No way was Peter getting away with our money. He was lucky I hadn't thrown a fit on the spot. Instead I felt a kind of strange calm. I had things under control. Dolce was in the dressing room and Jack was on his way. Wasn't he?

"I'll come with you," he said. Obviously afraid I'd call the cops from the office. Where were they? Why weren't they here? Go slowly, I told myself.

In the tiny office I fumbled with the desk drawer handle. I pawed through the papers until I found the checkbook. All the while Peter was glaring at me. There was a bulge in his pocket. Was he armed? Was he dangerous? All of a sudden I wasn't so calm anymore. As soon as I finished filling out the check, he snatched it out of my hand.

"You had to kill MarySue, didn't you?" I blurted. "And take her shoes so you wouldn't be found out."

"You're the clever one, aren't you?" he said snidely. "I warned Dolce about you. You think you know fashion, but you know nothing about how it works. You think you can pick up a pair of shoes from a boutique, charge someone who can't afford them an arm and a leg. And yet you have no idea how those shoes got there."

"I didn't know then, but I know now. I know that poor children are used so people like you can make money off them."

"People like me?" His voice rose to a crescendo. "You're just as guilty as I am, little Miss Snotnose. I know what you did. How you tried to get the shoes back. MarySue told me how you went to her house, threatened her. You're angry because I succeeded when you failed. I got the shoes and you didn't. I didn't have to threaten her."

"Then how did you do it? You killed her, didn't you?"

"I didn't kill her, not on purpose. I gave her a little pill, well maybe two or three or four in her champagne, just enough to put her to sleep, because she refused to turn over the shoes to me. I never meant to kill her—why would I kill the goose that laid the golden egg, so to speak? MarySue Jensen was one of my best customers. I just had to get the shoes back before someone recognized them as the ones in the magazine."

"The *Vogue* magazine?" I asked. "Now I get it. You bought shoes made by little kids in third world countries who were paid a penny an hour. They looked good, those silver stilettos. You sold them through fancy boutiques and ateliers, and you made plenty as long as no one knew what you were up to, but you were afraid someone would recognize those shoes at the Benefit. You had to get them back."

"And I did, no thanks to MarySue."

I could just imagine how MarySue, who'd planned and schemed to get those shoes, would have refused to turn them over to Peter that night. I couldn't believe what I was hearing. "So you're saying killing MarySue was an accident?"

"Of course. How was I supposed to know you can't mix a few drugs with a little alcohol? These society bitches do it all the time. I thought she'd have a headache, that's all. Now I'm outta here," he said. "I'm stopping at the bank on my way out of town. And if there's a problem with this check, I'll be back." He reached in his pocket and pulled out a small gun. "I know how to use it. See?"

I felt the blood rush from my head. He was going to shoot me. Now that he didn't need me anymore. "Why?" I said, my lips too numb to say anything else.

"Why would I shoot you? Because you know too much. Because I don't want you calling your boyfriend the cop. I thought the shoe box in your garbage would be a warning. But you didn't get the message, did you? Now I'm leaving the country, but I need time to get to the airport."

"I won't tell anyone," I said earnestly.

He laughed again, a high, hysterical laugh. Suddenly I heard the voice of my teacher Yen Po Wing in my ear: "Fluid and rapid movement. When in doubt, use the Northern Method." That's what he'd always told us. Easier said than done, of course, but I had to try. I should never have quit those classes, but who knew I'd need to defend myself from a shoe supplier? I leapt in the air and gave Peter one fluid, rapid and powerful kick in the groin. He doubled up and groaned loudly. I heard a crash, and I fell to the floor. I wondered if I'd been shot or just fainted. From the floor where I was lying faceup, I saw Dolce bravely rush toward Peter with some kind of weapon in her hand that looked like a coat hanger. At the same time Jack Wall burst into the room through the front door and ran into Peter on his way out. Jack grabbed him and twisted his arms behind him.

Dolce helped me up in time to see Jack put handcuffs on Peter.

"I heard the whole thing," Dolce told Jack. "Peter Butinski killed MarySue. He said he didn't mean to."

"Thank you, Dolce," Jack said. Then he turned to me. "You okay?"

I nodded weakly. "I thought you'd never get here."

"I'd like you to come down to the station and give us a statement. Both of you." He nodded at Dolce.

"Now? Tonight?" I asked. I was shaky and weak. I wanted to go home.

"If you wouldn't mind," he said. "You know where the station is."

Dolce and I locked up after Jack took Peter away. Then we went across the street to the bar for a drink. Believe me, we needed it. No sense in facing the law without fortification first.

"You were very brave," Dolce said to me after a few sips of her San Francisco cocktail made with two kinds of vermouth, gin and orange bitters.

"Not me. I fell down. Was that a coat hanger you were holding when you came out of the dressing room?" I asked as I reached for a deep-fried mozzarella stick on the bar.

"It was sturdy cherrywood with a trouser clamp. I could have done some damage with it. I just had to have something in my hand. I was so worried about you. So was your policeman."

"Do you think so?" I meant to say he wasn't mine, but it didn't matter. "I guess we'd better go give our statements."

Too nervous to drive, and maybe under the influence of those tasty cocktails we prudently took a cab to Jack's station. Alone with him and a recorder in his office, I went over my actions of the day, including the scene in the bookstore.

"That's how I knew Peter was involved, when he ripped the magazine out of my hands and bragged about what a super salesman he was, getting MarySue to order the shoes."

"Do you still have the magazine?" Jack asked.

"Of course. It's back in Dolce's office. You can use it for evidence. But Peter already confessed. At least to me, and Dolce heard him from where she was hiding in the dressing room. That's enough evidence, isn't it?" I asked. "What is it, involuntary manslaughter?"

"Not sure yet. Not your problem," he said. "But I will want you to testify."

"Of course," I said. "But not now I hope. I'm a little tired."

"I'll get someone to drive you and Dolce home."

"Thanks."

"I'll be in touch," he said. "You did good today."

I smiled. A word of praise from Jack was worth a lot. I wondered if I'd get anything else, like a medal of bravery. Instead, I got a dinner invitation for Saturday night.

"Same place?" I asked.

"My place," he said.

"You cook?" I asked. I couldn't believe this. I'd gotten the shoes back, and a tough big-city cop had invited me to dinner. Just a thank-you meal or the start of something big? Things were looking up. Before MarySue was murdered I'd been dateless, now I had three men in my life and I was going to do what I could to keep them around. Besides Jack there was Dr. Jonathan with his primo bedside manner. I owed him big-time for all the time, energy and money he'd invested in me. I owed Nick the gymnast as well, for all he'd done for me. Besides cooking up some *zama*, he'd been willing and able to help me shape up. When MarySue was killed we lost a good client, but I'd gained a social life. That might sound heartless but I did keep my promise to her to find her killer. It was the least I could do for her. I had to hope that MarySue was okay with it and that now we were even. RIP.

FASHION TIPS FROM DOLCE

Must-Haves for Fall

PANTS—Sleek, slim and super-sexy. You can't have too many skinny black pants in your wardrobe. Warning—Order one size down because they DO stretch. Buy several pair, wear to work or for any occasion that calls for Business Casual. Pair your skinny pants with chunky wedges or boots and you're good to go.

COLORS—Soft neutrals and non-offensive beige are in. No more over-the-top bold colors and retro designs. Afraid you'll be boring? Not if you mix it up with a fresh silhouette, fabrics and the new longer length.

VESTS—Now's the time to buy a faux-fur vest. No mistaking it for the real thing, but that's OKAY! No apologies please. Just wear and enjoy the look and the compliments coming your way. The cropped style is actually quite flattering.

SHOES—Yes, you can look fab on a budget! Mix and match budget items with high-end brands. Here's what I love—rough boots with flowery flirty dresses or pumps with ripped boy-friend jeans.

HAIR—Bangs. A great look for fall. They work well with the teased updos and the retro makeup. Natural waves? Scrunch your bangs while damp for more texture and roughness, that's what makes them curly. OR go natural—no straightening, no heat. Let your real texture out of the box. Bring back the bounce! "But what if my hair is straight?" you ask. Apply a leave-in conditioner while hair is damp to tame the frizz. Absolutely no wave at all? Get a cut with lots of layers. Scrunch hair while drying.

Aunt Grace's Dating Rules

DO's

1. It may sound boring and obvious, but do be on time. Showing up late or looking like you threw yourself together gives the impression that you don't care. Maybe you don't, but why bother going out with this person if that's the case?

2. Try to enjoy yourself. This is not a root canal or a final exam. It's a date for heaven's sake. Yes, finding your soul mate is serious business, but dating is supposed to be fun. At least act like it is.

3. Do compliment your date on his clothes, his car and/or his choice of venue. Both men and women put a lot of effort in trying to look good and it's good for us all to hear that all that effort has paid off.

4. Act like you're interested and interesting. Ask questions, share your thoughts and pay attention.

5. Do not play games. If you're not interested in seeing him again, don't string him along. It's selfish and isn't good for anyone. Let him down as gently and firmly as possible.

6. Date only men you're attracted to, no matter what your friends say. Otherwise you're wasting his time and yours.

7. Stay positive even when you have a terrible dating experience. Mr. Right may be around the next corner.

8. Be proactive. Whether you subscribe to an online dating site or your friends are setting you up. Dating requires action, planning and activity. Get out there and meet people.

9. Surround yourself with positive, like-minded friends. Share experiences, friends and good times. Good friends will root for you to succeed at love and will be there for you when you need support.

10. Don't give up. Stay upbeat.

DON'T's

1. Don't call, text or e-mail more than once a day to someone you've just started seeing. You'll come across as desperate.

2. Don't date the same kind of people you know are wrong for you. Many of us are attracted to the kind of guy who's not good for us, but now's the time to break the pattern.

3. Don't be late for dates. If you have a serious conflict, let the other person know. And always apologize.

4. Don't lie to your date unless it's to tell him you really like his shoes when you think they're dorky. The kind of lies I'm talking about are the ones you tell to try to impress him.

5. Don't be too available. I don't mean you should play games, but if you're free every night, you need to get a life other than dating. You've got interests. Pursue them. You've got friends. Call them.

6. Don't reveal your life story on the first date. Save something for later. Getting to know someone takes time.

7. Don't ignore your date. Concentrate on him instead of scoping out the hottie in the corner. Give the guy you're with the courtesy of all your attention.

8. Don't drink or eat too much. Everything in moderation.

9. Stay safe. Keep your cell phone charged and handy and tell your friends where you're going and with whom.

10. Don't give out your phone number or address on the first date.

11. No sex on a first date. It's much too soon.

12. Don't go out with married men. No matter how attractive. You deserve better.

Five Reasons Why Rita Likes San Francisco (Here's What, Where, Why, and When)

1. **WEATHER**—Rita loves the weather in San Francisco because (like her) it's so unpredictable. But it does make it hard for visitors to plan ahead. Yes, it's supposed to rain in the winter but there are gorgeous dry warm days all year round. Rita is always prepared because she never knows what weather the day will bring. That's why it's so important for a girl to dress in layers. Another fun fact is that the weather changes from neighborhood to neighborhood. The wind sometimes blows cold air and fog in off the ocean while a few miles away there can be warm sun on Telegraph Hill where Rita lives. The only things she knows for sure is that the sunsets over the ocean are spectacular, the fog creeps in "on little cat feet" under the Golden Gate Bridge and it never (almost never) snows except in 1887 when four inches of snow fell in San Francisco according to Meera who says she was there then, and there are (hardly ever) any April showers. Rita's advice to tourists—Come in the fall for the best weather and wear layers, layers, layers.

2. **WATER**—San Francisco is a city that's surrounded on three sides by water. The Pacific Ocean, the San Francisco Bay and

the Golden Gate Strait. Rita has a view of the Bay from her
flat on Telegraph Hill. The beaches can be a bit chilly for
sunbathing and the water downright cold even for the brav-
est swimmers, which Rita is not.

3. WALKING—San Francisco is a relatively small city, laid out
over a grid of 40 hills, which makes it both challenging and
exhilarating to walk around. Some of Rita's favorite walking neighborhoods are Pacific Heights with its stately historic
homes and spectacular views. She also takes out-of-town
guests on a steep hike up to Coit Tower on Filbert or Green-
wich Streets where they can get a peek into the gardens and
lifestyles of the people who live on the hill. Rita has yet to
walk across the Golden Gate Bridge but she wants to do
that, ideally holding hands with one of the men in her life
as they gaze at the beautiful city in the distance or the hills
of Marin County to the north.

4. FREE STUFF—Rita is always looking for a bargain, whether
it's clothes, shoes, accessories or entertainment. Fortunately
there is no entrance fee to the Golden Gate Park which was
created in the late 1800s according to our resident wannabe
vampire, Meera, who says she remembers when it was just
sand dunes out there. The park is even bigger than Central
Park in New York. Home to the DeYoung Art Museum, the
California Academy of Sciences and the Japanese Tea Garden, the park is a great place for Rollerblading, bicycling or
having a picnic. The museums require an entrance fee, so
Rita likes taking advantage of the free stuff like the Botan-
ical Garden, the Buffalo Paddock, Stow Lake, and the
Shakespeare Garden. There are also occasional free Sunday concerts in the outdoor band shell.

5. FOOD—Rita didn't come to San Francisco for the food, but
like so many others she is eating her way through the city.
She's not much of a cook but she has a healthy appetite and

the men she meets like to eat too. Obviously she came to the right place. Since she arrived, she's been introduced to Romanian food thanks to Nick Petrescu and his aunt, Meera. She's also eaten sushi, Vietnamese *pho*, cracked Dungeness crab, sourdough bread, clam chowder from a bread bowl, Korean tacos and much much more. It's a wonder Rita can still fit into her favorite Lucky brand jeans; it must be all that walking up and down the hills that keeps her a perfect size 4.

Recipes

Meera's Stuffed Cabbage Rolls—
Galumpkis
(With thanks to "Angelinaw")

Serves 4 Romanians or 6 Americans

Meera learned to make *galumpkis* from her grandmother in the medieval town of Brasov, where her family lived near the historic castle of Bran, a Gothic fairy-tale kind of palace. No wonder Meera has the spirit of the vampires in her blood. (If not the real thing.) Grannie used to fill Meera's head with tales of Vlad, the fifteenth-century prince who was the inspiration for Bram Stoker's *Dracula*. No surprise that Meera is a self-described vampire. Vampire or not, she's a great cook!

This *galumpkis* is the perfect dish when the weather gets cold in Romania or wherever friends gather to eat and drink. The tomato sauce is often described as a sweet-sour sauce.

TOMATO SAUCE

*1 ½ quarts crushed tomatoes (or you can use 1 can of
tomato juice)*

> *2 tablespoons white vinegar (apple cider vinegar will make it more tart)*
> *1 tablespoon sugar*
> *2 tablespoons garlic, minced*
> *1 teaspoon pesto*

CABBAGE ROLLS

> *1 head cabbage*
> *1 onion, chopped*
> *1 pound meat (traditionally done with ½ lb pork, ½ lb beef—but I use venison)*
> *2 tablespoons garlic, minced*
> *1 large egg*
> *2 tablespoons parsley,chopped*
> *1 ½ cups white rice, cooked*
> *salt and pepper to taste*

Core and boil the cabbage first. You are boiling for about 5 minutes—just to make the cabbage leaves pliable.

While the cabbage is boiling, prepare the tomato sauce.

Sauté the garlic and pesto in a skillet for 1 minute.

Add the tomatoes and cook, stirring occasionally for about 5 minutes.

Add the vinegar and sugar and simmer until the sauce thickens (this is a good place to taste the sauce—we like ours a little tart).

Season with salt and pepper and remove from heat.

By now your cabbage should be done.

Take the cabbage out of the water, run under cold water, and gently start taking the leaves off of the head. (If you overboiled your cabbage this will result in the leaves shredding.)

Lay out the leaves flat (like sheets of paper).

Cut out the vein from the backside of the leaf (this will make it really pliable).

The bigger leaves will be used for the bottom of your pot and the top of your pot, so put those really big leaves aside.

MAKE THE FILLING

Sauté the onion and garlic until the onion is soft (if you can caramelize them a little this adds extra flavor to the filling).

Stir in the parsley and a little of the tomato sauce (about ¼ cup).

Combine this mix with your meat in a large bowl.

Add the egg and cooked rice.

Mix well with your hands, seasoning with salt and pepper if desired.

Take the mix in small palm-sized chunks and place one chunk in the middle of a cabbage leaf. Roll the end up so it curls around the meat and then tuck in each side, covering the meat, and then roll the cabbage leaf up completely. (You should not see any meat.)

Continue rolling until all of your meat mix is gone.

Dividing the big leaves in half, place the big leaves in the bottom of your pan.

In Romania they use a big stock pot or dutch oven on top of the stove for cooking. In America Meera uses a Crock-Pot, or she bakes them in the oven in a cast-iron, porcelain-enamel French pot.

Place the cabbage rolls on top of the big leaves.

Pour the sauce over the rolls and add water if needed to cover the rolls completely.

Place the other big leaves on top of the rolls, tucking them in.

Cook for about 3–4 hours on low heat.

POFTA BUNA!

Zama De Pasole Verde
(Meera's Green String Bean Soup)

Guaranteed to cure the common cold, allergies, sore throat and ease the pain of minor concussions or the agony of unrequited love.

> 2 pounds string beans, cut in short pieces
> 3 pounds spring chicken, cut into pieces
> 2 tablespoons lard, oil or butter
> One onion, chopped and sautéed
> 1 teaspoon red pepper or more to taste
> 1 garlic clove
> Bunch of parsley and dill weed, chopped fine
> 1 ½ teaspoons flour
> 3 quarts water

Place lard or substitute butter in a heavy pot and sauté together with the flour until you have a roux, 3 to 5 minutes. Add red pepper, water and chicken and cook until chicken is firm. Cook green beans, garlic and onion in a half cup of water separately for a half hour then add to the chicken pot and cook the whole thing for 45 minutes or more. Add parsley and dill weed at the end.

Turn the page for a preview of
Grace Carroll's next Accessory Mystery . . .

Died with a Bow

Coming soon from Berkley Prime Crime!

April in San Francisco is all about layers. Not the layers of fog that blanket the ocean beaches, not the layers of cake at bakeries like Miette or Tartine. I mean layers of clothing, from a sleeveless tunic worn over a polo neck to pairs of leggings with ballerina flats or plain pumps. Under no circumstances should you wear a tight shirt or sweater with your leggings. The overall look must be balanced: the top must be roomy and the leggings must be fitted. It's simple really.

That's what I'd been telling the customers at Dolce's, the boutique where I've worked for the past year. Because in our city surrounded on three sides by water, chilly fog and a brisk wind can sweep over the town without notice in any month, and you have to be prepared for them. Sometimes it's a burst of brilliant, warm sunshine followed by damp mist or, in winter, a heavy downpour. If you asked me, and many customers did, I would recommend wearing a narrow

fitted top under a classic belted trench coat with dangling
earrings and, in this case, knee-high socks over tights.

Today I was wearing all gray, which looks softer next to
the skin than black or navy and is not as boring as it sounds.
With a boyfriend blazer over a tank top under a thin Alexander Wang sweater I love, I carried a striped canvas tote.
Wide-legged pants and strapped loafers made me feel ready
to take on the world, or at least Dolce's regular customers,
the rich and well-connected to the city's social scene.

One thing I was not ready for was to be greeted by a
stranger at the door of the Victorian mansion Dolce had
converted into an exclusive shop.

"Hello!" The young woman in satin shorts so full I
thought they were bloomers, along with tights, a ribbed long-
sleeved T-shirt and patent leather wedge sling backs invited
me inside as if I were a customer and she worked there. It
turned out she did work there.

"I'm Vienna Fairchild. Welcome to Dolce's," she said
with a dazzling smile. So dazzling her teeth must have
recently been laser-whitened.

"Hi, Vienna. I'm Rita. I work here."

"Rita," she said, looking puzzled for a moment while she
scratched her head. "Where have I heard that name before?"
Which made me wonder, was she kidding or wasn't I in the
right place? Had I landed in an alternate universe? "Oh, I
know. Dolce mentioned you."

Mentioned me? Me, her right-hand girl? That's funny, I
thought, because she hasn't mentioned you to me.

Right away I could tell things were different, and I'd only
been gone for two days. I'd taken Saturday off to move into
a smaller, more affordable apartment, and Sunday, the shop
was closed. While I was gone the accessory section had
been moved from the foyer and jewelry had taken its place.

Racks of new clothes were pushed against the far wall of
the great room, and our mannequins wore bright, bold
spring outfits that I'd never seen before, and if I had, I would
never have worn them or dressed anyone, even a fiberglass
model, in them. I knew the theme was citrus colors, but
someone had gone way too far. I mean, who wants to look
like a grapefruit?

I looked around, feeling a chill of apprehension. Vienna
was rubbing her slender, ringed fingers together, looking at
me as I looked around. Was she thinking, why is Rita wearing so much gray today when clearly spring is in the air?

"How do you like it?" she said. "Don't you just love, love
what I've done?"

"You did this?" I asked.

She nodded, waiting for me to go off into ecstasy.

"It's stunning," I said. It was. I was stunned. But not in
a good way. "So Vienna, are you . . ."

"Working here? Yes, I am. Isn't it amazing? Last week I
was wondering what to do with myself, just out of school
with a degree in marketing and nothing to market. I thought
I'd be perfect as a personal shopper for celebrities who don't
have time to shop for themselves. Or should I be a buyer for
a store like Saks or Nordstrom? Then my stepmother, I
believe you know Bobbi, suggested I move to the city. Next,
I land a job here at her favorite boutique. How perfect is
that? Works for them, and it works for me. I mean the suburbs where my parents and their significant others live are
way too quiet for me. Borrring. So I came in for an interview on Friday night, got hired and Saturday was my first
day." She sighed, no doubt exhausted from this long speech,
and spread her well-toned arms out wide. She beamed at
me and said, "And here I am."

I tried to beam back, but all I could come up with was a

weak smile. How on earth was there going to be room for both of us and my boss, Dolce, in this chic little store? I got my answer before I could say Diane von Furstenberg when Dolce came down the stairs from her apartment above the store.

"Rita, I see you've met Vienna." More beaming, this time from Dolce, who was wearing business casual—a magenta ruffled top with a tweed jacket and some sleek straight pants. "I knew you two girls would get along. And having Vienna here will free you up for some important work I need you to help me with," she said to me.

The work she had in mind was unpacking boxes of clothes, pressing them and hanging them on racks. The kind of thing you would ask the new girl to do, I thought. But no, Dolce, ever tactful, said she trusted only me to handle the new merchandise. Which made me feel good for about ten minutes. Then I missed my old job of being out front. The question was, didn't the customers miss me too?

As I worked by myself in the back room sorting endless boxes of new clothes and accessories, I could hear the sound of voices out in front. There was laughter and gossip, but I wasn't part of it anymore. That hurt. How long was I going to have to play the role of the backstage understudy? Once I overheard a customer saying, "Where's Rita?" I stopped and straightened my shoulders, ready to pop out and say, "Here I am," but then I heard Vienna say I was busy today and ask if she could help her.

Of course, it was her first day, and she was excited and eager to prove herself without me around to show her up. I could understand that. Tomorrow would be different. How, I wasn't sure. Would Vienna be willing to do this kind of work when the fun of the job was finding the right outfit for the right customer for the right occasion? I suspected the answer was no, she wouldn't.

After we'd closed that evening and Vienna had left with her boyfriend, Geoffrey, a tall, lanky guy she pointed out to us when he stopped in the street to pick her up on his BMW motorcycle, Dolce explained that Vienna was working on commission only.

"It's the only way I could afford to hire her," Dolce told me. "And why she has to work up front with the customers she promised to bring in. If she isn't selling anything, she isn't earning any money. Whereas you . . ."

She didn't have to say more. I had a salary. It wasn't very much, but it was enough to live on as long as I got a big discount on my designer clothes and didn't go out to eat unless someone took me. Which hadn't happened lately. And which used to happen more frequently when I was the new girl in town. There was no guy on an expensive motorcycle outside waiting for me today. No guy at all.

Only a few months ago I was juggling dates with Nick, an athletic Romanian gymnastics instructor, Jonathan, a gorgeous ER doctor, and Detective Jack Wall of the San Francisco Police Department, but my phone had stopped ringing after I helped Jack solve a murder. It seemed to be a case of No Good Deed Goes Unpunished.

Maybe Dr. Jonathan Rhodes was dating one of those attractive nurses I'd seen the last time I was at the hospital to have my sprained ankle examined. They'd have more in common with him than I ever would. I couldn't discuss sprains or infections in a meaningful way, if that's what he was looking for in a date.

Maybe Nick the gymnast was busy giving classes in competitive trampoline, introduction to the beam bar and so forth. He'd wanted me to sign up for one of his classes, but instead I'd joined Alto Aquatics, a swim club where I got my exercise swimming laps and learning floatation and water safety techniques from the swim coach. Maybe it's because I was born under the sign of Aquarius, the water bearer, that I'm more at home in the water than at a gym. What I do know is that I'm a typical Aquarius in that I look good in turquoise and I'm tolerant of others' viewpoints. To a certain degree.

It might be time to check up on my favorite police detective, I thought, though I knew my aunt Grace strongly disapproved of women chasing men. At age eighty, she's so with-it, she even has a Facebook page. At the same time, she has such strict rules she doesn't approve of calling or texting men unless they contact her first. She definitely wouldn't approve of going to the neighborhood where a certain man worked and having dinner at his favorite Vietnamese restaurant just in case he dropped in. I could just see her shaking her head, the curls in her bold blond updo quivering at the very idea.

It was possible the sexiest cop in the city had been transferred out of town, or he'd gotten disillusioned with law enforcement and quit, or he was wounded in the line of duty, or . . . It was only common courtesy for me to find out if he was okay.

"Date night?" Dolce asked me hopefully before I left. She'd probably noticed there'd been a drop in the number of men in my life from three to zero, and maybe she guessed I was eager to leave the shop, where I didn't exactly feel important today.

"Not tonight," I said brightly, as if every other night was booked. She knew better. She knew I'd tell her if I was going somewhere, and she'd get a kick out of dressing me up for whatever the occasion.

"You know there's the Annual Bay to Breakers Bachelor Auction coming up," she said. "I bought tickets today from Patti for you and me and Vienna. All the money goes to support the San Francisco Art Museum. It's a black-tie gala at the Palace Hotel. Every eligible bachelor in town will be on stage. We'll all get dressed up and go ogle the beefsteak," she said with a youthful gleam in her eye though she always said she was too old to lust after men.

I wasn't too old to lust, but I was too poor to have fun bidding on men I didn't know. It would be no fun losing out on the good ones because I'd be outbid by women with more money than I had. But it was kind of Dolce to get me a ticket and help me dress up for it.

I thanked her, said good night and walked outside. Now what? I couldn't stand the thought of facing an empty flat, even though it had a deck and a sliver of a view of the Bay Bridge. After a day of unpacking boxes at work, I wasn't in the mood to unpack my own belongings. I also didn't feel like facing an empty refrigerator in my empty flat. The police district where Jack Wall worked was only a bus ride away. Or I could hop a different bus and drop into the gym where Nick taught classes. But what would be my excuse this time? I'd already observed his class, signed up for lessons, which I never took, and stopped in for a smoothie at the snack bar. It was his turn to call me.

There was that voice inside my head that kept repeating, "Don't pursue men. If they want to see you, they know where to find you." So I took the bus straight home and called Azerbijohnnie's, a gourmet pizzeria recommended by one of our customers.

The woman who took my phone order had a distinct foreign accent, one that was vaguely familiar. When I gave my name she said, "How are you, Miss Rita? I haven't seen you since the funeral of that woman who was murdered."

"Meera?" I said, recognizing the voice of Nick's Romanian aunt, who I hadn't seen since she crashed a "celebration of life" party at a tavern across from the cemetery. Shy, she was not. "What are you doing there?"

"Filling out for a Romanian friend," she said in her distinctive Eastern European accent. "Who had to return to our country on family business. I didn't want him to lose his job here. I help out and I get free pizza. And some vodka he promised to bring when he returns."

I was surprised that mattered to Meera, a self-proclaimed vampire. Romanian vodka was not a delicacy according to my Romanian professor at college. He called it rotgut. As for pizza, I thought Meera only ate traditional Romanian specialties like *sarmale*, *salata boeuf*, and *papanasi*. "What about your job leading tours?" I'd taken her vampire tour of San Francisco with Nick a few months back, which was interesting as long as you didn't take seriously Meera's claims that she was a hundred-twenty-seven-year-old vampire herself.

"Friday and Saturdays only. You must come again. I have some new sites and information to share with you. Bring a friend. Half-price because I like you," she said. I noticed she said nothing at all about her nephew Nick. Did that mean he, like Dr. Rhodes, had another girlfriend? Someone who was in his adult gymnastics class who was more flexible than I was? If he did, I didn't want to hear about it, and I was glad I hadn't pursued him. But a minute later I heard myself say, "How is your nephew Nick?"

"Not so fine. He had an accident on the high beam and tore his ligament."

"I'm sorry to hear that," I said. Though I was glad to hear he had an excuse for ignoring me.

"He was doing a demonstration when he had a miscalculation, and now he has to stay off the leg, so I bring him food after work. I am sure he would like to see you at his flat on Green Street, number seventeen-forty-two," she said pointedly.

Actually, I owed her nephew because he showed up with food for me when I fell off a ladder a few months ago. "I'll go see him," I promised. And I would, but not tonight. I was in no mood to cheer anyone up but myself.

"What about your pizza?" she asked.

"I'll have the daily special," I said looking at my take-out menu. "Rainbow chard, red onions, feta cheese . . ."

"Why not try the Romanian special instead?" she asked. "My personal favorite, which I am making myself when not taking telephone orders. It comes with cabbage, tomato sauce, and grilled carp."

"I'll stick with the pizza of the day," I said firmly. Grilled carp might be delicious, but on pizza?

She sounded disappointed, but she confirmed my order, and I said, "*La revedere*," and hung up.

The pizza arrived an hour later—it was delicious with a glass of Two-Buck Chuck merlot, which I sipped and congratulated myself on being sensible and frugal. Tomorrow would be better. Tomorrow I would sign up for cooking classes somewhere. If Meera could make pizza, why couldn't I learn to cook too? Maybe the California Culinary Academy, or a smaller, more intimate place like Tante Marie's Cooking School, where I'd learn basic French techniques. I would unpack my dishes, buy a set of pots and give little dinner parties instead of sitting around waiting for men to call and invite me out. Yes, tomorrow had to be better.

But it wasn't.